TUESDAY'S SOCKS

———◆———

ALISON RAGSDALE

TUESDAY'S SOCKS

ISBN-10:0990747808
ISBN-13:978-0-9907478-0-2

TUESDAY'S SOCKS

CHAPTER 1

---◆---

Founder and sole employee of Mere Accounting, amateur bee-keeper, and aspiring mountaineer, Jeffrey Mere was a nice man. At sixty-four years of age, he lived in a nice stone, semi-detached cottage on a nice quiet street, in the town of Pitlochry, Perthshire. However, according to Agnes, his mother (ninety-one and counting), who lived in the old folks' home in town, nice was not all that it was cracked up to be. Nice was, in fact, the kiss of death for a single man of his age.

Jeffrey shared his cottage with a spoiled, agoraphobic cat called Ralf, a collection of vinyl records, and a set of days-of-the-week socks that Agnes had knitted for him. When he stood with his feet together he could see "Mon" stretched across the arch of the left foot and "Day" across the arch of the right. The same letters circled the ankle at the top of each sock.

Jeffrey's retirement loomed in nineteen days. Having never done anything particularly adventurous in his life, he planned to equip himself with everything he needed to climb Ben Macdhui, in the nearby Cairngorms. Technically, a mountain only had to be 600 meters, so according to Jeffrey's calculations, Ben Macdhui, the second tallest peak in Britain at 1309 meters, was a very respectable height. Besides, if Queen Victoria could do it — in a dress, no less — then so could he. Not in a dress, of course. But he could climb the mountain.

He'd never been very far from his home, but this trip would shake the nice right out of him, he hoped.

Jeffrey took out a small porcelain bowl and filled it with the only cat food Ralf would eat. He sat it on the tablemat, the only place Ralf would eat it, and tapped the spoon on the dish several times. As he waited for his elusive housemate to appear Jeffrey recalled his mother's reaction when he'd told her of his plans.

"It'll take mare than climbin' a mountain, laddie." She'd cackled, choking on the phlegm that permanently resided in her throat these days.

"Thanks for the vote of confidence, Mum."

"Sixty-four years and *now* you decide to venture outside your seventy-mile radius?" She cackled again. "Better late than never, I suppose."

Agnes was not cruel, exactly, she just saw life through stark, if impossibly thick, glasses. Jeffrey, on the other hand, always saw the rose-tinted best in people. He knew better than to hope for miracles, but he still believed in happy endings, even for himself.

The chart with his climbing plan hung on the wall behind the kitchen table. The map of the Cairngorm Mountains sagged a little in the middle, as he'd run out of drawing pins. He didn't care that he'd made several small holes in the wall. This was the time for throwing caution to the wind, after all. Lengths of red wool marked the route he was going to take, and little yellow flags, cut out of sticky notes and folded around cocktail sticks, showed the stops he'd make to rest and camp. He planned on spending one overnight on the way up and one on the way down. Several notes were taped around the edges of the map, listing all the items he planned to take with him.

Ralf sprang onto the table and, turning his fluffy backside deliberately towards Jeffrey, started to eat.

"Good boy," Jeffrey said, as he tossed the empty cat food can into the bin. "You'll be all right here for a few days, won't you?"

The cat ignored him and thrust his backside higher into the air, cleaning the last of the food out of the bowl. Jeffrey sat at the table and waited patiently; then, when Ralf jumped down, he picked up the bowl and put it in the sink. He was late for his visit with his mother, so he needed to get a move on.

Grabbing a packet of ginger snaps from the cupboard, he headed for the door. He never liked to go empty-handed to see Agnes, and she never liked him to arrive that way, either. She could be a crotchety old thing, but despite her sharp tongue, he knew she loved him dearly, as he did her.

"See you, Ralf," Jeffrey called into a vacuum. The cat was nowhere to be seen as he put his coat on and let himself out of the house. It didn't look like rain, so he wouldn't worry about taking an umbrella. Besides, he needed to get himself more conditioned to coping with the elements, as there'd be no umbrellas on his climb. Umbrellas were for tourists, anyway.

In twenty-three days, he'd be setting off. The walking boots he'd bought specially pinched and had rubbed two large blisters into his heels. One blister was filled with fluid and the other had burst, so every step he took hurt in one way or another. He supposed he should have started to wear in the boots sooner, but if he persevered and wore them daily for his walk to the old people's home, he was sure they'd feel like gloves by the time he left. Joe MacFarlane at the mountain sports store had assured him of that, and Joe had no reason to lie.

It was a bright evening, and he picked up his pace, despite the pinching boots. He'd only be five minutes late for Agnes, and maybe she wouldn't even notice.

"So it's late you are, is it?" Agnes sat in her favorite chair in the sunroom. A faded tartan rug was tucked around her bony knees. Her milk-bottle glasses on her nose, she hunched over her latest knitting project, a thick waistcoat for Jeffrey's climb. He'd told her he didn't need one because he'd bought an expensive fleece-lined walking jacket, but Agnes insisted that none of those fancy modern materials could beat Shetland wool.

When he'd protested, she'd waved a crooked finger at him.

"The weather on Ben Macdhui will dae ye in, if you havn'y got the right clothes."

Jeffrey knew she was probably, and infuriatingly, correct.

"So when are ye off?" Her needles clacked, along with her false teeth, as she spoke.

"Twenty-three days," he replied, smiling at one of the nurses as she passed the door.

"Aye well, I'll be finished by then." Agnes nodded at her lap and the growing pile of orange wool.

"Great," Jeffrey said.

"Tell me again why ye're doing this?" Agnes raised her eyes to his and her needles froze mid-purl.

"I've told you, Mum. I've wanted to do it for years, just haven't had the time." Jeffrey fidgeted in his chair.

"Aye." The needles moved again. "There's never enough time tae dae all we want tae, son."

"You're always saying I need to venture out, aren't you?" Jeffrey leaned over and wrapped his idle hand over her busy ones. "You OK, Mum?"

"Fine. Now, on ye go, I know ye're itchin' to get back to that bastard cat." Agnes cackled, then a hard cough rattled up through her ribs. Her torso quivered with the effort of refilling her lungs. A single tear made its way down her left cheek, and she wiped it away with a shaky hand.

"I can stay for a bit longer." Jeffrey watched as she slowly regained her equilibrium. He didn't want to leave. She seemed so small in the big chair, dwarfed by the wings on either side of her little white head.

"Aye. Stay a bit. You don't want to miss Mary, do you?" Agnes winked at him from behind her thick lenses, then smiled and bit into a new biscuit. Jeffrey shook his head at her and blushed.

Agnes liked Mary Ferguson. In fact, she was her favorite nurse at the home. She always took time to talk, and Agnes appreciated it. Mary didn't patronize her, either. She always called her Mrs. Mere, instead of "love" or "pet," and didn't shout when she spoke like some of the nurses did. She didn't try to make her eat cartons of cold custard, nor did she ask inane questions like "How are *we* doing today?" She addressed Agnes as an intelligent human being and even asked her opinion on things. Agnes liked Mary a lot.

She'd noticed the way Mary tended to wait around when Jeffrey was due to visit. Mary thought Agnes didn't notice, but she did. Not much got past her, even at ninety-one.

There were many things that irritated Agnes about getting old, but some things weren't so bad. It was annoying that her body betrayed her when her mind still felt so sharp. Her back and knees gave her trouble, her eyes played tricks on her daily, she didn't hear too well on the left side, and of course, the waterworks weren't what they used to be. One cup of tea was all she could handle, and then she'd have to hope no one made her laugh until she could make it to the bathroom.

On the upside, she got to read all day if she wanted, sleep in late, eat and drink whatever took her fancy, be quiet one day and opinionated the next. She could feign deafness if someone bored her and even pretend at sleep if she needed to avoid answering uncomfortable questions. Getting old had its perks, too.

Seeing Jeffrey shift uncomfortably in the hard-backed chair, Agnes took pity on her son.

"Nah, off ye go, son. It's fishcakes for tea, and Mary will be coming to get me presently. I think I'll have a nice bath tonight, then an early night. Nae mare Highland dancing for me." She winked, and her flash of humor released him. He kissed the top of her head.

"See you tomorrow, then, Mum." He waved as he walked out the door.

"Thanks for the biccies," she called back.

As he headed out into the hallway, Mary was walking towards the sunroom.

"Hi, Jeffrey. How's she doing out there?"

"Oh, OK. She's still got that nasty cough, though." He stared at his feet so as not to look Mary in the eye. She was always friendly towards him, but Jeffrey didn't want to mislead her. Mountaineers had to be careful of that kind of thing and keep their distance. There should be no shenanigans of any kind before a climb. Or did that apply to boxers before a fight, or maybe it was sprinters before a race? Anyway, Mary was lovely and all, but he had to stay focused at the moment. Ben Macdhui beckoned, and nothing was going to distract him from his mission.

As Mary watched his tall frame and broad back walking away from her, she sighed. So shy, and yet there was something intriguing about Jeffrey Mere. Mrs. Mere had told her that he was retiring soon. What would he do with all that spare time? Agnes had also mentioned something about Ben Macdhui, but Mary was sure the old dear had got it wrong. The little she knew about Jeffrey Mere so far would indicate that mountain climbing wasn't something he'd take to. Mary tucked a stray curl behind her ear, turned, and walked out to the sunroom. It was time for Mrs. Mere to eat something other than biscuits.

On the walk home, the rain battered down on Jeffrey. He wiped it from his glasses as he turned the corner into Willow Street. Momentarily annoyed at the betrayal of the weather, Jeffrey had finally resolved that this was nothing more than good training. After all, he needed to get used to being out in adverse weather conditions for the climb. He even considered walking around for a while longer, but at the thought of potentially catching a cold, he'd gone straight home. It was time for his tea, anyway, and Tuesday was his favorite dinner of the week: Scottish meat pie with baked beans and then a small bowl of vanilla ice cream.

Yes, Tuesdays were good days.

Ralf was, as usual, invisible when Jeffrey padded through the house. His Tues-Day socks were dry, but the bottoms of his trousers were soaked, and he left a snail-like trail across the kitchen tiles. The blister-making boots sat in the vestibule, banished to sit on the doormat until they dried out.

A wee dram would be just the ticket to warm him up, so Jeffrey turned back into the living room and poured himself a snifter to take up to the bath. His pie was warming in the oven, leaving him twenty minutes to soak in the warm water.

Once in the bath, Jeffrey placed his whisky glass on the wire rack that bridged the tub. Nestled between the lumpy loofah and a bar of soap, the inch of amber liquid was by far his favorite thing in front of him. A wet flannel lay heavy on his chest, and he wound the plug chain around one big toe, wondering if he could manage just one more twist before he pulled the plug out and the cooling water seeped away. The smell of his dinner meandered up the stairs. He was hungry.

Standing in his bedroom, Jeffrey wondered if 8:25 was too early for pajamas. He had no intention of going out again and wasn't expecting any visitors. Did he ever? Deciding it would be fine, he dressed in his favorite red tartan pair and, with his sheepskin slippers on his feet, made his way down the stairs.

As he passed the front door, he noticed something protruding from the letterbox. How had he not seen that when he got home from visiting his mum? Jeffrey pulled the yellow paper inside, and glancing at the thick print, he padded in to the kitchen.

"Come and meet your neighbors at a street party to celebrate the birth of Bonnie Prince George. Toast the health of the wee lad on Saturday from 6 to 8 pm. BYOB and see you there."

Jeffrey tossed the paper onto the table and went about preparing his dinner.

With his plate balanced on his knee, he turned on the TV. Tonight was *Antiques Roadshow* and then *Lonely Planet*. A fitting bill for his evening's entertainment, he thought, munching on his pie. *Antiques Roadshow* for an antique and *Lonely Planet* for… No, he stopped the thought. He mustn't be maudlin. He had a good life, a comfortable life. He had no complaints. Well, not many, anyhow.

As he scraped the last of the tomato sauce onto the last bite of pie, Jeffrey, not for the first time, wished he had someone to share his impending ice cream with. Walking into the kitchen, he recognized the lump of regret that still occasionally formed in his throat at moments like this. The lump was one of resignation, a physiological reminder of his surrender to the notion that he'd be alone for the rest of his days.

Shaking himself out of the daydream, he said out loud, "Silly to dwell." Besides, he had Ralf. Where was that cat?

CHAPTER 2

❖

Winding down Mere Accounting, in preparation for his impending retirement, had not been a complex task. As the sole employee, Jeffrey had occupied a small rented office above the dry cleaner's in the high street for the past twenty-eight years. It comprised one large room with rickety floorboards and a big bay window overlooking the town. He had use of a small kitchen in the hallway, which he shared with the only other tenant, Mrs. Freeman, a tailor.

He had informed all of his clients, six months before, of his planned closing date. He helped them all transition to new accountancy firms in good time for any upcoming deadlines, and he felt good about making sure they were all comfortable with their new situations. Only one client had refused to move his business despite Jeffrey's protestations. Sid Friendly, the owner of Friendly's Funeral home, was stalwart in his support of Mere Accounting. Sid said that he'd stick with Jeffrey until the very last day of his working life. Such was the quality of the service

Jeffrey had afforded him, and his business, over the years. Jeffrey, while flattered, had made light of things, asking if he might use his "good credit" with Sid to reserve two nice plots at the crematorium for himself and his mum. Sid had replied with a totally straight face.

"Absolutely. That's the least I can do."

Sid's response had popped Jeffrey's bubble, as he hadn't truly considered his mother's end, never mind his own.

Jeffrey walked along Belmont Street and headed for his garden allotment. It was Saturday. Only fifteen days to retirement and nineteen until his departure for Ben Macdhui.

Today he needed to check on his bees, as there was no nectar flow at this time of year. He had rigged up a feeding contraption at the opening to the hive and carried two large bottles of sugar water with him, swinging them in opposition to his legs as he walked. Jeffrey hummed a tuneless song and marveled at the lovely weather for the time of year. September could be wonderful in Perthshire, or it could be pure hell. Today was of the wonderful variety, and there was a lilt in his step as he thought about the day ahead.

Joe MacFarlane, from the mountain sports store, had called him the previous evening to tell him that the tent he'd ordered from Aberdeen had arrived. Jeffrey was excited to see it and hoped it was as good-looking in real life as in the catalogue. He couldn't afford to be seen in anything shabby, on the slopes of Ben Macdhui. He wanted to do the mountain proud.

Turning down Strathmore Street, Jeffrey swerved quickly to avoid a little girl on a pink tricycle.

"Watch out, wee one."

He jumped into the street to let her pass him on the pavement. The child's white-blonde pigtails were long and flapped over her ears. Her face was pink from both the breeze and exertion.

"Saw-reeeee." She called over her shoulder as, hunched in effort, she pedaled furiously away from him. Red tassels fluttered from each handle of her bike, and her little legs pumped with all their might.

Jeffrey chuckled to himself and continued on his way. He'd loved his own bike as a child, and until the Big Spill (as his mum had called it), he'd ridden it everywhere. He'd never been quite the same after the Big Spill and even now, all these years later, his jaw ached at the memory.

Jeffrey had been eleven at the time and riding hard on Coltness Road, heading home from the Boy Scouts for his tea. There was a stack of Buster comics he'd collected strapped to the rack over the back wheel, and his pullover was tied around his waist. His front wheel had been wobbly for a few days, but his dad had had no time to look at it, spending long days at the distillery, minding the huge copper kettles of whisky. His mum had the time to look, but no idea what to do with it, so he'd ignored the wobble.

Coltness Road was bumpy at the best of times, and Agnes was always telling him to be careful there. On that day the coal van had just driven along it, leaving a trail of dust and black pebbles in its wake. Jeffrey wasn't concentrating on the road too much as it was Wednesday, and Wednesday was fish and chips day. His mum would let him eat it out of the paper after he drenched it in malt vinegar. He could almost taste the bite of the vinegar when suddenly, his front wheel hit a lump of coal. He felt the jolt as the wheel slid out of its mounting, and in slow motion, Jeffrey went

12

barreling head first over the handlebars. He landed in a heap, the pavement coming up to smash into his jaw. The bike fell on top of him and as he lay, seeing the surface of the road under his right eye, he remembered pages of his prized comics fluttering silently down and settling over him like a layer of confetti.

He wasn't sure how long he'd lain there before the hurt started, slowly creeping through his bones. First it was in his right elbow, which was tucked awkwardly under his chest, then his right knee, which ached as if a thousand bees had stung him in the same spot. Then, it was in his jaw.

As he followed the pain, sprouting its achy rosebuds around his body, Mrs. Fraser, who owned the sweetshop in town, came running towards him, waving a tea towel.

"Oh my, Jeffrey. That was quite a tumble. Are you OK, love?"

Jeffrey remembered his manners, despite his discomfort, and tried to lift his head to tell her he was fine. The odd sensation that followed would remain with him to this day. With a herculean effort he'd lifted his head, but his lower jaw refused to come with the rest. It felt like an anvil, dangling under his face.

He managed to release his left arm and help Mrs. Fraser push the bike away. His hand went to his face and he gathered his jaw up and held it in his palm. This was weird. He tried to talk, to tell Mrs. Fraser that he was OK, but the sound that came out was more of a mew than a word.

Despite needing to hold up his bottom jaw, fear didn't take over from the pain until he saw Mrs. Fraser's expression. He'd heard of the color draining from people's faces, on TV and in books, but he'd never witnessed it until that moment. As she got a good look at his face she staggered, shoved the tea towel in her mouth and took two steps back.

"Oh, Jeffrey," she mumbled through the towel. "You poor wee thing."

With his free hand, Jeffrey pushed himself up to a sitting position. Coltness Road had started to spin in a disconcerting way and the sky was above him, then below him, then above him again. Mrs. Fraser knelt down beside him and put her chubby sweetshop-arm around his shoulder. She smelled of cinnamon.

"You sit still. I'll be back in a jiffy. Now don't move, do you hear?"

Jeffrey had tried to nod as the road continued to wiggle beneath him. It seemed like she'd been gone for an entire day by the time Mrs. Fraser came back. She was carrying a blanket and Jeffrey wondered why she was feeling cold, on such a nice day. As she reached him she draped the blanket across his shoulders and he had to admit, it felt good. Once it was wrapped around him he began to shiver.

"I called your mum, pet. She's on her way with the car."

Jeffrey tried to speak. Again the mewing came, instead of words. What about his fish supper? Would Mum bring it with her, so it didn't get cold or go to waste? Mrs. Fraser shushed him.

"Don't try to talk, love. Just sit quiet for now."

Again Jeffrey nodded, his hand remaining under his jaw. He knew if he let go, the bone would go crashing to the ground, like in a Tom and Jerry cartoon. As he tried to sit still, he noticed that his arms were shaking, each little judder causing new needles of pain to stab his face. He glanced over at his bike. It was badly misshapen. The bent frame sprawled brazenly, half on the pavement and half in the street. The front wheel was nowhere to be seen. As Jeffrey stared at what was once his favorite thing in the whole world, the twisted metal frame took on a new, sinister

14

significance. His trusty bike had let him down. Badly.

Three days later, as he lay in Pitlochry Community Hospital, his broken jaw pinned and wired, and his right arm in a heavy cast, fish and chips were the last thing on his mind.

The *tring-tring* of the little girl's tricycle bell snapped Jeffrey back to the present. Once again he stepped out into the street to let her pass him on the pavement. Her cheeks flushed, she raised a hand and waved.

"Thank yoooooou," she shouted, as she sped away from him.

"You be careful, now," he called after her.

The Big Spill had certainly been a whopper of a fall and had left him bike-less, and fearful, for the rest of that year.

CHAPTER 3

———◆———

Mary tucked the sheet tightly around the empty bed. Mr. McDougal had passed away in the night, and she felt the cold new absence in the room. She was always sad when the old dears gave up the ghost. No matter how long she worked in elder care, she never got used to it. She tried not to get attached to her patients but, it seemed, she was incapable of not making special connections and, inevitably, having her favorites.

Agnes Mere was one of those favorites. The old biddy was bright as a button, with a wicked sense of humor, and Mary had grown very fond of her. Mrs. Mere always had a ready snipe or gibe about one of the other old folk, which would have Mary giggling, despite her disapproval.

Mary looked forward to their chats and found the old lady interested in some surprising things. She often asked Mary to read the newspaper to her and then would wax lyrical about politics, the struggling economy, and the shocking price of petrol (though she had no car and hadn't driven in years). There had been an article in the *Herald* a few weeks back on the cave art found at El Castillo in Spain. Supposedly, Neanderthals had created the paintings. Mrs. Mere had told her that she'd always wanted to visit the Niaux Cave in France. When Mary asked about it Agnes had explained that it was one of the most impressive Paleolithic rock galleries in the world and was said to be 14,000 years old.

As Mary smoothed the bed cover, she recalled being deeply impressed, on more than one occasion, by the old lady's active mind. She also knew that Mrs. Mere was very keen that she get to know Jeffrey better. Mary did find him intriguing, if a little awkward and diffident. He was kind and patient, and obviously devoted to his mother. What would it feel like to have good a man, like Jeffrey, in her life?

Her history with men had been limited and unsuccessful. Her ex-husband, Jimmy, had been more eloquent with his fists than his voice, and the memory of his fits of anger and abuse still made her shudder. She'd lived in fear for seventeen years in their Glasgow tenement flat. Watching him walk up the path each evening, the set of his shoulders had been enough to tell her what kind of night she'd have. Would she be scraping stew off the floor and walls or laughing nervously with him at some inane comedy on TV?

There was no way she'd ever put up with a man who resorted to violence again. She had moved on from that, having relocated to Pitlochry four years before. After Jimmy had tracked her down to the hospital in Edinburgh where she'd worked for nearly two decades, she was proud to have escaped him once more and re-built herself a good life.

Agnes Mere was the only person in Pitlochry that she'd told

about Jimmy. He'd been a bad'un from the start. Her own mother had warned her against him, which of course served to propel Mary towards him with more force than she had herself intended. The forbidden fruit being predictably sweeter, she had dived into marriage at sixteen, after only a few months of courtship. Escaping from her revolting and lecherous stepfather, William, had just been a bonus. However, she'd learned to regret her decision faster than she'd ever dreamed possible, and the toll those years with Jimmy had taken was still visible to her when she looked in the mirror.

Mary glanced at her reflection in the window behind the bed. She wasn't bad for her fifty-six years, but she could see the shadows of the past in her face, even if no one else could. Life was cruel sometimes, but she'd survived.

She loved her job and this pretty little town, and now, after the long probation, typical of small communities, she finally felt as if she belonged. The old people's home was well-run and the people friendly. For Mary, it was a sanctuary that she enjoyed spending her days in. She prided herself in making all the elderly in her care feel valued and relevant. So what if she had a few favorites?

CHAPTER 4

The bees were quiet when he got to the allotment. He kept his hive here, rather than in the small back garden at home, as a service to all the gardeners whose vegetables and flowers grew next to his. The bees were their resident pollinators and everyone's produce flourished, thanks to their efforts. Jeffrey harvested the honey a few times a year and shared it with his fellow gardeners.

"Hello, bees." He spoke quietly. Bees didn't take to being surprised, and he had a healthy respect for their moods, having been stung numerous times over the years. He didn't hold with all that pricey equipment other beekeepers used. Jeffrey had an old netted pith helmet that he kept in the shed, along with a soft wide paintbrush and a pair of yellow rubber gloves his mother had been going to throw away. So far, this equipment had been adequate for his beekeeping, and until such time as it wasn't, he was quite happy.

Working slowly and methodically, he filled the feeder with the sugar water and replaced it, brushing a few curious bees gently back into the hive with the brush. Happy that they were safe and stocked with food, Jeffrey tucked his gloves and helmet away in the shed and walked home humming "Flower of Scotland." The boots were not so painful today, so things were looking up on that front.

It was another lovely day. The blue sky stretched overhead, and a light breeze ruffled his hair. As he turned back onto Willow Street, he was surprised to see people setting up folding tables. Some were wrapping lampposts and draping their doorways with Union Jack bunting. Others were dragging chairs out onto their driveways. Of course, today was the street party. He had forgotten about it completely. Perhaps it would be fun to go along for an hour or so? It had been a while since they'd done anything together, as a street, and he knew there were a few newcomers. He would pop into the corner shop across the road and get a bottle of wine.

Fred and Matilda from next door were hanging bunting around their window as Jeffrey approached.

"Jeffrey, are you coming out for a drink later?" Fred's round red face jiggled behind his glasses. If there had been call for a Santa Claus to make an appearance at the street party, Fred would be the man for the job.

Jeffrey raised the bottle of wine he'd just bought and waved it.

"Aye, I'll be there."

He smiled at Matilda, who looked lovingly up at her husband.

"I've got to go back into town in a bit to pick up my new tent, but I'll join you this evening."

"Super duper," Fred called at Jeffrey's back as he walked inside his cottage.

Saturday's tea was quick and easy. Roasted cheese with sliced tomato and then a strawberry yogurt. Not the boring kind, but one of the ones with the fruit at the bottom. His stomach rumbled as he deposited the wine on the kitchen table and called for Ralf.

The cat, as ever, was nowhere to be seen.

"Oh well, just you hide, then," Jeffrey called up the stairs.

The tent was waiting, so he'd worry about Ralf later.

Jeffrey had walked past Pitlochry Mountain Sports many times over the years. Never having ventured in before two weeks ago, it felt like a foreign country to him. As he walked inside, the tightly packed store was dark. The ceiling hung heavy with walking sticks, fishing rods, ski poles, and thick coils of climbing rope. Jeffrey ducked his head at the last minute to avoid a rather disturbing suspended mannequin in a full ski suit, helmet, and goggles, which threatened to decapitate him with its skis.

"Hello?" Jeffrey called out. Joe MacFarlane was nowhere to be seen.

After a moment or two, the shopkeeper popped up from behind the long display cabinet. Joe was a tall, wiry man. His thatch of silver hair and youthful piercing blue eyes, in contradiction to each other, made pinning down his age difficult. Jeffrey guessed he was in his late forties. A keen hiker and climber himself, Joe had been delighted to welcome Jeffrey as a new customer.

"Hello there, Mr. Mere. Come to collect your tent?"

"Yes, indeed. That came in quickly, didn't it?" Jeffrey leaned against the counter and removed his cap, laying it on the glass surface.

"Aye, it did. I'll get it for you now." Joe walked into the back room, through the door marked "Staff."

Jeffrey looked around the shop. There was so much equipment, most of which he had no idea what to do with. Joe had helped him put together a basic kit for the climb, as Jeffrey didn't want to be weighed down with too much in his backpack. Apart from the tent and his new boots, he was taking a sleeping bag and pad, a small camping stove, a collapsible pan and plate, a spoon, a penknife, a lighter, two water bottles, a battery-operated lantern, a travel toothbrush and paste, some toilet paper, some clean underwear, and four pairs of socks.

Joe had stressed how important it was to guard one's feet when climbing, so Jeffrey had taken his advice and bought some expensive hiking socks. He wouldn't tell Agnes, of course. She would only get upset at him spending money needlessly when she could have knitted him a few more pairs herself.

"Here it is, then." Joe emerged from the back room carrying what looked to Jeffrey to be a very small package.

"Is that it?"

"It is. Amazing how wee it looks in the box. The challenge of course is getting it *back* into the box when you're done." Joe laughed.

Jeffrey took the package. It felt so light.

"And the frame is in there too?" He looked at Joe.

"Of course. It's all there." Joe walked back behind the counter.

"Well, that's amazing." Jeffrey shook his head.

Twilight was settling as he got home. He tucked the tent safely into the cupboard under the stairs and called the cat. Ralf had to be hungry by now.

As he sliced some of his favorite extra-strong Orkney cheddar, Jeffrey's mind wandered. Next weekend, he decided, he would have a dry run. He'd assemble the tent in the living room, just to make sure he knew how to do it, before setting off the following Saturday. His departure date was coming around quickly, and the thought of his climb made his heart patter.

He should also lay out all his equipment and take inventory, make sure he had everything he needed. Suddenly, he remembered his camera. Grabbing a sticky note from the drawer, Jeffrey wrote CAMERA on it and slapped it onto the map on the wall. There were so many things to remember.

The cheese ran off the top of the toast, flowing onto the baking tray like cheddar-lava. Jeffrey stooped to watch it in the grill. He hated when the edges of the toast got burned. It was a delicate business, making good roasted cheese.

After preparing a steaming cup of tea, Jeffrey tucked in to his molten dinner. Ralf's food glistened in the bowl, smelling faintly of tuna, but as yet the cat had not materialized.

By the time Jeffrey opened his front door, most of his neighbors were outside. Fred and Matilda waved as he walked down his driveway, and Fred shook a wine bottle at him.

"Fancy a wee glass then, Jeffrey? To toast the bairn?"

Jeffrey nodded and accepted a glass of wine. He handed Fred the bottle he'd bought. "You can add that to the bar, too."

"Lovely, lovely. Will do." Fred's cheeks jiggled. "Cheers to Prince George then."

"Cheers. Here's tae him." They all tapped their plastic glasses and then took a sip.

"So, Jeffrey. How are you? Not long until you go off to conquer Ben Macdhui, eh?" Matilda smiled, her rotund, apron-covered body reminding him of a floral babushka doll.

"That's right. Just a couple of weeks away."

"Well, that's nice. I'm sure you'll have a wonderful time." She nodded, then sipped her rosé. Her feet, encased in checked woolen slippers, moved from a twelve-o-clock position to a ten-to-two position as she rocked backwards on her heels.

"I'll bake you some scones to take with you. Can't have you getting hungry, up the mountain." She sipped some more. The rosé was seeping up into her cheeks.

"That'll be lovely, thanks." Jeffrey smiled at the kindly woman. She'd always talked to him as though he were her son, when, in truth, there were only a few years between them.

"So, have you met the new neighbors in the street yet?" Matilda offered Jeffrey a paper plate covered in small, triangular sandwiches.

"Not yet." Jeffrey shook his head at the sandwiches. "I just ate, thanks, Matilda."

"There's that young Indian couple with the twins, over there, at number 56. Nice people, though I canny really understand him. Such a queer accent."

Jeffrey swallowed his wine and felt his cheeks warm. He had no reason to be, but found he was embarrassed by Matilda's gauche remark.

Undeterred, she went on. "Then there's that lovely nurse from the old folks' home. Mary, her name is." She nodded down the street towards the river. "Number 61. Moved in about two months back. Nice lady."

Jeffrey started at the name.

"Mary, you said?" He pulled at his collar and did his best to look uninterested.

"Aye, Mary Ferguson. She works at the old folks' home. She probably knows your mum?"

Jeffrey coughed and then took a big swallow of wine. How was it possible that Mary had moved to Willow Street and not told him? Didn't she know he lived here, too? If not, then surely his mum would have told her?

Jeffrey finished his wine in one more gulp. This was strange. He liked Mary, but he didn't really know her. Would it make a difference to the price of eggs if she lived on Willow Street? He wondered why he was feeling rattled by her new proximity. He looked around, suddenly feeling trapped and awkward.

As if to order, the strip of Union Jack flags around Matilda and Fred's doorframe flapped violently in a gust of wind. The edges of the paper plates on the table lifted skywards like corrugated wings, the sandwiches not heavy enough to keep them down. Suddenly, red-white-and-blue napkins, egg mayonnaise, and bread triangles were flying into the rose bushes that lined the driveway as Matilda let out a squeal.

"Oh, jeepers. Fred. Grab that. Och, nooo."

Jeffrey and Fred scrambled to pick up some of the sandwiches, laughing at each other as they piled the spoilt food back onto one plate.

"Oh, well. Just as well you'd already eaten, eh?" Matilda shrugged, deflated. "There was half a dozen eggs in those." Her face hung.

Fred reached over and silently patted her back.

"Sorry about that." Jeffrey wasn't sure what he was sorry for, the wind itself, or for laughing at the food catastrophe. Why did he always do that — apologize for something he had no control over? He really needed to stop that.

"Oh, to hell with the sandwiches." Matilda's smile was back. "Let's have a spot more wine."

Jeffrey spent another hour at the party. He walked all the way down the odd side of the street and back up the even side. There was no sign of Mary at number 61 or anywhere else. Her door had a Union Jack garland hanging on the knocker, but no other signs of life.

Jeffrey said hello to all the familiar faces he passed and introduced himself to the young Indian couple. He had to focus determinedly on the husband's mouth as the young man told him their name. He didn't want to ask him to repeat it more than twice. The Subramanians seemed a shy family who smiled a lot. The twins, a girl and a boy, circled him on their matching trikes, listening to the adults' conversation. Jeffrey noticed that their teeth were all marvelously white against the wonderful creamy amber color of their skin.

He'd have liked to have a more exotic complexion himself. His Celtic skin and pale blue eyes left him vulnerable to the sun, whenever it decided to show up in Perthshire. In the Indian summer of 1976 he'd been roasted, just sitting out in the park during the town fête. He'd learned his lesson that day, but at least sunburn was one thing he wouldn't have to worry about up on Ben Macdhui.

CHAPTER 5

———◆———

The day had come. Jeffrey was closing the office and handing back his keys to Frank Duff, the landlord. He recognized that he was both sad and excited as he picked up his ficus plant and briefcase and walked down the warped stairs for the last time. He knocked on Frank's door and waited.

"So you're off then, Jeffrey?" Frank stood in the doorway, his wool-clad stomach protruding farther into the hall than the rest of him.

"Aye. Today's the day, Frank." Jeffrey replied, shrugging behind the plant. "We're all square on the rent though?"

"Aye, certainly. We're all square." Frank nodded slowly. "We'll miss having you upstairs."

"Thanks. I'll still be around. Perhaps we can have that dram we've been talking about for years." Jeffrey laughed.

"We'll do that, Jeffrey. We will." Frank extended his hand. "Best of luck to you."

Jeffrey juggled the ficus. He was glad he had it to hide behind as he shook Frank's hand. He wasn't good at goodbyes.

"I'll be seeing you soon then, Frank. Thanks for everything."

Jeffrey walked along the high street. As he waited at the zebra crossing, he caught sight of his reflection in a shop window and smiled. He looked like a giant alien walking along, all legs and arms and leaves.

Today was Friday. Friday was breakfast-for-dinner day. He'd drop the ficus off at home, then pop over to see Agnes. If she was feeling chatty, he'd make it back home in time for *Coronation Street*. If she was tired, then he'd be home in time for the six o'clock news. Either way was fine by him, as he'd just be eating off a tray in the lounge.

"Ralf. I'm home," Jeffrey called up the stairs.

He dropped his briefcase under the hall table, then put the plant on the lounge windowsill. What would he take to his mum today? Scanning the kitchen cupboard, he spotted some Jaffa Cakes. Perfect.

When he got to the home, Agnes was in the sunroom again. Facing away from him, the top of her head was barely visible above the chair back. Her hair was purple. He could have sworn it hadn't been purple yesterday? He could see the ends of her knitting needles sticking out on either side of the chair as she worked away.

"Hi, Mum."

He walked around in front of her and patted her knee. Agnes looked up.

"Jaffa Cakes — yummy." She smiled a watery smile and shoved her heavy glasses back up her nose. "What's the time?"

"It's 5:15. What're you having for your tea tonight?" Jeffrey pulled a chair across the tiled floor and sat opposite her. The lavender hair was distracting.

"Is this Friday?" she asked.

"It is."

"Well, its gammon and pineapple then, isn't it?" Agnes resumed her knitting. "How long 'til you're off?"

"Next weekend, Mum. A week tomorrow."

"Right, well, y'er waistcoat is ready to try. I'll just cast off and you can see what ye think."

Jeffrey eyed the bulky orange heap on her knee and took a deep breath.

"Okie dokie," he said, standing up.

Agnes reached into the sewing basket at her feet for scissors. Snipping off the strand of wool, she held the article up in front of herself.

"Looks good to me."

Jeffrey took his jacket off and slipped the waistcoat on over his shirt. It was a good fit, if a little thick, but the Shetland wool prickled maddeningly, its scratchiness making him wriggle.

"Stand still, boy," Agnes snapped as she hauled herself up out of the chair. Standing at full height her purple head came up to the middle of his chest.

"Turn 'roon.'"

Jeffrey obeyed and then turned back again to face his mum. She tugged at the front, then yanked at the bottom of the waistcoat.

"Good fit." She looked up at him. "Just need to put the buttons on it, and it's done."

29

"Brilliant." Jeffrey slipped the waistcoat off and handed it back to Agnes, who was bending forward, her little backside searching for the chair. Jeffrey held her arm and settled her back onto the seat.

"So you've got everything you need, then?" She eyed him over her glasses.

"I do. I'm all set. I picked up the tent today."

"Y'er dad was a great camper. Never was ma' cup o' tea, though." She coughed, a rattling cough, then put her hand up to her mouth to nudge her teeth back into place. "Couldn'y be doin' with all the fuss. Packing this and that, cooking outside in the rain. Och, the rain just seeped into y'er bones." Agnes stared out the window into the little garden.

Jeffrey knew she preferred to sit in the sunroom, rather than in the common room with the big TV. She liked to watch people passing in the street. Beyond the road was the river. Sometimes, on sunny days, the swans would gather on the banks and laze about. She often pointed them out to him and remarked on their peaceful expressions.

Jeffrey looked at his mum. Drowning in the big armchair, she seemed to grow smaller with every visit these days. Was she shrinking? He'd once called her Mrs. Pepperpot and had received a cuff to his ear in return. He'd not make that mistake again.

"You know, the best holiday we ever had was in Oban. Dae ye remember, son?" Agnes's voice was wistful. Not sounding much like Agnes at all.

Jeffrey looked at her, the super-thick glasses heavy on her little nose, the false teeth that seemed to have become too big for her face, the new purple hair. Was this tiny creature his sturdy mum, the same woman who'd have taken on a drunken dockside worker if he'd threatened her family?

"I do remember, Mum. That was the year of the sandcastle competition, right?"

Agnes nodded and wiped a single glistening tear from her left eye.

"Aye. That was some marvel you and y'er dad built. Looked like Scone Castle." With that, she giggled and rocked back and forward a little in the chair. "That wee woman was steamin' when her boy got second place for his stupit sand mermaid." Agnes's eyes wandered back to the riverbank. She seemed transported into the memory.

Jeffrey laughed and patted her knee.

"I do remember her. She was a nasty piece of work."

Mother and son laughed together, and the moment became suspended in time. Neither of them wanted to leave it and return to the overly warm room, which was now beginning to smell of gammon.

"Jeffrey?" She was staring at him.

"Yes, Mum."

"You know y'er going to be fine, son, don't ye?" She scanned his face.

"Of course. I've got all the right equipment, a good map, the right shoes, I'll be absolutely fine."

Agnes was still, her eyes not leaving his face. Slowly, she nodded, and he felt as if her small smile was a private one that he'd caught sight of by mistake.

"Aye. Ye'll be fine." She reached out and put her tiny hand over his. "Ye're a good boy."

Jeffrey smiled at her. She was getting sentimental in her old age.

"Well, I'd better be off, Mum. Got to feed the cat. I'll see you tomorrow, OK?"

Jeffrey rose and put his jacket on. "Don't scoff all the Jaffa Cakes at once." He winked at her.

"That'll be right. Ma stomach'll revolt if I dae." Agnes picked up the waistcoat and folded it into an orange cube on her knee.

"Thanks for the waistcoat, Mum. It'll be great for Ben Macdhui."

She waved him away.

Having been dismissed, Jeffrey padded out through the hallway and nodded at the receptionist. They were very good about letting him come and go, to visit. There were official visiting hours, he *was* sure, but for some reason they didn't seem to apply to him.

"Jeffrey?" The voice came from behind him. Turning around, he saw Mary.

"How's she doing today?" She stood close to him now. He could smell lily of the valley.

Mary was quite a tall lady. Had he noticed that before? Standing in front of him she almost looked Jeffrey in the eye. With her red curls like a bright cap on her head, her eyes a startling green and a smattering of freckles across the bridge of her nose, she was a Celt through and through.

"Oh, she's fine. Just getting a bit sentimental." Jeffrey nodded towards the sunroom.

"Oh, really?" Mary stood her ground and watched his face. "All OK, though?" She sensed his mild concern.

"I think so. She's just reminiscing a lot these days."

"That happens." Mary nodded as she spoke. "Shouldn't worry about it too much." She reached out a hand and placed it lightly on his arm.

"Yeah. Thanks. I mean, I won't. Thanks." Jeffrey stuttered. She was touching him. What was he supposed to do now?

Mary, feeling his discomfort, dropped her hand.

"Well, I'd better let you go, then."

"Right, well, I'll see you tomorrow, then." He made to leave, then stopped and turned back. "Oh, Mary, I heard you'd moved to Willow Street. Is that right?"

She nodded. "I did. A couple of months ago."

"Well, welcome." He smiled and felt his face suddenly warm. "Hope you'll like the neighbors."

"Oh, I think I will." Mary winked, raised a hand in goodbye, and walked away.

CHAPTER 6

—◆—

A week later, all Jeffrey's equipment lay strewn around the living room. The tent was holding court in the middle of the floor, the coffee table having been shoved against the radiator. He had to admit, it looked impressive. Like a giant red-and-blue beehive with a zipped door panel, it had long red flaps that would be pegged snuggly into the earth. His cooking equipment and clothes were also lying in neat piles on the floor, and his clothes, all freshly laundered, were folded into another pile. He felt ready. He'd told his mum that he'd be checking his equipment, but she hadn't seemed terribly interested.

Agnes had been a bit maudlin that day. He frowned. Something was up with her, but he couldn't put his finger on it. When he'd arrived to see Agnes, Mary had been talking to her in the sunroom. Their heads had been close together, and he'd felt as if he were intruding. As he got closer, he guessed they were talking about him.

"He's never been the type to take risks," Agnes whispered.

"Well, there's a lot to be said for caution and reliability." Mary replied.

"Aye, well, good that ye think so, lass." Agnes nodded her little purple head and at that, Mary had looked up and seen him.

"Oh, Jeffrey. Ears burning?"

"Apparently, they should be?" Jeffrey winked as he spoke.

"I'll go and let you chat to your mum. See you later." Mary put a hand lightly on his shoulder as she passed, like she was handing the Agnes-baton to him.

"Bye, Mary." He watched her walk away, and felt oddly lonely.

Agnes had not been very talkative, so his visit had been brief. He'd left a packet of custard creams for her and beaten a hasty retreat, knowing he had to do his inventory. He worried about leaving for Ben Macdhui, but knew Mary would keep an eye on Agnes for him.

He'd arranged for Matilda to come in and feed Ralf while he was away, and he'd take care of the bees himself before he left. All else could wait for the triumphant hero's return. He smiled to himself and began gathering his equipment to take back upstairs. Now, how did the tent come apart again?

Two hours after Jeffrey had left her, Agnes shifted in the floral armchair in her room. She wanted to see the nine o'clock news, but she also wanted to write a letter. It was a very important letter, and Mary had said she'd help by bringing her some nice paper and an envelope. Not the thin stuff they gave you here at the home. That stuff you could spit peas through. She wanted something good quality, that held up well over time. This was a letter that she intended Jeffrey to keep.

The sky was already black outside, and glancing at the clock, she saw it was 8:50. Her little TV screen flashed, dragging her gaze from the window, and Agnes tutted at the parade of nonsense they put on these days. There were hardly any good programs anymore. Thank god for the mute button.

Mary went off shift at nine and had promised to stop by before she left. Agnes looked anxiously at the door.

Mary knocked as she walked into the room, breathing heavily. She looked at her watch. "Sorry. I'm cutting it a bit fine, aren't I? I wanted to get here earlier, but Mr. Smethers took a bad turn, and we had to call an ambulance."

Agnes cackled. "There's nothing wrong with that auld bugger. He just likes all the attention." She pushed her errant teeth back into place and patted the bed for Mary to sit.

Mary perched on the edge of the thick mattress. The pink bedcover trailed on the ground as the bed sagged a little.

"I can't stay long, but I brought the writing paper." She handed Agnes a small white plastic bag. Inside were four sheets of ivory-colored paper and a single envelope, all with a thin gold line around the edge.

"Oh, lovely." Agnes smiled. "You're a gem. How much do I owe you?"

"Nothing. It's no bother at all," Mary replied, adjusting her bag on her shoulder. "I'd better get going, though. Are you OK until tomorrow?"

"I'm fine, love, thanks." Agnes smiled, her glasses reflecting the TV screen as she watched the younger woman walk towards the door.

"Got a hot date th'night then?" She winked at Mary.

"No." Mary giggled. "I should be so lucky. Just a date with my washing machine."

"Och, never mind. Maybe tomorrow, eh?"

"Maybe tomorrow, Mrs. Mere. We live in hope." Mary waved over her shoulder as she left.

Agnes pulled the heavy paper out of the bag. This was perfect. Tonight she'd skip the news and write her letter.

Mary strode down Willow Street. The wind was picking up and her coat, which had seemed like the right choice when she'd left the house at lunchtime, felt light and inadequate. She was probably just cold from weariness. It had been a long week, and she was glad she had a couple of days off coming soon. She needed to sleep late, read the paper in her dressing gown, and watch all the recorded TV programs she loved. She also needed to wash her windows, catch up on letter writing, and pay some bills.

As she passed Jeffrey's house, she slowed down. Not that she was nosy, but the lights were on, and Jeffrey seldom pulled his curtains, she'd discovered. He was standing in the living room. Just above the windowsill she could see something blue and red. It looked like the top of a tent. As she moved under the street-light, Mary ducked her head, hoping he wouldn't notice her watching and think she was spying. He looked happy. He was nodding and his lips were moving. He seemed very pleased with the tent. She smiled to herself as she realized what he was doing. He must be testing it out for Ben Macdhui.

As she continued into the shadows, Mary looked back over her shoulder. He was a sweet man, Jeffrey Mere. What you saw

CHAPTER 7

Jeffrey tapped the bowl with a spoon again. The cat food was turning rancid, and he wanted to go to bed.

"Ralf? Last chance, boy," he called into the silence.

No response.

Jeffrey stirred his hot chocolate and gradually turned off the lights as he moved through the hall and up the stairs. He had four days until leaving for Ben Macdhui on Sunday, and he wanted to take Agnes to Inverness for a nice lunch on Friday. She didn't get out that much anymore, and he knew she loved the steak and kidney pie at the Fort Hotel on the Black Isle at Inverness. Last time he'd taken her there, she'd vacuumed up the pie with a pile of mushy peas and chips, then had eaten a large plate of sticky toffee pudding and custard. To his amusement, she had washed it all down with a pint of Guinness. He chuckled to himself at his mother's capacity for food. She was a waif of a thing with the appetite of a sailor. She could swear like one, too, if pressed.

Yes, Agnes was quite a woman.

She'd really become his hero after his father had died. Jeffrey had only been fourteen when it happened. No one had expected Angus Mere's forty-eight-year-old heart to stop. Certainly, no one had expected him to fall headlong into one of the huge copper whisky kettles at the distillery, poaching himself into the bargain. Jeffrey was sure his dad would have been mortified at spoiling an entire batch of the precious fluid, had he known.

So, at forty-one, Agnes had become a widow but, despite her heartbreak at losing her best friend, she'd pulled up her proverbial bootstraps and moved on. She'd gone to work at the fishery so they could stay in their house, and had tried to maintain as normal a life as possible, for Jeffrey's sake. He missed his dad terribly, but with Agnes there, staunchly in his corner, he'd never felt neglected. She wasn't the lovey-dovey kind of mother, but he knew she cared for him deeply.

As he walked into his dark bedroom, Jeffrey flipped on the light switch and noticed a lump under the duvet. Had he left his hot water bottle in there? He placed his cup down on the bedside table and patted the lump. A shrill meow made him jump.

"Jeepers, Ralf. What're you doing?" He laughed and pulled back the quilt. The cat lay low on its stomach, its ears folded flat against its head in protest at the disturbance. Glaring at Jeffrey, Ralf slowly resumed his toilette, working at his front legs with his tiny pink tongue, while a dark oval hairball glistened beside him on the sheet.

"Charming." Jeffrey shook his head. "Thanks, friend."

When Jeffrey came back from the bathroom with a wad of tissues, Ralf was gone. Having disposed of the gooey gift, he climbed into bed. He was too tired to change the sheets now, so he slid over to the other side of the bed, taking his hot chocolate with him.

He propped himself up against the pillows. The room felt different from over here, the door farther away and the window closer. As he stretched his feet out towards the end of the bed he wondered, as he had many times, what it would feel like to share it with someone. How would it feel to see a person curled up next to him, perhaps stealing the covers or even snoring? How strange it would be, and yet, how wonderful. The pillows over on his usual side lay flat and pristine. Feeling tired, and resigned to his customary aloneness, he drained the mug and set it on the bedside table.

Just four more nights and he'd be sleeping on the mountain. He felt sure that he'd not feel lonely there, out in nature, surrounded by great hills and valleys, the starry sky stretching overhead. He'd not be lonely then.

In the corner of the room, his tent and sleeping bag lay on the floor, his boots standing to attention next to them. He'd always loved camping. He and his dad had gone on several trips, leaving Agnes at home. They'd pack Angus's little Ford with the ancient canvas tent and rusty camp stove. Their sleeping bags always smelled of camphor from the mothballs Agnes insisted on storing with them in the attic. Jeffrey was in charge of map reading, and Angus would stick red dots along the route they planned to take to make it easier for him to trace. They'd sing car songs like "Ten Green Bottles" and "Old MacDonald" and count the Highland cattle along the way.

Another of Jeffrey's responsibilities had been to administer ginger biscuits and salted crisps, which he'd cram into Angus's mouth while his dad kept his eyes on the road. Once they'd eaten through the pile of cheese-and-pickle sandwiches Agnes always packed for them, Jeffrey would pick out all the yellow and orange Opal Fruits for himself and save the red and green ones for his dad. Those were happy times, and Jeffrey had loved having Angus's undivided attention.

This would be the first time he'd ever camped alone, and up to now he hadn't actually considered that fact. His new sleeping bag smelled of the mountain sports store; the little stove was unused and shiny and the tent smart and clean, no mud caked onto the pegs or holes in the netting over the door. Would it feel the same? Whatever it felt like, he was sure it would be great to finally do this, to make the climb. Somewhere deep inside, he knew that Angus would be proud of him for doing it, too.

Jeffrey leaned over and switched off the light. He'd sleep well tonight.

CHAPTER 8

—◆—

Agnes licked the envelope and pressed down hard on the seal. The letter was done, and she felt a lightness in her heart that had been missing for a while. When a body has something on their mind, it's best to get it out; that's what Angus had always said. He'd told her that things bottled up would fester and rot their container from the inside out. Agnes smiled at the memory of her husband and glanced at their wedding picture on the chest of drawers. She'd been robbed of Angus far too soon. It had been difficult not to be bitter but she'd done her best and overall had had a good life — and she'd had Jeffrey.

He'd seemed excited tonight; his trip was approaching and she noticed him fidgeting in the chair. She knew he wanted to get home and so had remained mostly quiet during his visit, letting him think she was tired. He'd kissed the top of her head as he left, and she'd smelled the Lux soap he favored. Jeffrey was nothing if not a creature of habit, and she'd have died from shock if he switched to another brand or did something radical like comb his hair in the opposite direction. That just wouldn't be Jeffrey.

This trip he'd planned had come as a bit of a shock. Agnes had tried not to be snarky when he first mentioned it, believing that it would go the way of the holiday in Spain he'd talked about eight years earlier, but never took, or the theater weekend in London he'd planned but didn't go on.

This time, however, things were different. He really seemed to be set on climbing Ben Macdhui, and Agnes, better than anyone, knew what a huge step this was for her son. She wondered if Jeffrey even recognized that himself. She also wondered if he knew that this was the sign she'd been waiting for for a long time. Jeffrey was finally taking steps, moving outside of his microcosm. He was being bold for the first time since he was a young boy, for the first time since the Big Spill. As she thought of him climbing the mountain, she visualized him walking away from her, his back heavy with a pack. Would he turn and look back?

The colder nights were drawing in, and she shivered. She needed to get those buttons on the waistcoat. Mary had bought them for her in town, and they sat in a brown paper bag on the table. She'd stitch them on in the morning, as her eyes were tired now. Tomorrow would do fine.

CHAPTER 9

Jeffrey helped Agnes out of the car and, with a hand tucked under her arm, steered her back inside the home. Mary stood in the hall and smiled at them as they walked in.

"How was lunch?" She stepped forward and took Agnes's extended hand.

"Brilliant." Agnes nodded as she spoke. "Best steak and kidney pie in Scotland."

"Good to know." Mary giggled then said, "Did you not bring me any back?"

Agnes looked up sharply, suddenly concerned. Mary patted her hand.

"I'm kidding, Mrs. Mere. Relax."

Agnes let her shoulders drop.

"Och, I should'a brought you some. The pud' was the best, too."

"Stop torturing me." Mary laughed as they walked slowly

towards Agnes's room.

Jeffrey watched his mum's small rounded back and marveled at the obvious connection between the two women. As soon as Agnes had spotted Mary, he was all but forgotten. He was glad of it even if, at times, it made him feel superfluous. He knew Agnes needed a friend aside from himself, and he was glad Mary was that friend. If he could have chosen a companion for his mum, he couldn't have done better than Mary.

He trotted behind them, wanting to talk to Agnes before he left her. Mary was waiting to help her into her chair for a nap.

"Can I have a minute with my mum, Mary?" Jeffrey stood on the doorway.

"Aye, sure." Mary smiled and slipped past him into the hallway. "Don't keep her too long, now. She's done in." She spoke quietly, close to his ear.

Jeffrey crouched down opposite his mum as she leaned her head back against the chair. Her eyelids were heavy with fatigue, but her eyes were smiling behind her glasses.

"I'm stappit foo'." She patted her non-existent belly.

"No idea where you put it, Mum. There isn't a pick on you." Jeffrey smiled.

Agnes looked at him expectantly. She was tired and wondered what he wanted to say.

"Are you OK, Mum?" Jeffrey scanned her wrinkled face.

"What de ye mean?" Agnes eyed him.

"I mean, is everything OK?" He frowned.

"Aye, lad. Everything's fine. I'm just tired." She nodded as she spoke, as if convincing herself of the truth of her own words.

"Would you tell me if anything was wrong?"

"What wi'd be rang? I'm fine, I tell ye. If ye'd let me get to ma nap, I'd be even better."

Her familiar cackle once again reassured him. Perhaps he was imagining her silence and uncharacteristic solemnity of the past few days? She seemed OK now, and her appetite was certainly as healthy as ever.

"Well, see you, then. I'll be in tomorrow afternoon, and then Sunday morning I'm off early, so it'll be Tuesday before I'm back. OK?"

Her mouth gaped in a yawn then Agnes stuck her chin out as her eyes slid downwards, silently addressing his feet. Jeffrey obediently pulled up his trouser legs and showed her his Fri-Day socks. She nodded her approval.

"Night, son."

He kissed the top of her lilac head and left her to her nap.

CHAPTER 10

Jeffrey's equipment was all packed and ready. The bees were fed, Matilda had his door key, Ralf was nowhere to be seen, and his boots were on his feet. All was as expected. As a tribute to Agnes he wore his Sun-Day socks under the hiking socks Joe MacFarlane had sold him. His waistcoat was folded into his backpack, and he checked his old Boy Scout compass and the battery on his new mobile phone one more time. He'd taken Joe MacFarlane's advice and bought the phone for the trip. It wasn't something Jeffrey had felt the need for before, as he never went very far from home and when he did he'd always relied on maps for navigating but, as Joe rightly put it, if he got into trouble up on the mountain, a map wouldn't be much good to him for getting help. Joe had made sure to show him the points where he'd get reception, and Jeffrey had marked them on his map. He'd left his number with Mary in case Agnes needed him while he was away. It was only two and a half days in all, and he planned to be back at the home before she had her tea on

Tuesday.

He'd promised to go straight there so he could tell her all about his adventure. He packed his Tues-Day socks specially, as he knew she was bound to check what he was wearing as soon as she saw him.

It was eight am and a bright day. Jeffrey had eaten three eggs, some bacon, two slices of toast, and an apple to set himself up for the journey. He was excited as he packed the boot of his Mini. The map was folded on the passenger seat, and a paper bag with six scones Matilda had baked that morning sat on the back seat next to the rest of his food. He wondered how long the scones would last, bearing in mind that he could smell their floury goodness through the bag. It was something odd that always happened on car trips. He could eat an entire meal, then get into the car and be looking for something to munch within a few minutes. Perhaps it was simply boredom? Or perhaps it was just the proximity of the food, conveniently sized and packed, making it irresistible? He wasn't sure, but he was sure the scones wouldn't make it to Ben Macdhui.

With a full petrol tank, a full boot, and a full heart, Jeffrey drove towards his first port of call, the Cairngorm ski center, where he'd be logging his climb and leaving the car. The weather report was encouraging, light winds and good visibility for the day. He knew that could change, and quickly, but for now, there was nothing standing in his way.

The sixty-five-mile journey to the ski center was over in a snap and aside from getting stuck behind a tractor pulling a trailer of hay, for a good ten miles, Jeffrey had had a relatively clear run. He hadn't wanted to hassle the farmer, so he'd sat quietly behind the trailer, keeping a safe distance. With his window cracked, he had enjoyed the fresh scent of the hay. Strands of it blew onto his windscreen, but he didn't mind. It was all part of the journey, and he smiled to himself as he watched the scenery begin to change around him.

The gorse thinned out as he passed, and the hard edges of fences gave way to the beautiful symmetry of dry stone dykes. Low shrubs along the verges shivered in the breeze, and behind them, gentle hills that swept away from the road grew gradually closer, gathering momentum and transforming themselves into steeper and steeper slopes, blanketed in lush green. The remains of the season's pink and purple heather, scattered here and there, provided a touch of contrasting color.

Jeffrey was aware of the increase in altitude when his ears popped. He only stopped once, next to a crystal-clear waterfall that tumbled down a rock face next to the road. He poured himself some hot tea from the thermos he'd packed and, of course, sampled Matilda's scones, which were as wonderful as he'd expected. She'd sliced each one and filled them with slivers of butter and a generous helping of strawberry jam. The eating of them was a little messy, but the resulting sticky fingers and chin were totally worth it. He saved three of the half dozen, but knew they'd be gone by the time he pitched his tent that night.

The trees along the way were bending slightly, leaning away from the breeze. The sun shone weakly, and Jeffrey kept his eye on the gathering clouds overhead. They looked ominous, but he was determined not to let the potential for rain spoil his mood.

At 10:10, having parked in the upper lot at the ski center, Jeffrey noted that the wind had picked up quite a bit. On the first stage of his climb, the trail that would take him to the summit of Cairn Gorm ran to the left of the funicular railway. Jeffrey watched groups of people moving around, many of them circling their cars and adding layers of clothing, waterproof jackets, and hats. There were several groups pushing mountain bikes, calling to each other and nodding politely as they passed him.

Outdoorsy people generally acknowledged one another, or so he'd heard. He supposed it was a bit like dog owners, always smiling and saying hello to other dog owners they encountered on their walks, as if they were all part of some secret society. He smiled at the notion that *he* was now part of an elite group, being a hill walker — no, a mountaineer. For some reason, his legitimacy inside a clique made him feel valuable, more so than he ever had before.

As a shiver made its way up his back, he was glad of the extra clothes he'd thrown into the boot at the last minute. Opening his backpack, he rummaged around inside, his fingers instantly feeling the scratchiness of the woolen waistcoat. He pulled it out and slid it on over his sweater. Even with Agnes's bulky orange creation on, he still had plenty of room inside his heavy outer jacket. He stuffed his gloves in his pockets and his woolen hat and a long scarf into his pack. As he looked around at the wonderfully dark, towering peaks topped with snow, his excitement grew.

Locking the car, Jeffrey checked his equipment one last time and then, hoisting his pack onto his back, set off to register at the ski center.

As he started his ascent, the trail climbed a steep ridge. He quickly felt his heart rate pick up and, within a few minutes, was timing his strides with his breaths. Taking long and steady steps, keeping the pack in the center of his back, as Joe MacFarlane had told him to, he walked on.

He passed two other hikers and four young men on mountain bikes. *Rather them than me. Too tough on the legs to bike up this hill.*

By the time he'd reached the 850-meter marker, the terrain had softened, the slope becoming gentler. Jeffrey looked at his watch. It was 11:06, and as he only planned on going as far as the summit of Cairn Lochan before setting up camp for the night, he felt confident that he had plenty of time.

Before he set off, he'd checked the weather forecast again on his phone, as Joe had showed him. Apparently, the chance of wind gusts of up to 50 miles per hour was 62%. That could be a problem. As he looked at the landscape sweeping and rolling around him in giant folds of green, his excitement became tinged with fear. What had he been thinking? He should have chosen an easier climb for his first attempt. Could he, and his tent, withstand a 50 mile-per-hour wind? Jeffrey felt a film of sweat suddenly coat his face, and he pulled open the collar of his jacket. Was this whole thing a bad idea? If he turned around now, he figured he could make it back before dark. He could go home, unpack, and stay put until Tuesday. No one need even know he was there.

As he thought about hiding out inside his cottage, an image of himself crawling combat-style, slithering on his stomach under the lounge window flashed before his eyes. A laugh broke loose from his throat, taking him by surprise as it floated away down the hillside. He had not come all this way to turn back at the first hurdle. He'd get himself moving, and if the weather got too bad, then he'd just set up camp earlier in one of the sheltered saddles between the peaks. He'd be fine, he hoped.

Jeffrey packed away his map and set off again. He surveyed the path ahead, which cut through the starkly beautiful landscape. This route would take him close to the edge of the cliffs, so he needed to keep his wits about him and focus on enjoying the scenery one section at a time. After all, he didn't want to miss anything on his way up.

Time passed unnoticed and, mesmerized by the landscape undulating beneath his feet, he picked his way through the crystal streams that ran down from Coire na Sneachda. This was exactly how he'd imagined it. This was why he'd come.

Jeffrey stopped intermittently to take pictures. Agnes would want to see this, and he wanted to keep a visual journal of his climb, both for her and for himself to enjoy over and over again. He imagined them sitting in the sunroom at the home, sipping tea and eating ginger snaps while he talked her through the series of shots, describing each section of the ascent and descent. She'd enjoy that.

As the climb became gradually steeper, Jeffrey's heart began to patter under his waistcoat. A wave of heat rose up his chest, and he considered shedding his jacket, but then thought better of it. He'd read about how easy it was to suffer from hypothermia, even at this time of year, so instead he dampened his handkerchief in the stream, dabbed his flushed forehead, and wiped the back of his neck, letting the cool touch of the fabric refresh him. His boots were feeling only slightly heavier on his feet than when he'd set off, but as far as he could tell, they were not rubbing additional blisters into his newly hardened heels. All seemed well in the boot universe.

By 12:49, he'd reached a rubble-covered plateau that seemed like a good spot to stop for a bite of lunch. Jeffrey shook off his pack and settled himself on a flat slice of rock. The wind did seem to be picking up. Should he check the weather forecast again, or wait until he was closer to Cairn Lochan? Deciding that he needed to refrain from draining his phone battery, he resolved to have faith that Mother Nature would not go out of her way to thwart his long-awaited adventure. Well, not this soon, anyway.

Checking the map, he confirmed that he was on the westerly summit of the cairn. While the wind nipped at his earlobes, reminding him who was boss, Jeffrey chewed on one of the doorstep-thick cheese-and-pickle sandwiches he'd packed and sipped water from his bottle. Why did food always taste so much better outdoors? With each cheddary swallow, he visualized his masticated lunch smothering the mild concern bubbling up in his belly. He wouldn't let his angst about the weather spoil his enjoyment of the beautiful view over the corries towards Loch Morlich.

Despite the wind bringing the temperature down, the sun still shone bravely between clumps of clouds. As he packed away his water bottle, Jeffrey's full stomach relaxed. He could do this.

He knew he needed to continue south and keep following the trail towards the summit ridge of Cairn Lochan. As soon as he felt himself tiring, he'd pick a good spot to set up camp, making sure to give himself time to pitch the tent, explore a little, sort out some hot food, and get settled before the mountain drew the curtain of darkness around itself. He'd read that mountain darkness was thick as treacle, leaving one in no doubt that nature had the upper hand. He felt a rush of excitement at the prospect and another simultaneous twinge of fear in his stomach.

CHAPTER 11

———◈———

Jeffrey forged on, and the clouds gathered more closely overhead. He glanced up nervously every few steps, and as his
temperature gradually rose inside his heavy clothes, his anxiety
followed suit. Recognizing the signs of increasing panic, Jeffrey
focused on breathing steadily in and out of his nose (another
tip from Joe MacFarlane) until he gradually felt his equilibrium
return.

Before long, he could see the summit of Cairn Lochan ahead.
The leeward side would offer him more shelter, so after checking the direction of the wind, he headed left towards the Lairig
Ghru. His pack was feeling extremely heavy now, and his feet
hung like boulders on the ends of his shaky legs. It was time to
set up camp, eat something, and rest.

He picked his way carefully across the rocky terrain, hoping
for an easy ascent, but the pitch was steeper than he'd expected
as he got closer to the Lairig Ghru. His breathing became more

labored, so he unzipped his jacket. Just as he was beginning to think of turning around, the landscape flattened slightly, and on his right a tidy little plateau, just big enough for a camp, offered itself up to him. A nearby stream added the required element he was looking for, making this an ideal campsite. Flooded with relief, Jeffrey moved towards it, scanning the ground to see if he could successfully pitch his tent. It looked as if he could tuck himself in close to the base of the peak behind and be protected from the wind that was now gusting past him worryingly.

With each blast of cold mountain air, Jeffrey felt himself propelled forwards, as if a big cold hand in the small of his back was pushing him on. Suddenly, his feet were lifted slightly from the ground and he skipped forward a step or two to steady himself. He was top-heavy. His large pack, reaching beyond the top of his head, threatened to topple him over.

Catching his breath, he laughed out loud, imagining the comic scene (had anyone been watching) of this lone climber falling flat on his face in the rocks, pinned down by his unwieldy backpack. He pictured his own arms and legs squirming from beneath the bright orange pack like those of a giant spider in its death throes.

Setting up camp was fairly quick and mercifully smooth. The tent basically assembled itself, like a pop-up igloo. Once he'd secured its tapered fingers deep into the ground with the six long metal pins and the wiry guy ropes supplied for the purpose, Jeffrey crawled inside to sort out his stove and cooking utensils. He then unrolled his bedroll and sleeping bag. He hadn't slept in a sleeping bag since he was a boy, and the thought of wrapping himself up in it like a cozy pupae appealed to him as the sides of the tent were suddenly buffeted in towards him.

Once his provisions were stacked neatly, and his bedroll

prepared, Jeffrey shoved his camera into one pocket and his phone and headlamp into the other. He pulled his hat over his head, put his gloves on, and tied his scarf snugly around his neck. It was time to explore and take some snaps that he could share with Agnes. What would she be doing now? Glancing at his watch, he saw it was 3:03. She'd have had her lunch and would more than likely be snoozing in the chair in the sunroom. Sunday lunch was her favorite.

As he wriggled through the opening of the tent, thinking about Agnes, Jeffrey could almost smell the old folks' home, the oppressive heat mixed with the perpetual smell of cabbage that permeated the entire place. How was it that that cloyingly sweet cabbage aroma made its way into everything, when they only cooked it for the residents once a week?

He'd heard that as people aged, their bodies became less capable of disposing of sugars. Apparently some foods, like wheat, literally fermented inside them, giving off a sweet odor from the skin and on the breath. He'd noticed that lately with his mum, but had been too polite to mention it. Besides, what was she going to do about it? At ninety-one, she wouldn't be interested in a cleansing high-fiber diet or any of these newfangled colonic treatments. At the thought of his mother's colon, Jeffrey shuddered. What on earth was he thinking?

Standing up to his full height, he stretched out his back. The wind seemed a little less fierce now, and looking around him, Jeffrey breathed in his surroundings. With the map tucked safely inside his jacket, he set off towards Cairn Lochan.

The summit of Cairn Lochan was totally worth the scramble. As he was in no particular rush, Jeffrey had taken his time and enjoyed the views stretching out around him as he climbed the gravelly slope. By 4:45, he was sitting on a slab of rock looking down on what many called God's country. Well of course, anyone from Scotland knew that this *was* God's country. Why would he or she want to be anywhere else?

According to his phone, sunset was estimated at 4:58, so his timing was perfect. He pulled his camera out, and as if in response, the cliffs began to glow an eerie red in the fading light.

South of his position, the Cairngorm plateau slipped gradually into the darkness below. As he clicked the shutter on some shots that he hoped would make Agnes nod her head in approval, Jeffrey felt a sudden sadness. He worried about his mum. She rarely complained, but he knew that she struggled these days. Her arthritis gave her terrible pain; her eyes were shutting down, making reading, and her beloved knitting, increasingly difficult. Even her new hip (replaced nine years ago, but Agnes still referred to it as new) ached when she walked now. She'd told him that it was a strange thing to be trapped inside a decrepit body when the mind wasn't ready to be done with you.

She kept herself busy with knitting and played Scrabble with Mary during her shifts, but he knew that her restricted existence frustrated her. She had apparently told Mary that the world was shrinking and that sometimes she felt crushed by its walls coming in towards her. He was grateful to Mary for telling him that, but in some ways he wished she hadn't. It was one thing to suspect that Agnes wasn't entirely happy, but quite another to know it for sure.

His mother was a bright woman with an inquiring mind and more fortitude than anyone else he knew, but despite his best efforts, he couldn't find things to interest her anymore. He'd tried to get her to look at his new phone with him, to no avail.

"What the hell di' I want wi' that thing?" she'd snapped. "Tek' it away."

He'd asked her if she wanted him to bring her books on tape, but she'd laughed at him, saying that her hearing was worse than her eyesight, so she'd stick to the large-print paperbacks, thanks all the same.

He wished there was something he could think of to get her out of herself a bit. He missed the forceful woman who'd bullied him countless times into trying new things. But that Agnes existed back before the tables had turned, before he had become the carer.

Scanning the horizon, Jeffrey watched as the redness of the mountains bled slowly sideways into the surrounding sky. The colors changed before him as he took picture after picture, hoping that his battery wouldn't run out before he captured this incredible sight. The sky over the Munroe Range was on fire and he, Jeffrey Mere, was here to see it. Who'd have thought it? This magnificent display of nature was worth all the worry, the planning, and the momentary fears he'd felt. This was perfection.

Using the map, he pinpointed the peak of Ben Macdhui. It seemed to glow even redder than the surrounding hills, as if deliberately drawing his attention. It was clearly showing its reluctance to surrender to the darkness or to allow the moon to rise behind it, sending its slopes into the creeping shadows.

However, the persistent moon rose in the south, and as the final slivers of red faded from the sky, Jeffrey shivered. It was a full moon tonight, the perfect time to be here, and another nod to his meticulous planning. As the silver button glowed in the sky, Jeffrey rose and stretched out his legs. There was light enough to see clearly so, stuffing his camera away, he turned and headed back towards his tent.

By 5:50, he was descending the low gravel slope towards the plateau where he'd set up camp. He could see the top of the red-and-blue tent as it bent dangerously in the wind. It struck him as odd that higher up on Cairn Lochan, there had been less wind than down here. It was strange how mountain weather worked. Joe MacFarlane had warned him about that, and so had the various books he'd read. Jeffrey knew not to take anything for granted in the mountains, either here or up on Ben Macdhui the following day.

Feeling ready to shed his boots and break out his evening meal, he stepped over a gap in the rocks and approached the tent. Unless his eyes were deceiving him, right in front of the entrance lay a long dark shadow. It stretched across the width of the tent, flat to the ground, rising towards the front much as a wedge of granite might. Jeffrey slowed to a stop and held his breath. The shadow moved, raising its large head up from the bulk of the body. As he focused his eyes on the dark form, he thought he saw a tail stretching around the side of the tent.

The ancient forests, rivers, lochs, and glens of the Cairngorms were home to several rare and endangered species, and he had hoped to spot a red squirrel, or perhaps an elusive capercaillie, on his climb. This creature, whatever it was, was way too big to be either of those. It was likely not a reindeer either, as from what he could see, there were no antlers on that huge head.

He'd read about rare sightings of wildcats up here, but surely he couldn't be so unlucky as to come across one of those today? Standing still, Jeffrey tried to focus his mind on what to do next. He suddenly had an overwhelming desire to talk to someone, to let someone know where he was and what was happening. Who would he call? No point in calling Agnes, or even Mary, as they couldn't help him out of this particular jam. Would his phone get a signal here? The ski center at Aviemore would be closed now, and before Mountain Rescue could get to him, he could end up wildcat fodder. He'd make a nice meaty dinner for this one, if it so chose.

His heart clattered in his chest. Knowing he had to do something, with his eyes fixed on the dark shape, Jeffrey slowly lifted his left hand and slid it into his pocket. He pulled out his phone as carefully as he could, but despite his efforts, the flap of his jacket caught on it. As if in slow motion, his lifeline fell from his gloved hand, bouncing on the rocks at his feet. Damn — now he'd have to bend down and get it. His heart raced towards a new crescendo as he looked down, frantically scanning the ground for the familiar shape of the device. Just then, the creature heaved itself up on its four legs and waited, standing its ground. Jeffrey watched as its tail began to move menacingly from side to side.

Now, Jeffrey knew as well as anyone that when a cat wags its tail, that's not a good sign. Ralf only wagged his when Jeffrey bathed him in the kitchen sink or was changing the litter box.

Jeffrey concentrated on not moving as the creature took a tentative step. The moonlight was casting great shadows around him, and he struggled to focus on the animal, trying to make out its shape more clearly. Suddenly, it bolted forward. Jeffrey turned to run, but his foot slid into a crack in the rock beneath him. His body tumbled forward, and he felt the impact on his elbow as he landed hard on his right side. Instinctively raising his arms, he wrapped them around his head, protecting himself from the claws and teeth that were about to bear down on him.

He heard the footfalls, heavy and close. He held his breath.

This was it. Within a few seconds, the creature was at his side. He could smell its rancid breath, and feel it as well, moist on his hands as they cupped his face. If he had been one to pray, this would have been a good time to do that.

Just as he was readying himself for the excruciating pain of his predator tearing into his flesh with its hungry teeth, he felt a wet tongue on his neck. There was no pain, just an odd musky smell and then cold wetness. Terrified, Jeffrey lay motionless. The creature continued to bathe him with a rough tongue until Jeffrey felt a heavy paw placed on his side. Suddenly, the licking stopped, and as there had still been no tearing or clawing, he gingerly lowered his arms.

Sitting next to him on the rock was a massive dog. Its coat was long and matted, and damp dreadlocks hung over its face, all but obscuring its eyes. Its feet were the size of tea plates, and the one that it had placed on his side remained there, heavy and insistent. The dog was sitting down, and its tail swished slowly back and forth across the gravel. If he'd been one to give thanks, this would have been a good time for that, too.

Rolling slowly onto his back, he shrugged the massive paw away and then sat up cautiously. The dog stayed put, watching him through its dreadlocks.

"OK. Good dog." Jeffrey spoke tentatively, and in response to his voice, the dog's tail wagged more vigorously.

Feeling slightly more confident that he was not going to be torn limb from limb, Jeffrey pushed himself backwards a little, craving some air that didn't smell of wet dog.

"Well, you're a grand beast, aren't you? Where did you come from, eh?" He kept his voice low and even.

The dog remained still, watching, as Jeffrey slid his feet

underneath himself and slowly stood up. He carefully put weight on his twisted ankle and was relieved that he could stand on it without too much pain. He had to get back to the tent, so as the dog seemed friendly enough, he made his move.

As he walked towards the red-and-blue igloo, the dog rose and padded behind him. When it stood up, its head was almost level with Jeffrey's waist, which he calculated was approximately three and half feet from the ground. This was a big dog, indeed.

"You can't come with me, pup." He leaned down and spoke to the top of its head. "You need to go home now."

No sooner were the words out than Jeffrey realized how ludicrous they sounded. Go home? Here they were, at almost 1100 meters. The only other people he'd passed had been down on the initial slopes, the mountains having felt as if they belonged exclusively to him since then. There had been no lodges, camps, or homes to speak of since he'd left Aviemore.

Looking down at the shaggy coat, Jeffrey noted the absence of a collar. Disappointment gripped him, as he had hoped to find that this large, forlorn soul belonged to someone. He felt sorry for the creature, and as he walked carefully back to the tent, he let his hand drop to his side until it made contact with the matted shoulder. The animal didn't pull away; on the contrary, it leaned into Jeffrey's hand, increasing the pressure of the connection. Jeffrey felt his heart twinge. The poor thing. Who knew how long it had been up here, wandering around, lost and alone.

As he reached the tent, Jeffrey felt his stomach rumble. He was suddenly starving, and as a big gust of wind shoved him abruptly toward the entrance, he reached down and unzipped the door.

"Well, night-night, then." He crawled inside the tent and turned around to see the dog sitting down. Two dark eyes were focused on him as the beast slowly lowered itself onto its stomach, front paws extended, sphinx-like. Gradually, the dog's big head came down and rested on its front paws, and it exhaled loudly through its nose. Blinking under the matted hair, it studied Jeffrey intently.

"I'll be closing the door now." Jeffrey reached for the zip. "You take care."

The dog lay motionless, barring the tip of its tail that twitched as the cold wind gusted over the long body, parting the dirty hair along its back.

The zip went around smoothly, closing out the night, and Jeffrey quickly turned on his travel lantern, casting a yellow glow inside the tent. With a shiver, he located the little stove, a can of soup, and the fold-away pot. He needed to get something warm inside himself, and then he'd settle in for the night.

The soup was tomato. He emptied the can into the pot and set it on the stove. Joe MacFarlane had suggested packet soups, but Jeffrey hated the powdery stuff, so had plumped for cans, despite the extra weight. He'd swithered as to what flavors to bring, but tomato and cream of chicken had won the day. He'd keep the chicken for tomorrow's evening meal, along with the last round of cheese-and-pickle sandwiches and the packet of HobNobs.

Large pink bubbles popped across the surface of the soup as the edges of the pot gathered heat. Jeffrey ate two sandwiches while he was waiting. The last of Matilda's scones would make the perfect pudding, with a nice cup of mountain water from the flask he'd filled earlier. The smell of the soup reached his nostrils, and he stirred the thick liquid with his spoon. As he set the tin mug on the edge of the stove, something moved in his peripheral vision. He turned to see the shape of the dog pressing itself along the outside of the tent. The animal made its way around to the sheltered side and appeared to lie down, wedged between the tent and the base of the mountain.

Jeffrey felt more than a touch of guilt as he poured the hot soup into the mug and then carefully wriggled inside his sleeping bag. His boots stood at the doorway and his hat, scarf, and gloves were neatly folded on top, ready for the morning.

He sipped the scalding soup, burning his tongue.

"Damn," he said into the night, his breath escaping in a thin smoky wisp.

It was colder outside than he'd thought September would be, so as he waited for the soup to cool down a little, he decided he'd put on some extra socks and another sweatshirt so that he could sleep.

He unzipped his sleeping bag and crawled over to his backpack. As he reached inside it to find his extra clothes, the heavy body of the dog rolled towards him, making the side of the tent bow inwards. The wind was whistling now, plucking the tent's thin guy ropes into a weird song. Underneath their ethereal voice, he thought he could hear whining and as he watched, the bulk of the dog shifted, apparently curling up into a smaller ball. There it was again, the whining.

Jeffrey moved over to the entrance and unzipped the door just enough to stick his head out. The wind was bitter and cut into his exposed face like an ice pick. He knew that dogs were hardy creatures, many of them used to sleeping outside in all weather. However, this dog didn't seem to be used to the biting wind, obviously seeking shelter with the only human being within several miles. What was he to do? Could he leave the poor thing outside all night? Would he be able to live with himself if he found a big, frozen, shaggy carcass in the morning? Shaking his head, Jeffrey unzipped the flap completely and called into the wind.

"Come on. Come inside, then."

Instantly the dog roused itself, rounded the tent and scurried in the door, almost knocking Jeffrey off his knees.

"Whoa, there. Take it easy." Jeffrey chuckled at the cold, damp creature, disheveled and shivering inside the tent. Its head reached almost to the roof, and its big dirty feet were planted squarely on top of Jeffrey's sleeping bag.

"Hey. Get off there." He reached over and grabbed a handful of fur, pulling the dog off his bed. The creature complied, moving to the opposite side of the tent, then, accepting this as its place, curled up in a tight ball. With its nose tucked under one paw, it eyed Jeffrey.

He closed the flap again and returned to his bedroll. Just as he was about to pull on his sweatshirt, he spotted the scones. The mutt must be hungry. How could he sleep knowing that its stomach was empty, while his was full of sandwiches and soup?

Jeffrey grabbed the scones and crawled back into bed. His soup cup still steamed as he lay the paper bag by the side of the bedroll. He opened it up and pulled out a scone.

"Are you hungry, pup?" He reached out his hand towards the dog, the floury round balanced on his palm.

The big mutt raised its head and sniffed the air.

"Come on. You can have it." Jeffrey shoved the scone closer to the dog's muzzle.

Crawling across the gap between them on its stomach, the animal tentatively sniffed the scone, then stuck its pink tongue out to lick it.

"Take it. It's OK."

The dog picked up the scone in its teeth and, in two fast gulps, swallowed it whole.

"Well. You were hungry." Jeffrey laughed as the animal licked it lips. Even Agnes would have taken four bites to demolish a whole scone.

"All right, then. You can have the other one, too." Jeffrey reached into the bag and gave the last scone to the dog. It took it gently from his hand, and the last of Matilda's masterpieces vanished into the shaggy mouth.

Realizing the mutt must be thirsty, Jeffrey poured some water into the pot he'd heated his soup in. He swirled it around, then crawled over and unzipped the door a crack. He carefully poured the soupy liquid out on the ground, away from the entrance. The icy wind pulled at his hair, making him shudder as he closed the tent flap. He filled the pot again with clean water then placed it under the dog's nose. The animal drank deeply and messily then raised its sodden nose, leaving a trail of droplets on the ground-sheet.

Jeffrey got back into his bed. Then, feeling compelled to pat the dog's head, he leaned over and extended a tentative hand. Unsure whether the animal would welcome his overture, he hesitated; then, much to his surprise, the dog shuffled on its belly across the floor and shoved its head up under his palm.

"There you go," Jeffrey said, patting. "Settle down now and get some sleep."

The dog, seeming to understand, lowered itself down next to Jeffrey's bedroll and, turning its back on him, resumed its ball-like position, nose under paw.

Jeffrey moved the lantern up near his head so he could read. He wanted to be sure to remember to turn off the lamp, so as not to waste the batteries, as he'd need it tomorrow night as well.

Snuggled inside the heavy bag, Jeffrey soon felt the warmth his body was generating permeate all the way down to his cold feet. The dog lay heavy against his side, but he found its presence comforting rather than annoying as he lifted his book and began to read.

Outside, the wind gusted and the little tent's guy ropes whistled and sang, but Jeffrey felt fine. In fact, he felt better than he could remember feeling in a very long while.

CHAPTER 12

Jeffrey woke at 4:10 am. The dog was still by his side, breathing heavily into the damp atmosphere of the tent. Sunrise was estimated for 5:20, and he hoped to find a good spot on the mountainside from which to witness the start of the new day. As he shifted inside his sleeping bag, Jeffrey marveled at his internal alarm clock. How did the body know to rouse itself at a certain time, with no specific external stimulus? It was a mystery indeed, but a useful one.

He wriggled out of the warm bag, noting that he had slept remarkably well, considering the hard ground under his bedroll, the noise of the wind, and the fragrant and unexpected guest he'd acquired. He pulled on a clean pair of hiking socks, then his Mon-Day socks over the top. It was only right to give a nod to Agnes on the next day of his climb.

He'd brought plenty of bread and some tea bags for his two breakfasts. A packet of bacon and a jam jar of milk were wrapped in an ingeniously thin cooling sleeve that Joe had recommended. He also had a bag of dried apple slices and a tub of raisins. It was definitely time to eat.

Jeffrey picked up the pan and mug, then shimmied outside the tent to wash them in the stream of icy water pattering down the side of the nearby slope. The morning was still dark and chilly, but the mountains were clearly visible around him. The view promised to be just as impressive today as it had been in the blood red of the sunset the night before.

As he walked around the tent to the south side overlooking the glen, Jeffrey caught his breath. Clouds were literally floating, like a great fluffy river, through the Lairig Ghru, hundreds of meters below him.

Squinting into the distance, he felt excitement rise at the thought that he might actually witness an inversion. As his *Mountain Climbing for Beginners* book had informed him, inversions occurred when an overlying layer of warmer air prevented the colder air underneath from rising. Sometimes, at high altitudes, cumulus clouds could become trapped, condense, and spread out under the warm inversion layer, forming an eerie white carpet. The mountaintops would be visible above the layer, like ghostly pyramids rising out of a fog. Even seasoned climbers weren't often lucky enough to see this natural phenomenon. He'd seen pictures of it, but hopefully today he was going to take some of his own.

Hurrying back to the tent, Jeffrey decided to eat the remaining sandwiches rather than waste time cooking. He drank two cups of water and stuffed a somewhat dry triangle of cheese and pickle into his mouth as he gathered the equipment he'd need to climb Ben Macdhui. He really wanted to see the inversion from up there, to look south from Britain's second-highest peak and soak in the wonder of the experience.

While he moved around the small tent, the dog roused itself and scratched its ear.

"I've got to go, pup." Jeffrey patted the big shaggy head and, quickly opening the HobNobs, laid four on the ground in front of it.

"Come on — eat your breakfast."

The dog nudged the biscuits with its nose, then picked them up surprisingly delicately, eating them one at a time. It licked up all the remaining crumbs, then looked at Jeffrey expectantly.

Confident that he had everything he needed, Jeffrey crawled outside the tent with the dog close at his heels. He closed the flap securely and, checking his phone, map, compass, water bottle, and camera, nodded to himself and slung the pack on his back. He was all set.

After making a pit stop to relieve himself — where, much to his amusement, the dog followed suit — Jeffrey filled his two water bottles and headed south. The climb would only take about an hour, and all being well, he'd be at the summit by 5:15, just in time to find a good spot to see the sunrise hitting the promised inversion.

The dog stayed a few paces behind him as he climbed. Jeffrey remained focused ahead and, with intermittent checks of the compass, felt confident that he was on track. This was going to be a great start to a great day, perhaps the greatest day of his life, when he made it to the top of Ben Macdhui.

With a light breeze and the morning chill surrounding him, Jeffrey started to whistle "Flower of Scotland." It was a cheery tune, one that always made Agnes smile. He whistled in time with his steps and before he knew it, he was approaching the summit. The sun was beginning to rise, sparkling tantalizingly across the massive peaks stretching west across the Lairig Ghru. With the top of Ben Macdhui within his grasp, Jeffrey felt his heart grow light and the backpack even lighter. His legs felt strong, the boots were like a second skin, and even his Mon-Day socks felt good inside them.

Stopping to take in the spectacle before him, he ran a hand over his rough chin. He'd not thought to bring a razor, but for once in his life, he supposed it didn't matter if he went unshaved for a day or two. He was sure the mountain would not take offence. Perhaps he'd even grow a beard? Some of the greatest mountaineers had beards, after all — think of Sir Edmund Hilary. Jeffrey chuckled to himself and pulled his hat lower over his ears as the breeze bit at them. He swiped at his nose with the back of his glove, then reached down and stroked the dog's head.

"You're a good dog," he said, smiling at the mutt as its tail swooshed from side to side, tapping the back of his boot.

"Let's go then, eh?"

Jeffrey adjusted the pack on his shoulders and set off up the last few yards to the summit.

As he crowned the mountain, what he saw brought a prickle to the backs of his eyes. The inversion was like nothing he'd ever witnessed before. The sea of clouds beneath him, stretching north of the summit, was everything he'd hoped for. It looked like he could have stepped out onto it and walked his way across to the horizon.

Reaching his arms out wide from his sides, Jeffrey took a deep breath. The cold air felt raw in his lungs, and his hands tingled.

He stomped his feet and let out a yell.

"Helloooooooooo world. This is Jeffrey Mere here."

The dog jumped at the sudden noise and began circling Jeffrey's legs excitedly.

"Don't worry," he laughed. "Everything's all right."

In response, the animal dropped down on its front paws, leaving its backside up in the air, and barked.

"Well — you have a voice too, eh, lass?" Jeffrey ruffled the dog's rear end and then turned his attention back to the spectacle below.

An hour and dozens of photos later, Jeffrey felt his backside numb from the hard mountain beneath it. Up to now, any discomfort had been forgotten in the magic of the sights and sounds of the morning. The sun was now fully risen, and the mountains glowed in the soft yellow light of the new day.

The dog lay close to his side and snored unabashedly. The animal was so trusting, so accepting of its fate, that Jeffrey, for a moment, wished that he could take a leaf out of its book. Why must he worry about life so much? Why did he turn away from things he'd like to do, finding reasons and excuses not to do them? Life was short and too precious to waste on *what ifs* and, worse still, *if onlys*. As he watched the light build across the mountains around him, Jeffrey resolved to make changes. He'd take more risks like this one, make bolder choices, and to heck with the consequences. He'd made it this far unscathed, after all. The world was his for the asking, and Jeffrey planned on asking.

At the thought of this diversion from the norm, Jeffrey imagined Agnes's reaction. She would undoubtedly cackle when he told her of his revelation. She'd maybe even mock him, doubting his sincerity. But deep down, he knew that, despite all her teasing, she wanted him to live more boldly. However, he also knew that behind her rolled eyes and muttered rebukes was the shadow of fear that with each step he took outwards, she might lose him to the world. The idea that his mother was afraid of being alone cast a momentary shadow over his jubilant mood.

Shaking the dark thought from his mind, Jeffrey inhaled deeply. He would make her proud of him yet. Even in his sixties, he could become the son she'd hoped for and could brag about to her friends. It was never too late to change, and he knew that he wanted to — not only for Agnes, but also for himself.

Feeling the cold seep up into his back, Jeffrey rose, then bent down to touch his toes. It was good to stretch out the taut muscles and feel the pull down the backs of his legs. Resigned to leaving this spectacular perch, he turned and made his way down the mountain. Nothing had prepared him for the wonder of what he'd seen, and nothing could ever erase the memory he'd made.

The dog trotted behind him, sliding down the loose gravel slopes. Jeffrey kept an eye on it, making sure it stayed close by. Within forty minutes, he saw the top of the tent and smiled to himself. He'd made it up Ben Macdhui, and he felt sure that life would never be quite the same again.

CHAPTER 13

❖

The second night passed as peacefully as the first, the wind having dropped and the temperature remaining steady. Jeffrey and the dog had snored happily together after a warm meal of soup, toast, and bacon, all washed down with copious amounts of tea. They'd shared the remaining HobNobs, and Jeffrey had read out loud from the *Mountain Climbing for Beginners* book until they both fell asleep.

The following morning, with the tent disassembled and everything stored away in his backpack, the two companions made their way swiftly down the mountain. Jeffrey only began to worry about what to do with his new pal when he saw the Aviemore ski center ahead. He'd have to report the dog as lost, and he wondered if they'd have any facilities to care for the mutt until its owners could be found.

Reaching his car in the upper car park, Jeffrey unloaded the backpack into the boot. It felt good to be without its weight on his back, but he also missed it instantly. It had made him feel grounded and purposeful, carrying his home on his back for a couple of days.

He patted the pack down flat and closed the boot; then, beckoning to the dog to follow, he walked towards the ski center. He was sure he probably smelled a bit ripe, having had no shower for two days, but as long as he kept his jacket on, he shouldn't offend anyone.

He saw that a tiny woman wearing a National Park Service shirt manned the information desk. Her eyes peeped, owl-like, from behind thick glasses, and her ruddy complexion spoke to her love of the outdoors.

"Can I help you?" She looked up at Jeffrey and smiled.

"Good morning. I climbed Ben Macdhui yesterday." Jeffrey heard the statement leave his mouth and instantly blushed. He was sure he wasn't the only first-time climber to have been so full of his own accomplishments, and that this woman would probably laugh at his childlike blurting.

She looked at him for a second or two, then said kindly, "Well, congratulations. And didn't you pick the perfect day for it, with that beautiful inversion and all?"

Jeffrey nodded and cleared his throat.

"I was wondering if you could help me? I came across this dog, up on Cairn Lochan. She has no tags or collar and seems to have been up there a while. She's pretty dirty and thin." Jeffrey looked down at his side, but the dog was gone.

The lady rose and leaned over the desk, looking down at Jeffrey's feet.

"Dog?" She sat back down and stared at him.

"Yes. She was here a second ago." Jeffrey turned and scanned the long reception area, searching for the matted animal. There was no sign of her.

"She must be outside. I'll go and find her and come back." Jeffrey turned and walked out to the car park. Pacing up to his car, he expected to find the dog sitting there, possibly curled up into a ball, maybe even asleep as it waited for him to return. But his companion was nowhere to be seen.

Suddenly worried, Jeffrey weaved his way between all the parked vehicles calling to the dog. "Here, girl. Where are you, lass?"

After a few minutes, he spotted a family unpacking bikes from a camper van and walked over to them.

"Excuse me. Have you seen a big shaggy dog anywhere around? She was with me, but she's disappeared now."

"Sorry, mate. Huv nay seen any dogs th'day." The man replied as the woman silently shook her head and shrugged.

"OK, well, thanks." Deflated, Jeffrey walked back to his car. Where on earth had it gone? He hoped to goodness that no one had backed over it by mistake. Could it have run away down to the main road and been hit by a car? A wave of sadness and loss took him over, and he crouched down on his haunches. How daft to be so affected by a stray mutt. It hadn't been his to start with, but now, at the thought that it was gone, Jeffrey felt oddly bereft.

Two hours later, having had no luck in finding his messy pal, Jeffrey filled in a small white card for the notice board in the center. With a heavy heart, he wrote:

LOST DOG!! Very large with a brown coat. No distinctive

markings. No collar. If found please call J Mere 01632 963811. Thanks!

As he pushed the drawing pin into the soft board and straightened the little card, Jeffrey was annoyed that he hadn't taken even one picture with the dog in it. If he had, he could at least have left a photo with the center in case someone found the dog after he'd gone.

Resigned to his pal having left him, Jeffrey returned to his car and, stowing his heavy jacket in the back, set off for home. As his Mini bumped down the road, he resolved to call the ski center in a day or so to see if the dog had turned up. Further to that, there wasn't much he could do. It was time to get back to Agnes and share his experiences with her. He knew she'd love the snaps of the sunset and, of course, the magnificent inversion.

As the road slipped gently by him, the landscape transformed itself from the wild spareness of the mountains to the flatter, more managed lowlands. Pitlochry was only fifteen miles away now, and he felt a tingle of excitement about getting home. He considered going back to the cottage and taking a shower first, but then decided to go straight to the old folks' home, as he knew Agnes would be watching the clock and expecting him. He had so much to tell her, and with a flush of his newfound confidence, he imagined their conversation, her response to the pictures, and her admiration of a job well done on his part.

Half an hour later, as he walked into the home, the atmosphere was heavy. It was oppressively hot, as always, but this was different somehow. There was no one at the reception desk, and as it was Tuesday, Jeffrey thought it odd. Had the desk been abandoned on a Sunday, he'd have understood that.

Making his way past the desk, he turned right, heading down the corridor to the sunroom. Agnes would probably be out there knitting, waiting for him.

Just as he was about to open the glass-paneled door, he heard his name. He turned around to see Mary walking towards him.

"Jeffrey, you're here." Mary held her hand out to him. He thought it frightfully formal, but reached out as if to shake hers in return, when she suddenly clasped his tightly between both of her own. It felt nice, but was not how she usually greeted him. He'd only been gone two days, so this was quite a welcome. Perhaps he needed to stay away more often, if this was how it turned out?

"Jeffrey, I'm glad you're back. Can we go into the day room for a wee chat?" Mary had not let go of his hand. Her face looked flushed and her eyes watery.

"Sure — but hadn't I better say hello to Mum first?"

"Come with me, Jeffrey. Let's sit down for a minute."

For the first time since walking in the door, Jeffrey felt a pinprick of worry. Why was Mary delaying him like this? What was going on?

Settling herself in an armchair in the day room, with its densely flowered wallpaper and mismatched furniture, Mary sniffed into a white hanky.

Jeffrey lowered himself into a chair opposite her and took a deep breath. He knew now, with shattering clarity, exactly what was going on.

"She's gone, isn't she?" His voice flat, Jeffrey watched as Mary nodded silently and wiped her nose.

Just as it had started to make its presence felt, his shiny new "climbed-the-mountain" confidence circled the room like a balloon that had been burst, wheezing and spluttering around him until the empty membrane settled on the floor at his feet.

Tears flowed freely now over Mary's cheeks, and she gulped ferociously, trying to control herself.

As he watched, having no words to offer her, Mary straightened her back, ran a hand through her hair, then lifted her gaze to his.

"She passed away on Sunday night. It was very peaceful, Jeffrey. She'd had her dinner, and we played Scrabble for an hour or so, then she said she was tired. I was on a late shift, so I helped with her bath and tucked her into bed." Mary looked at his impassive face, clearly gauging whether she should continue. Jeffrey nodded, mutely, letting her know to keep talking.

"She wanted me to read to her for a bit, which I thought was unusual, but it wasn't a problem. We read a few pages of the Sunday *Telegraph*. I left her around nine pm. She just slept away. The night nurse, Ginny, checked on her at ten, and she'd gone. They called me back in, and I met with the doctor on call. It was declared natural causes. Her heart just stopped." Mary was sobbing now.

Jeffrey rose and walked over to the chair. He knelt down in front of Mary and wrapped his arms around her. She leaned forward, dissolving into his shoulder, and as he felt the wetness of her tears against his neck, Jeffrey's own dam broke. They clung to each other and shared their sadness at the loss of a woman they had both loved.

He wasn't sure how long they were in the day room, or how long he'd knelt, holding Mary, but gradually they pried themselves apart and made their way to the kitchen to brew some tea.

As he watched Mary fill the pot and lay out two mugs, Jeffrey's throat opened itself up enough for him to speak.

"Mary — can I ask why you didn't try to call me on Sunday? The cell phone worked on most of the mountain." He spoke levelly and quietly, no accusation in his voice.

"She left instructions that we were not to contact you if anything happened to her. It was as if she knew. I think she just decided she was ready, Jeffrey." Mary turned to look at him, her nose and eyes red as cherries.

Jeffrey accepted the cup of tea she held out to him and leaned back against the counter.

"She left a note addressed to me on her bedside table. That's why Ginny called me back when she found her. There was one for me and one for you." Mary reached into her uniform pocket and pulled out a thick, ivory-colored envelope with his name on it. He recognized Agnes's spidery scrawl. Jeffrey took it from Mary's hand and held it loosely at his side. The envelope weighed heavy in his palm, and even heavier on his heart.

"Her note to me said not to call you under any circumstances, but to let you have your adventure. She also asked me to be the one to tell you when you got back, and then she said some other stuff that was personal, I mean, just for *me*." Mary sniffed.

Jeffrey sipped the hot tea. He hadn't asked for sugar, but Mary had added some nonetheless. He guessed it was her prescription for shock, and although it wasn't his custom, the unusual sweetness was welcome today.

"She also left a package for you in her room, but said you needed to read the letter before you opened that." Mary took a sip of tea, then beckoned him out into the corridor, back towards the day room.

Jeffrey followed obediently, noticing that there were no other staff members padding around in the usual manner.

"Where is everyone?" he asked as Mary closed the day room door again.

"They're just giving us privacy. They're all about the place, though." Mary smiled weakly and sat on the edge of a corduroy sofa that had seen better days.

"Do you want to be alone to read your letter?" She hugged her cup close to her chest.

Jeffrey nodded, and felt the weight of the envelope renewed in his hand.

"Right — well, I'll be out here whenever you want company."

He watched silently as she rose and walked to the door.

"Jeffrey. I'm so sorry I fell apart. I meant to be strong for you, and there you are comforting me." She shook her head as if scolding herself.

"It's fine, Mary. I know you loved her, too." Jeffrey smiled a half smile at her as she left the room.

He put his tea down on the coffee table and then blew his nose in one of the tissues Mary had given him. A lump of sadness lay tight across his throat as he slid his finger under the seal and opened the letter.

Dear son,

I hope this finds you well. You'll be back from your climb up Ben Macdhui now, and no doubt you had a ball. I'm sorry I won't be here to hear all about it, but you can tell Mary in my stead. She is a bonnie lass and cares about you, Jeffrey. Perhaps you can even take her up there sometime, to see it for herself?

So, now on to what I have to tell you. You mustn't be angry that I told them not to call you. I knew that it was my time and it was all I could do to hold on long enough to finish your waistcoat and see you off. There was no point in dragging you back just to deal with my old bones.

Son, all your life, you've chosen the proven route. You've been so careful with your life, your work, your money, and your heart. When you were a wee boy, I sometimes wished you'd venture out a bit more and not be so fearful of everything, but I knew that you'd come to it in your own time. I know the Big Spill set you back, but I always believed you'd find your feet again.

Well, sure enough, Ben Macdhui fit the bill. The mountain represented everything you'd doubted you could manage, all wrapped up in one big package. The day you told me that you were going to climb it was the day I knew that it would be OK to leave you, that you were going to be all right on your own.

I know you'll miss me for a while, but you'll be fine, son. Time heals, and soon enough you'll be happy again. Remember that time marches on and all things change with the tide.

These past few years, you've taken good care of me, better than any mother could wish for from her son. I've always been proud to be your mum, Jeffrey, and not all mothers can honestly say that about their children. You were a good wee boy, and now you're a good man, and that's something you can be proud of.

Well, I'm tired now, so I'll sign off. Don't forget to eat your vegetables, get regular haircuts, and always take care of your feet. I've left you a package in my room that I hope you'll enjoy.

Have a wonderful life, son. Though I may not have said it often, you were the light of mine for many years, and now it's time you became the light in someone else's.

Speaking of which, please give Mary a hug. She is a bonnie lass and made my time here much more pleasant. Play the odd game of Scrabble with her so she doesn't miss me too much. While you're at it, take her out to dinner at the Fort Hotel. Maybe she'd enjoy the sticky toffee pudding as much as I did? It is the best in Scotland, after all.

Your loving mum,

Agnes Mere.

P.S. Mr. Stuart in town has my will. Don't forget to call him, and he'll sort everything out for you. I don't have much to leave you, but I know you'll spend it well.

P.P.S. I want to be cremated. Mr. Stuart will give you all the details. Now, don't listen to Mr. Friendly if he tells you there's no room at the crem. I know he keeps slots aside for folk he likes. Don't let him bully you.

P.P.P.S. Say hello to that bastard cat when you see it.

Jeffrey folded the thick pages along the creases and pushed the letter back inside the envelope. Agnes's loss was raw and heavy, made all the more painful by the fact that she'd known, when she said goodbye to him, that it'd be the last time she saw him. If he'd known that, would he have done anything differently, he wondered? Why did it seem that whenever he let himself enjoy something, whether it be riding his bike too fast or climbing a mountain, bad things followed?

He opened the door to the corridor and walked along to Agnes's room. The bedspread was folded in a neat pile along with the flannelette sheets she loved. Her dressing gown hung on the hook behind the door, and her slippers were tucked tidily under the bed. The sight of her belongings brought a fresh wave of pain as he wandered around the empty room. On the bedside table was the wedding picture: Agnes and Angus in their early twenties. They were smiling at the camera, the edges of the picture brown with age and the frame battered with handling. Jeffrey reached down and picked it up. He would take it home.

On the end of the bed was a brown paper package. Once again he saw his name, this time printed in big capital letters. It looked as if Agnes had gone over each letter at least three times, just in case anyone thought this was for someone else. Jeffrey smiled as he ran his finger over the letters. He could see his mum, her eyes screwed up behind her thick glasses and her tongue sticking out as she concentrated on writing this, the pressure of the pen all but piercing the paper with the force of her intention.

He flipped the package over and tore open the paper. Inside was a pile of dark socks. There were four pairs, and as he picked them up, he saw that four of the socks said "Any" across the arch and around the cuff and the other four said "Day." At the sight of the scratchy offering, Jeffrey felt new tears fill his eyes. He looked down and pulled up his trouser legs. He'd been sure to wear Tues-Day's socks today, as he'd known she'd ask about them when she saw him.

He spoke into the quiet room.

"Thanks, Mum. These are great. I've got Tuesday's on, as you can see."

As he stood looking down at his feet, Mary tapped the door lightly and waited for him to turn around.

"Are you OK?" She hesitated in the doorway.

"Aye. I'm OK, Mary. Come in if you like."

Mary walked across the room and glanced down at the socks on the bed. On a reflex her hand went up to her mouth and she stifled a giggle. Suddenly, thinking better of it, she blushed.

"Oh, sorry, Jeffrey. It's just..."

"Don't worry." Jeffrey smiled. "That's Mum for you. She had the last laugh, as always."

CHAPTER 14

The crematorium was gradually filling up. Wool-clad Pitlochry folk were wandering in, nodding to each other and speaking in hushed tones. Jeffrey stood at the door and shook each wrinkled hand that passed him.

"Thanks for coming. Thanks very much for coming." He spoke by rote, aware of the vague smell of mothballs lurking in the parade of Sunday-best coats and hats that had come to pay their respects to Agnes.

Her entire knitting circle was here, as well as most of the dominos league, the women's institute, the bingo club, and several of the nurses from the home. Jeffrey scanned the many faces, searching for Mary's. He'd seen her arrive a while ago, but she'd since disappeared.

When he finally spotted her again, he noticed that she'd taken on the role of usher and was directing people to seats. She was helping Mrs. Barnes from the bakery into a chair next to Fred and Matilda. He liked Mrs. Barnes. She'd always given him an extra treacle tart or piece of mincemeat pie for Agnes when he'd stopped in to buy a granary loaf each Monday. She was a kind woman with a weakness for Bingo, much to Agnes's delight. His mum used to call Mrs. Barnes her partner in crime when they'd escape on the bus to Aviemore once a month, to play at the community center.

Catching his eye, Mary smiled. Her pretty red hair was tied back in a black bow, and her dark coat was long, swinging around her shapely calves. Feeling momentarily guilty for noticing Mary's calves on a day like today, Jeffrey smiled bashfully back at her as another warm hand was pressed into his.

"So sorry, Jeffrey. A great loss indeed." Frank Duff, his old landlord from the office, smiled sadly.

"Thanks, Frank. She was a force of nature, that's for sure."

"Aye, she'll be missed at the kirk, right enough. Nae-b'dy tae argue with the vicar about organizing the fête or whether to have booze on the tombola stand." Frank chuckled; then, correcting himself, he frowned and said seriously, "She was a grand lady."

Jeffrey watched as Frank walked over and sat down next to the Subramanians. It was so kind of them to come even though they didn't know Agnes. It was a generous show of support for him, and he was grateful. He wondered momentarily what an Indian funeral would be like. Didn't Hindus also burn their dead?

As Jeffrey watched the last few people filter in from the cold, the vicar nodded his silvery head towards the back of the room. As if by magic, the double wooden doors closed silently, ghostlike, on the small group within. It was time to get started.

The vicar's voice hummed low and steady as the Pitlochry folk bent their heads, wiped their noses, and nodded at the appropriate pauses. As Jeffrey looked around the room, he wriggled his toes. His feet were freezing. The room was warm enough, so he couldn't understand it. He had worn his Thurs-Day socks and heavy-soled shoes, so there was no reason for him to be feeling the cold like this. Perhaps it was shock? Perhaps he just needed a nice hot cup of tea and his slippers to take the chill off the day and out of his bones?

He closed his eyes momentarily and imagined sitting at home in the cottage, his feet pressed up close to the fire. As he listened to the vicar's words, describing his mother, many of them sounded fitting and comfortable. *Kind* — yes, Agnes could be kind. *Selfless* — yes, he could agree with that. *Loving* — in her way, she *was* a loving person. Agnes showed it in practical, day-to-day ways, like making his favorite banana sandwiches for his packed lunches and being proud of the fact that he had the whitest collar on the playground. While she never was one to shower him with sloppy affection, Jeffrey had always felt loved.

As the vicar's soliloquy on Agnes's virtues continued, the sharp edges of truth began to blur somewhat, to Jeffrey's mind. *Supportive* — was Agnes supportive? He supposed so, if she agreed with the cause. *Community-minded* — now that was a bit of a stretch. *Tolerant* — now, hang on a minute. Jeffrey coughed loudly at *tolerant* — he had to draw the line there.

As if sensing his proximity to thinning ice, the vicar calmly introduced Jeffrey and stepped down from the small podium, taking a seat next to Mary in the front row.

Jeffrey had written a speech for this day. He had even rehearsed it in front of Ralf, and in the bathroom mirror, as he really wanted to do Agnes proud. Now that he was up here, being stared at by all these expectant faces, his throat felt suddenly tight and unyielding. Swallowing over a walnut, he began.

"Thanks, Reverend, and thanks to everyone for coming. Mum would have been touched, right enough." His voice sounded weird inside his own head. Tinny, thin, and not like himself at all.

Matilda sniffed loudly, and Fred slipped his arm solicitously around her shoulder. Jeffrey paused, momentarily distracted, while Mary reached into her handbag and discreetly handed Matilda a fresh tissue for her leaky nose. Good old Mary.

"So I won't keep you long. Just wanted to say a few words about my mum, Agnes Mere. She was a good wife, mother, and friend. As most of us know, Mum had a way of getting to the heart of the matter in no time flat. You always knew where you stood with her, and that is a rare thing."

Pausing, Jeffrey adjusted his tie, which was tight across his Adam's apple.

"When she met my dad, she left Glasgow and made her life in Pitlochry. She always said she was happy here. I know she'd have loved to travel a wee bit, see the world, but instead she chose to make her world here as honest as she could. After we lost Dad, she took up the challenge of life alone and raised me with all the strength and caring she could muster. I never wanted for much, and I will always be grateful to her for that."

Matilda blew her nose and shuddered violently. Fred patted her broad back, then locked eyes with Jeffrey and shrugged in apology. Jeffrey took a deep breath, preparing to continue.

"Many of you helped to make Mum's last days easier, happier. I especially want to thank all of you who were there at the end." As his eyes met Mary's, Jeffrey felt his voice begin to betray him. He'd not been there. He'd been up a mountain, sleeping soundly with a stupid big dog in his tent, while Agnes took her last breath. He'd finally decided to take a long-awaited leap of faith, venture outside of the seventy-mile radius she teased him about so mercilessly, and in the same instant had lost his mum, his rock, and his best friend.

Jeffrey felt a hot tear make its way down his cheek. Enough now. He swallowed hard.

"Let's sing her favorite hymn to send her on her way. Please join me and thanks again to you all for coming."

On cue, a tape-recorded version of the hymn Agnes had specified, "Courage, Brother, Do Not Stumble," began to play from somewhere behind the curtain at the back of the room. The group of mourners rose, lifted their wilted song sheets, and began to sing.

The beech coffin, draped with his mum's favorite freesias, jolted slightly as the belt underneath it began to move. The delicate flowers vibrated oddly, as if Agnes were laughing underneath them as she rolled away towards the furnace. Jeffrey watched the coffin slowly disappear and heavy green curtains sweep around the gaping hole that had swallowed his mother whole. The notion was too painful. The Agnes he loved wasn't inside that box. She could never be contained by *any* kind of box that he knew of.

Jeffrey closed his eyes as the hymn drew to a close, and when he opened them, Mary was at his side.

"Come on. Let's go." She slipped her hand through his arm and guided him gently towards the door. Obviously sensing that he was done in, Mary stepped into the foyer of the crematorium and addressed the gathering group.

"Friends. Refreshments will be served at the Old Forge Inn.

Please come and join Jeffrey there, if you're able."

Jeffrey nodded, mute, as people filtered away. He looked down at Mary and smiled gratefully.

"Well done. Well said. I mean, thank you, Mary."

"Welcome. Let's get you over there, and I think a wee dram is in order?" She squeezed his arm encouragingly, and they walked out together into the frigid air of the difficult day.

CHAPTER 15

Jeffrey's life had taken on a gray pallor since Agnes's funeral. The early winter weather matched his mood as he trudged up and down to the allotment daily to feed the bees. It was time for the little workers to lock down the hive and protect themselves from the bitter cold to come. He supposed he was much like the bees in this respect.

Aside from shopping for food and the occasional stroll down to the fish ladder to watch the salmon leap, he'd become reclusive. Ralf was his usual grumpy self, so there was no change or company to be found there. Mary had begun popping in a couple of times a week on her way to and from work. She'd bring a packet of biscuits, a pie, or an interesting article she'd found on beekeeping. She obviously hoped to engage him in conversation, but even her visits couldn't snap him out of his dour mood. The last time she'd come, he'd sensed an edge of irritation in her voice as she asked, again, if he'd cooked himself a proper meal that week.

"I did. Beans on toast." He'd shrugged.

"Jeffrey, beans on toast does not constitute a balanced meal."

It might not have been a balanced meal in Mary's book, but to Jeffrey it was adequate. Besides, that day he just hadn't felt up to the usual Monday fare of grilled chicken, mashed potatoes, and sweet corn.

She'd offered to come over and cook for him, but he'd declined, saying he didn't think he'd have the pans she needed and besides, he'd hate her to go to any trouble.

He watched her walk away, her shoulders more rounded than usual, and regretted his obstinacy. She was a lovely lady, Mary, and in truth he'd really wanted her to stay, spend some time with him, and put an evening in. Why had he all but pushed her out the door?

As he drew the curtains on the darkening sky, Jeffrey felt the familiar dread of another night spent alone with a meal, the TV, and his heavy conscience. He felt his punishment, albeit self-inflicted, was just. If he allowed himself to feel even remotely better, Agnes's passing might take on less significance than it deserved. If he moved on, began to think of the future or, god forbid, laughed at something again, who would remember her as she needed to be remembered? He, after all, had left her alone to climb a mountain. He should have waited. After all the time he'd spent with her, visiting her in the home every single day, she'd slipped away the one time he wasn't there.

He'd read her letter over and over throughout the month that had passed since the cremation, but despite her words and admission that his leaving had given her the out she needed, he couldn't forgive himself. His punishment was just. He'd be alone, and that would be that.

The newspaper lay on the arm of the sofa, reminding him that today was Wednesday. Wednesday was fish and chips day, which meant a walk into town. He glanced at the clock. 6:14. Time to get his coat and make the trip to the fish bar for his customary haddock and chips.

As he slipped his heavy coat on in the hall, a sharp rap at the door startled him. Standing on his front step was Matilda. She wore her ever-present slippers and a raincoat thrown loosely over her wide shoulders, showing glimpses of her floral apron underneath.

"Hello, love. I brought you a pie. Steak and kidney." She pushed a dish towards him, its top tightly tucked under a layer of tinfoil.

"Oh, thanks, Matilda. You didn't need to do that." Jeffrey accepted the dish and stepped backwards, as if to invite her in.

"I made enough for two, in case Mary was popping in tonight." Matilda searched his face and shuffled her slippered feet.

"No, not tonight." Jeffrey heard his own voice, forlorn and flat.

"Well, all the more for you then, pet." Matilda winked, and her attempt to lighten his mood touched him. "Fred's away this week visiting his sister in Skye. I'm at loose ends so, what do I do? I cook." She grinned.

"You're a gem, Matilda." He smiled and raised the pie in thanks as she turned and waved over her shoulder. "Twenty minutes at 350 and you'll be all set. Just let me have the dish back. It's my best one."

"I'll do that." He called after her as she rounded the hedge that separated their gardens and started back up her own driveway. Their semi-detached cottages, linked at the hip, were homey. Like two sturdy halves of a whole, they sat surrounded by their small gardens and low sandstone walls at the street. As he watched his friend approach her front door, Jeffrey felt guilty that he hadn't asked her to join him, but he simply couldn't bring himself to spend an evening making small talk. Feeling resigned to his lack of gallantry, Jeffrey waved with his free hand as Matilda disappeared inside her door.

The pie smelled marvelous. Even though it was Wednesday, and strictly fish and chips night, it would be great to have a home-cooked meal. And it would save him the walk into town.

Shrugging his coat off, Jeffrey draped it over the banister, made his way into the kitchen, and laid the pie on the stove. Peeling back the tinfoil, he could see the layers of Matilda's famous puff pastry sitting on top of the dish. He was hungry.

Jeffrey pulled out a plate, a knife, a fork, and a napkin and set them on his tray. Switching the oven on to 350, as instructed, he spotted his phone on the kitchen table. It'd be a shame to heat the entire pie, and then only eat one portion. Good food was best shared, or so Agnes always said, so he leaned over and picked up the phone. Dialing the familiar number, his stomach did a nervous flip-flop. Silly, really. He was just calling a friend to see if she wanted to share a meal. There was no reason to be nervous.

There was no answer. As Jeffrey prepared to hang up, he heard a click and Mary's voice on her answering machine. He left a short, awkward message and hung up. Of course she wasn't there. Why would she be? He'd had ample opportunities to see her, ask her over, or pop in on his way back from the fish ladder. Had he done anything about it? No. So, what did he expect?

An hour later, he wiped the last of the thick gravy up from his plate with a slice of bread. He'd made a respectable dent in the pie and still had enough for two meals the following day. The rich meaty flavor had reminded him of Agnes's cooking. She'd prided herself on her baking, and her puff pastry really was second to none. Matilda's was delicious, too, but to Jeffrey, there was nothing quite like his mum's.

After cleaning up his plate and watching an ancient episode of *The Sky at Night* on BBC2, Jeffrey yawned expansively. It was only 8:50, but he was ready for his bed. Taking the newspaper with him, he switched off the lights and headed up the stairs. He was too tired to shower, so he'd just get straight to bed, read the paper, and take care of all that in the morning.

His bed felt soft and welcoming, and within a few minutes, the heat emanating from his feet took the chill off the sheets. He really needed to get an electric blanket this winter. That'd make all the difference to his nights.

The newspaper was unwieldy, and within a few minutes, it fluttered to the ground as sleep overtook him.

CHAPTER 16

Jeffrey woke with a start. At the end of his bed sat the big dog, wet and filthy. The same odd, sweet smell he remembered emanating from its mouth when it had shared his tent on the mountain filled his nostrils, and he flinched. What was that smell?

Sitting up, he rubbed at his eyes. Was he seeing things? How had the beast found him here and then got into the house? Swinging his feet over the edge of the bed, Jeffrey was shocked to see water lapping beneath them. What was happening? Had a pipe burst? As he tentatively lowered one foot into the water, he heard his name.

He jerked his head up and looked over at the dog. He really was losing his mind. Had the dog spoken? The animal sat completely still — all except for its eyebrows, which twitched questioningly, as if asking Jeffrey what he was intending on doing about the water.

"Where did you come from, lass?" Jeffrey asked the matted creature. The huge head with the familiar dreadlocks lifted up and turned towards the window overlooking Matilda's back garden. The dog let out a sharp bark and then paced over to the window. Placing its huge dirty paws up on the sill, it began to whine.

"What's the matter, eh?" Jeffrey waded through the icy water to the window. As he leaned around the dog, he could see an orange light flickering from Matilda's garden. The dog continued to whine as Jeffrey tried to open the window to get a better look. As he wiggled past the big hairy body, he felt his foot catch on the edge of the bedspread, and suddenly the glass pane before him was gone and he was tumbling out the hole towards the damp lawn below. His body hit the ground with a thump, and his eyes shot open.

With a start, he realized he was still lying in his bed, warm and dry. There was no dog. There was no water. He'd dreamed it. Turning over on his side, Jeffrey tutted to himself. As he sat up to pat his pillow and turn it over, he glanced through the crack in the curtains. Was he imagining it, or was there a strange orange glow coming from Matilda's garden?

For a split second, he considered pulling the curtains tighter and going back to sleep. Then, for some reason, he thought about the dog's presence. What if it was some kind of sign or portent? Perhaps he'd just check on that light.

Stepping over to the window, he pulled the curtains back, opened the window, and leaned out into the frigid night air. Sure enough, there *was* a strange orange flickering coming from next door. What on earth was she up to?

Irritated, Jeffrey pulled on his dressing gown and headed down the stairs. Matilda may just have fallen asleep with the TV on, but something told him he needed to check on her.

As he rounded the hedge at the end of the driveway, Jeffrey could smell smoke. Panic gripped him, and as he reached Matilda's front door, he pressed the bell and slammed the knocker simultaneously. There was no response. The more he sniffed, the more he could smell smoke. Pushing open the letterbox, he could see into the hallway and there, clearly visible against the paneled side of the staircase, was the reflection of what looked like flames licking the paint.

"Matilda?" Jeffrey shouted as loud as he could into the letterbox. "Matilda, are you there?"

No response. Jeffrey twisted the doorknob, but the door was locked tight. He stepped back onto the driveway, instantly knowing what he must do. To save time, he pushed himself straight through the prickly hedge that separated their two gardens. He felt the barbs of the roses grabbing viciously at his clothes, and then he was back at his own door. Running inside, he grabbed the phone from the kitchen table and dialed 999.

By the time he got back to Matilda's door, dark smoke was oozing out from underneath the seal. As he pushed open the letterbox again, he could hardly see the staircase at all.

"Matilda! Matilda?" He shouted with all his might, but there was still no response.

Here he was, standing on her doorstep in the middle of the night in his slippers and dressing gown. The fire engine was on its way, but he had no idea how long it would take them to get here.

In a moment of clarity, Jeffrey reached down and picked up Fred's favorite garden gnome, the one with the fishing rod that sat at the edge of the tiny gnome-sized pond. He swung the smiling figure high over his head and then brought it crashing down on the glass panel in the door. Shards of glass flew in all directions, some landing on his slippers. He ran the gnome around inside the frame, trying to clear away as much of the sharp debris as he could. The hole he'd created was quickly filled with thick smoke escaping from the house as he reached inside and felt around for the latch.

His fingers found the metal shape they sought, and he pushed it downwards. Leaning hard on the door, he swung it inwards, allowing great bubbles of smoke to blow past him into the night.

"Matilda?" Jeffrey screamed at the top of his voice. "Matilll-llddaaaaa?"

His eyes were stinging and watering and he felt a burning sensation as the gluey smoke snuck into his open lungs. Jeffrey stepped into the hallway and batted at the acrid fog ahead of him that was separating him from the rest of the house.

The footprint of Matilda and Fred's house was identical to his own, just inverted. Feeling his way along the edge of the banister, he estimated the distance to the door into the lounge. Then, remembering all the films he'd seen about crawling along the ground in a fire in order to get below the smoke, he dropped down onto his stomach. He could just make out the tartan carpet beneath him and the bottom of the doors in the hallway. Spotting the opening into the lounge just where he expected it to be, Jeffrey shuffled snake-like along the floor, moving towards the back of the house and the kitchen. He didn't have enough puff to call to Matilda again, so he saved his breath and kept moving forward slowly instead.

As he slithered into the lounge, a little way ahead of him on the floor he caught sight of a tartan slipper, then another one. He moved closer and saw that inside the slippers were two thick ankles. Filled with both relief and terror, Jeffrey reached out and tentatively touched Matilda's leg. He didn't want to be forward, but needs must sometimes. Was she unconscious? Was she dead? *Please God, if you're listening, don't let her be dead.*

The ankles didn't move. This wasn't good, not good at all. He could hear flames crackling and popping in the kitchen, and their orange glow seemed to be becoming more intense. The heat was startling, and he began to sweat. Gathering himself up onto his knees, Jeffrey felt his way along the edges of the chair until he found a hand, then a chubby elbow. Leaning into the dark void of the chair, he stood up, hooked his arms under the elbow, and lifted up and back with all his might. Matilda's bulk flopped forward and followed him down onto the carpet with a thud.

The stinging in his eyes was becoming unbearable. Sitting back on his bottom, Jeffrey dragged Matilda towards him. Her back against his chest, he hooked one of his arms under each of hers. He closed his eyes tight against the advancing smoke, relying on his memory of the house's layout to shuffle his way back towards the front door.

After what felt like an age, he could eventually feel the chill of the night air on his back. Thank goodness. His eyes stung painfully and his lungs burned. He coughed great racking coughs as he shuffled and shuffled until he felt the cool metal strip of the doorframe under his hip. As he backed out the door, he could hear voices. There were several shouts and then a siren. Jeffrey was afraid to let go of Matilda or open his eyes. As a firm hand gripped his shoulder, he let himself fall backwards and was caught under the arms.

"Get her out. Is she out?" He spoke into the night sky, eyes closed and gasping for air.

"Aye, she's out. You can let go now, mister." Jeffrey felt one final, painful tear as another cough ripped its way up his raw chest. He gasped to fill his lungs, and then everything went black.

CHAPTER 17

———◈———

The room smelled funny. Why did his bedroom smell of bleach? Jeffrey lay still, his eyes tightly closed, and wondered why he felt dizzy. He was so tired, and his arms and legs ached. If he hadn't known better, he'd think he hadn't had any sleep at all. First the weird dream last night with the dog, then this feeling of floating. He really was beginning to worry about himself. He took a deep breath, deciding that he needed to get a grip and face the day. Just as he was about to open his eyes, he felt a warm hand on his arm.

Startled by the contact, Jeffrey opened his eyes and was shocked to see Mary sitting next to him. Her eyes were red and puffy, and she had her coat on.

"Mary?" His voice sounded bizarre, like when he had had laryngitis at nineteen. His hand flew up to his throat and covered his Adam's apple. Agnes had given him honey and lemon in hot water for it then. He'd have to make himself some of that now.

His eyes were stinging something rotten, and as he looked around, he realized he was not in his own bed. The room was white and all but bare, and the bed, a narrow single, was propped up at the head. He had a sheet and a thin green blanket over him instead of his puffy duvet, and where were his pajamas? Having uttered only the one word, Mary's name, he started to cough. The coughs came bubbling up from his kneecaps, through his thighs and stomach, and then into his chest. He couldn't stop, no matter how hard he tried. The caustic ripples took the strength right out of him. After a few moments, as the spasm subsided, he lay back onto the pile of pillows, his ribs quivering.

"Jeffrey. It's all right. You're all right. You're in the hospital." Mary's voice sounded odd, too. Did she have laryngitis as well? She squeezed his arm tightly and then stood to plump up the pillows behind his head.

As he watched her moving around him, Jeffrey began to recall the events of the night. They felt a little jumbled in his head, but he wanted to tell Mary what had happened. He tried to squeeze out the words in between bouts of coughing.

"Matilda... Is she OK? I saw the light...so much smoke ... but then her slippers and ... heavy, so heavy but ... thanks to the dog." He spluttered again, a fresh round of hacks taking his voice away completely.

"Don't try to talk, Jeffrey. We know what happened." Mary sniffed as he closed his eyes again. It felt better to keep them closed.

"You're suffering from smoke inhalation. But you saved her life. Matilda is going to be fine."

At this, Jeffrey opened his eyes and looked at Mary.

"I saved her?" His voice was breathy, like a whistle. The words he spoke were heavy in his mouth, but the sound of them in his ears was light and marvelous.

"You did indeed. She'd left something in the oven. At least they think that's what happened. She must've fallen asleep, then the smoke overwhelmed her and she... she could have suffocated, Jeffrey. Or worse. You are a marvel, really you are." At this, Mary dissolved into tears. Not the kind of tears that actresses shed in films, but the kind of tears that make your face swell up, your cheeks go red, and your eyes disappear into their sockets.

"Oh, don't cry," Jeffrey whispered. He placed his hand over hers and patted gently. "All's well that ends well, isn't that so?"

She nodded and sniffed, then rooted around inside her bag for a tissue.

"You're a hero, Jeffrey Mere. Everybody's saying it."

As he lay back, his whole body felt overwhelmingly heavy. A hero. Had he heard that right? Jeffrey Mere, a hero? Who'd have thought it? As the thought permeated, he suddenly felt sad. Other than Mary, there was only one person whose opinion really mattered to him, and she was gone. Just to have Agnes tell him that she knew what he'd done would have meant the world. She'd have nodded and then cackled while her teeth clacked. She might've said, "Well, lucky for Matilda you're such a light sleeper." She'd have played it all down, but he was sure she'd have been proud nonetheless.

Mary had gathered herself together and was taking off her coat. She pushed her red curls away from her blotchy face and tucked the already tightly tucked blanket under his thigh.

"The doctor is going to come back in a few minutes to check on you. I'll just go and tell him you're awake." Her voice now sounded all businesslike and nursey.

"No. Just sit with me awhile." Jeffrey patted the bed next to him and smiled at her. "He'll come when he comes."

Mary blushed, hesitated, then sat down, neatly smoothing her skirt over her knees.

"So Matilda's fine?" he repeated, his voice sounding a little less rusty this time.

"She is going to be fine. They've called Fred, and he's on his way back from Skye." She nodded and then smoothed her skirt again.

"You need to just rest up now. The doc says it'll take a few days for the effects of the smoke to wear off, so they'll keep an eye on you. Are you in pain?"

Jeffrey shook his head. She really had a lovely face. It was round where it needed to be round and sharp where it needed to be sharp. She had just about the most perfect face he'd ever seen.

Before he could stop himself, he reached up and stroked her cheek. Mary gasped and her face reddened, but she didn't pull away. Jeffrey felt exhilarated. Perhaps it was his brush with death that had given him the brass neck to touch her this way? Whatever it was, he was glad of it. Her cheek was soft, and he liked the feel of it under his fingertips.

"Mary?" He let his hand stay on her cheek.

"Yes, Jeffrey?" She looked down at him, her eyes still wide.

"I think I may need a bed pan."

CHAPTER 18

Jeffrey lay looking up at the speckled ceiling tiles while the little TV suspended from a bracket on the ceiling warbled with a midday chat show. He was still feeling a little woozy from the pain medication, but if he lay very still and concentrated on the picture of the Forth Road Bridge on the wall, the room would stop moving eventually. Lunch had been a dry ham sandwich with a cup of tepid tea and two digestives. He was still hungry but knew that Mary would be in soon with a scone or a fruit tart from Mrs. Barnes at the bakery. Mary was on early shift at the home today and had promised to pop in on her way back from work. She'd been feeding Ralf for him, and the idea of her inside his house made him smile. He liked the thought of her letting herself in the front door, walking through to his kitchen, and calling the cat, like she belonged.

He was hoping to go home the next day and was so looking forward to getting back to his own bed. The hospital was fine, but he missed his fluffy duvet.

The previous day, Mary had gone into Perth and bought him new slippers, a pair of pajamas, and a heavy toweling robe, his old ones having been ruined by the smoke. She'd brought the items into the hospital for him, and he'd been impressed with her choices. Nothing too gaudy, just a nice blue robe, some navy flannelette pajamas with dark green stripes, and a pair of size ten sheepskin moccasins. Perfect.

As he lay half listening to the TV, something moved in the corner of his eye. Turning his head to the side, expecting to see a nurse coming in to take his blood pressure for the millionth time, Jeffrey caught his breath. Just inside the door sat the dog. Its shaggy head hung low between its shoulders, and its tail swished noiselessly from side to side. He could just make out the familiar dark eyes behind the matted dreadlocks, and as he exhaled slowly, for fear of scaring it away, the dog's nose twitched.

"Hello, lass." Jeffrey rolled carefully onto his side. "What're you doing here?"

The dog was motionless, other than its swooshing tail.

"I doubt they allow dogs in here." Jeffrey propped himself up on one elbow and beckoned to the animal. "C'mere, then."

The dog rose tentatively and walked forward on its great tea-plate paws until its muzzle was lying on the blanket next to Jeffrey's hand.

Jeffrey reached out and stroked the huge head. "I've missed you. Where did you go, up on the mountain?"

The dog blew air out of its nostrils and shook its great head as if denying having disappeared. Jeffrey laughed.

"OK, OK. I'm just glad you found me. Are you going to stay around this time?" The dog leaned into his hand as he spoke.

"You're a good girl."

A loud cough at the door pulled Jeffrey's attention away from the animal. Mary stood with a brown paper bag in her hand and a questioning look on her face.

"Who're you talking to?"

"Well, the dog, of course." Jeffrey turned his attention back to where the dog had been standing, only to see an empty space. A slight impression on the green blanket was all that remained of the animal's presence.

"Dog?" Mary walked into the room and slid off her coat. She had on her uniform and her sensible nurse shoes that squeaked as she walked on the cold linoleum floor.

Jeffrey frowned, perplexed. What was going on with this dog? How come it kept appearing and disappearing?

"It was right here." Jeffrey pointed to the side of the bed. "Just a moment ago."

Mary frowned and picked up a vase of daisies the Subramanians had brought to the hospital. They needed fresh water, and Jeffrey seemed to be havering about a dog. He had mentioned a dog being up on Ben Macdhui with him too, but Mary hadn't thought that particularly remarkable, assuming the animal had simply been a stray that he had encountered.

He was worrying her. She needed to ask the doctor if hallucinations were normal after smoke inhalation. She knew the pain medication could cause odd side effects. Maybe that was it? He'd been though the mill, right enough.

"I'll get you some tea to have with your scone. Mrs. Barnes sent you a treacle one." Mary walked briskly out into the corridor.

Jeffrey loved treacle scones, especially with raspberry jam on them. Agnes had always made her own raspberry jam, and he'd enjoyed helping her wash and sterilize the jars each year in preparation for the new batch. The task, routine, mundane to some extent, had pleased him. Seeing the sparkling jars and new lids lined up on the kitchen counter had been satisfying for them both. He suddenly felt listless, thin, like too little raspberry jam spread over too much scone. He wished he could put his feet on the ground, really feel the earth under his feet, like he had on Ben Macdhui.

Mary walked into the waiting room and over to the sink. She carefully emptied the cloudy water out and refilled the vase. The daisies smelled aromatic, and she ran her fingers over the velvety petals. Jeffrey needed to rest and get his strength back. So much had happened to him in just the last two months that it was no wonder he was losing his grip on reality. He'd retired from accounting after forty years, climbed a mountain, lost his mother, and then run into a burning house to save his neighbor. He'd had a busy few weeks.

As she walked back into Jeffrey's room, she saw Fred sitting at the side of the bed. His girth was bigger than the spindly chair could accommodate, and he spilled over each side of it as he leaned in towards Jeffrey.

"I'll never be able to thank you enough, Jeffrey. You saved the old girl. She means the world to me." Fred sniffed and wiped his eyes.

Jeffrey lay back on his bank of pillows and shook his head slowly.

"It was nothing, Fred. You'd have done the same for me."

Fred's shoulders quivered as he reached for Jeffrey's hand.

"Shake my hand, pal. You're a prince among men, Jeffrey Mere."

Jeffrey took Fred's hand, and the two men looked at each other. Spotting Mary in the doorway, Jeffrey withdrew his hand from Fred's and coughed.

"Hello, Fred." Mary placed the vase on the small Formica table under the window, then turned to face them. "How's Matilda?"

"Oh, she's all right. They're keeping her sedated due to the smoke. Her lungs need to clear, they say, but the doctor says she'll be right as rain in a few days, thanks to Jeffrey here." Fred once again patted Jeffrey's hand with his own big, fleshy paddle. "He's a hero, right enough."

Jeffrey made a low grumble of protest as Mary nodded and touched Fred on the shoulder.

"I'm very glad, Fred. That's a blessing indeed. Now, would the pair of you like a nice cup of tea?"

"Oh, aye, that'd be grand." Fred smiled, and Jeffrey nodded silently. Mary smiled and walked out into the corridor heading towards the cafeteria.

"So, Jeffrey, is there anything you need? Can I do anything for you?" Fred rose and paced around the bed towards the window.

"No, Fred, I'm fine, really." Jeffrey felt wrung out. He really wanted his treacle scone, but now wasn't sure he could stay awake long enough to eat it. Why was he so tired?

"Mary is taking great care of me." He yawned, a great jaw-breaking yawn, and wriggled a little farther down against his pillows.

"Aye, I see that. She's a good lass, and kind of sweet on you, maybe?" Fred winked as he spoke, and Jeffrey felt his face get hot.

"I wouldn't exactly say that, Fred."

"Open yer eyes, man. It's as plain as the nose on my face." Fred chuckled and poked Jeffrey's leg through the green blanket. "She's a looker, too."

Jeffrey pulled the blanket up under his chin and smiled at Fred's words. Was Mary really sweet on him, or did she just feel sorry for him after everything that had happened?

Not feeling the need to talk any more, as two women might have, the men sat in silence. Fred stared out the window into the darkening sky, and Jeffrey stared at the crack in the ceiling tile above his bed. Theirs was a companionable silence, born from a new bond that had just formed between them. Sometimes words got in the way, and this was a time for simple contemplation.

After a few minutes, Mary came in, carrying a tray with three mugs of tea.

"Here we are, gents." She laid the tray on the bedside table and handed a steaming mug to Fred. As she turned to Jeffrey to give him his, she saw that he was fast asleep. His cheeks puffed out ever so slightly with each exhale, and his eyelids fluttered gently as he slipped into a deep slumber.

She picked up her cup and put a finger to her mouth as she looked at Fred. Fred, getting the message, nodded and then sat back slowly in the spindly chair, balancing the mug on his broad belly.

"Want a scone?" Mary mouthed at him and pointed to the paper bag on the table.

Fred nodded and gave her a thumbs up as a big smile spread across his face. The two ate in silence, sipped their tea, and watched their sleeping hero.

CHAPTER 19

---◆---

Mary's small car drew up outside his house and she turned off the engine. Jeffrey looked over his shoulder at her. It was unfamiliar, but nice, to be driven by someone, and even nicer to be driven by Mary.

"Ready to go in?" she asked, nodding towards the cottage.

Luckily, thanks to the sturdy stone wall construction between his house and Fred and Matilda's, there had been no damage to Jeffrey's home. His friends', on the other hand, was all but destroyed inside. While structurally it remained sound, the contents that hadn't burned were ruined by smoke and fumes.

Fred had arranged to have the whole place emptied, cleaned, and painted while Matilda stayed in hospital. In the meantime, he was sleeping down the street at his fishing pal Andy MacRae's house.

Fred's door was wide open, and there was a pile of rubbish on the front lawn that would have made Matilda furious. As he looked closer, Jeffrey could see that this wasn't rubbish; it was their belongings. He saw their couch, what was left of it, blackened at one end with comically large springs protruding awkwardly from where the cushions should be. The dining table had two legs left and was propped up on its side against the charred sideboard. Two dining chairs without cushions, equally black, lay immodestly on their backs. The living room curtains were heaped on the grass, and several books were scattered around, their singed pages fluttering in the cold breeze.

As he climbed out of the car, Jeffrey was struck by the reality of how quickly things could change. One forgotten pie in the oven and bingo, your life was transformed, your story scattered on the lawn for all the world to see. Yes, the message was loud and clear: life was fickle, and it needed to be given the respect that it deserved.

Mary carried a plastic bag with Jeffrey's new nightclothes in it. She followed him up the path, tutting at the sorry sight next door.

"Poor Matilda, to have to come back to that mess after everything she's been through."

They both knew Fred was doing everything he could, but by all accounts, it would take weeks to set their home to rights.

Jeffrey meandered towards his front door. Inside the cottage, he thought everything looked oddly normal. His walking boots remained at attention in the vestibule, his coat was draped across the banister where he'd left it. Having just passed the mayhem next door, the simple order before him didn't seem right, somehow. He had to admit, however, that it did feel good to be home.

Mary followed him in and placed the plastic bag on the hall table.

"Do you want me to make you a cuppa before I go?"

"That'd be great." Jeffrey smiled at her. He didn't want her to rush off, and a cup of tea would extend the length of time she stayed and breathed her cinnamon breath into his home.

Mary shrugged off her coat and hung it on the rack. As if on autopilot, she picked Jeffrey's up from the banister and hung it tidily next to her own. Smoothing her skirt over her hips, she walked into the kitchen.

Jeffrey looked down at his feet. He was wearing the new slippers she'd bought for him, and they felt cozy. As he considered his warm feet, he heard a meow. Craning his neck up the stairs, he called to the cat.

"Ralf, where are you, boy? I'm home."

As usual, there was no response, and the cat made no appearance at the top of the stairs. No change there, then? Shrugging, Jeffrey padded into the kitchen. The kettle was boiling, a seductive tendril of steam curling up towards the ceiling. His Union Jack teapot, two mugs, and a jug of milk sat on the counter. Across the room, Mary was in his favorite chair at the table. In her lap, curled into a ball and indulgently licking an extended front leg, was Ralf.

Jeffrey gasped. How was this possible? Ralf hated everybody, and yet here he was making himself comfy on Mary's lap. As Jeffrey watched her gently stroke Ralf's back, he imagined what it would feel like to have her touch him that way. Suddenly embarrassed by his own train of thought, he coughed. Mary looked up at him.

"Such a lovely cat. We've become good friends, haven't we, Ralf?" The cat pawed at her thigh and arched its back, luxuriating in the attention.

"So I see." Jeffrey nodded and slid onto the opposite chair.

Mary's red curls were tucked neatly behind her ears but sprang to unruly life again at her collar. He loved the way her hair had a mind of its own. Her shoulders sloped away from her neck in a graceful line, and as she talked to the cat, Jeffrey felt himself hypnotized by the sound of her mellow voice.

"Jeffrey?" Mary carefully put Ralf on the ground and stood up. "Jeffrey?"

"Oh, yes, sorry. What?"

"Shall I make you a sandwich, too?" As she spoke, Ralf wound his way theatrically between her ankles and then, if his ears were not deceiving him, Jeffrey heard purring. Well, if that didn't take the biscuit.

Mary stayed for a couple of hours. She'd been to the supermarket to get some provisions for him, so his fridge was better stocked than it had been since Agnes had died. She helped him prepare a chicken casserole and left him instructions on when to bake it. He'd asked her to stay and join him, but she'd said she had to get going. Jeffrey had been disappointed but knew that she'd gone out of her way to take care of him these past few days, so he thanked her graciously again and let her go.

His plate was now empty and balanced on the arm of the chair. His stomach full, he extended his feet close to the fire, which glowed satisfyingly. He hadn't put the lights on in the room, preferring to enjoy the reflection of the flames on the walls. Not wanting to pollute the peaceful atmosphere with the TV, he sat in silence. Funny how flames were so comforting now, having been so devastating and frightening next door, just a few days ago.

Fred had locked up and gone to Andy's for the night, so all around was peaceful. Jeffrey wiggled his toes inside the sheepskin slippers. As the events of the past few weeks began to run through his mind, he laid his head back and let the film reel play. So much had happened. So much had changed. Here he was, despite it all, safe and sound in his cottage as if none of it had really touched him. And yet, in his heart, he knew different. Not only had he climbed Ben Macdhui, but he had saved a life. How many people could say that? Not many in Pitlochry anyway, he was sure.

As the fire warmed his feet, Jeffrey felt the same glow of pride he'd felt at the top of the mountain. He'd achieved more than he'd expected already, and who knew what was yet to come? Jeffrey knew that in this moment, a simple homemade moment, a seismic shift had occurred. His life, the life he'd once lived, had been altered at its core. Everyone knew that in order to make something better, sometimes you had to break it first. Well, he'd broken something, all right. The mold he'd taken sixty-four years to make for himself lay in pieces at his slippered feet. And now, after everything he'd experienced, he wanted so much more from his life.

CHAPTER 20

The travel brochures were scattered all across the kitchen table. Jeffrey paced the floor in his slippers and chewed on a chunk of Orkney cheddar, eyeing the array of colorful pictures, which stood in stark contrast to the darkening December skies outside. So many places, so many towns and cities and airports, so many kinds of people, smells, and tastes. He had no idea where to go. He just knew he needed to go.

The cottage he'd lived in contentedly for so many years felt inexplicably small around him now, and he'd taken to driving in ever-increasing circles, venturing farther and farther outside of Pitlochry. He'd gone south to Edinburgh, west to Oban, and east to Arbroath, his little Mini humming along the unfamiliar roads as he watched the scenery change from hill to pasture to coastline.

He especially liked the shores to the east, in Angus, with their gentle sweeps, white sand, and tidy coves. The previous weekend, he'd even stayed one night in a rented caravan on the beach at Monifieth. He'd walked for miles along the front, nodding hello to the many dog walkers, pensioners taking their daily constitutionals, and pink-cheeked children on bikes. He'd stopped to sit on one of the famous dolphin-shaped benches, and buffeted by the salty wind, he hadn't felt like the only jagged rock on a pile of smooth pebbles, as he had for much of his adult life. Instead, he'd felt as if he fit into the new landscape just fine.

Each time he got home to Pitlochry from one of his excursions, all was exactly as he'd left it. Increasingly, rather than giving him comfort, the realization disappointed him.

Fred and Matilda were back in their newly decorated cottage, and the almost daily flood of thank-you gifts had, mercifully, begun to wane. Jeffrey was full to the gunnels with pies, stews, scones, and sugary fudge. He'd gained four pounds' worth of Matilda's gratitude, and much to his annoyance, had had to buy some bigger trousers. While he understood and appreciated her need to do something for him, the constant supply of food was weighing heavy on more than his waistline.

The local papers had made a big fuss about his saving Matilda, and he'd even been interviewed for the regional Morning Show on the radio. His picture had appeared in several papers and now, when he walked through the town, Pitlochry folk smiled and tipped their hats at him, nodding their approval, some even asking for his autograph. The previous week, he'd signed a copy of *Woman's Own* for a lady in front of him at the checkout in the supermarket. While these things were happening, Jeffrey would blush, downplay his role in Matilda's survival, and hide his pleasure at their gratitude. He'd never sought the limelight, and in the past the thought of it had always made him sweaty, but this felt surprisingly good.

After a couple of weeks, the initial flurry of attention had died down, even though the landlord of the Old Forge Inn had framed his newspaper interview and hung it behind the bar. The heading, "Local Hero Saves Woman from Blazing House," screamed from the wall. He was a celebrity, and there was nothing he could do about it.

Ralf mewed from somewhere up the stairs, snapping him back to the present. In Mary's absence, the cat had resumed its antisocial behavior, to which Jeffrey was once again resigned. Glancing at the clock, he saw that it was 5:30. Emptying a can of the only food that the cat would entertain into the customary dish, Jeffrey shouted.

"Come and get it!"

Today was Thursday, so his own tea would consist of a Scotch egg from MacLintock the butcher, a can of peas and carrots, and a caramel wafer for pudding. He had a few bottles of Santa's Swallie, his favorite Christmas Ale, in the larder, so he decided he'd treat himself to one.

As he waited for the crispy breadcrumb coating around the egg to warm in the oven, Jeffrey shivered and wandered back into the lounge. The fire crackled in the hearth, taking the chill off the room and his back. He moved the burned wood fragments around with the poker, then threw a new log into the grate. The nights were fairly drawing in.

As he watched the flames lick tentatively up and around the edges of the piney log, he wondered if it would be a long winter. This would be the first Christmas without his mum, and to tell the truth, he was dreading it. He hadn't even thought about putting up the little tree that lay in a box in the cupboard under the stairs. It just didn't feel right to do it, somehow. He wished he could go away somewhere and just avoid Christmas altogether this year. Even the thought of seeing Mary wasn't enough to cheer him on the subject.

A few minutes later, he walked into the lounge holding the copper-colored ale and watching the breaded egg roll precariously across the plate. The little heap of peas and carrots admirably did the job of stopping the golden ball from descending directly onto the carpet, so Jeffrey settled himself in his armchair then turned on the TV.

As the screen flickered into life, he took a long swallow of ale. A man with thick silver-gray hair and a polished English accent was walking along a cobbled street, describing what he saw. Little mopeds buzzed around, and behind him rose a mammoth structure that Jeffrey recognized. It reached up many stories above the man's head and had row upon row of empty windows and sections of crumbling stonework where one could see the bright blue sky behind.

The presenter indicated around himself as he spoke into the camera, addressing Jeffrey directly.

"Perhaps the most quintessential of all ancient structures in this city of Rome, the Coliseum stands stalwart, despite the centuries of war and turbulence it has witnessed. This architectural wonder is a symbol of both civilization and barbarism. It is as spellbinding today as it must have been when, with a flick of the thumb, emperors decided the fate of gladiators before crowds of spectators all those centuries ago."

Jeffrey swallowed a mouthful of the spicy egg. Rome, now that would be an adventure. When he was a boy, Agnes had read him many stories about the Roman armies that had passed through

Britain. She'd been very proud of the fact that they hadn't managed to conquer all of Scotland, retreating behind Hadrian's Wall. He remembered her cackling at the idea that the Romans had called the Celts Barbarians. They'd been so afraid of them that they had supposedly sent diplomats into the Celtic lands with valuable gifts for the important leaders, as encouragement for them to stay friendly.

"It'd tek mare than a few trinkets for us t'let thay Eye-ties intay oor country." She'd laughed.

When he was eleven, Agnes had taken him on the train to the National Museum in Edinburgh to see an exhibition of ancient Roman coins, tools, weapons, and jewelry. Imagine if she knew he'd been to Rome, actually stood on the roads they'd read about, climbed the Spanish Steps and walked around the Coliseum? Rome would be a real adventure, all right.

As he swallowed again, a big piece of egg got caught in his throat, and Jeffrey coughed. He gulped at his beer and felt the lump slide painfully down.

A passport. He'd need a passport. He supposed the post office was still the place to go for that, so he'd check with Mrs. Henry when he went in to get his paper in the morning.

He was going to walk up to the allotment in the afternoon and check on the bees one last time before the drones closed up the hive entrances, ready for the winter. He had a few remaining potatoes, leeks, and beetroot that he could dig up, and then he'd turn the earth over and leave it until spring. He hoped Mary liked beets; there were so many that he'd never be able to eat them all.

He and Mary had arranged to go the cinema the following evening to see a film she had recommended. He didn't mind what it was, really, as long as he got to sit in the dark little theater with her, feel her shoulder pressed up close to his, and eat Maltesers.

As he watched the streets of Rome and the gray-haired Englishman, Jeffrey's plan unfolded. What would Christmas be like in Rome?

CHAPTER 21

———◆———

Mary had almost finished her shopping. The cart rattled, one wheel pulling stubbornly to the left, and her shoulder ached from tugging it against its will. She'd had a long shift at the nursing home and was looking forward to a hot shower and a change of clothes before meeting Jeffrey at the cinema.

She'd been seeing him a couple of times a week since the fire, and while she felt them becoming closer, it was happening more slowly than she would have liked. It could never be said that Jeffrey Mere was rash, but she'd have welcomed a big dose of rashness right about now. How long was she supposed to wait? How many dinners was she to cook and how many walks along the river was she to take before he made his move? He'd touched her arm a few times, brushed a curl away from her face, but that was it. She was getting frustrated with the pace of their developing relationship.

Something inside her had told her that Jeffrey would change

after the fire. The fact that he'd saved a human life should have puffed up his ego a little, given him a boost of self-confidence, surely?

She pushed the trolley along the aisle, grabbing a packet of ginger snaps as she passed the display. She knew Jeffrey loved them, just as Agnes had. She missed Agnes. Her sage old friend with the acerbic wit had been sharp as a tack until the night she'd decided that she was done and had closed her eyes on the world, once and for all. It was typical of Agnes to choose the timing of her own passing with such specificity. Mary felt a tug of sadness as she wheeled the trolley to the checkout. She missed the long conversations they'd shared, the little secrets they'd exchanged. Agnes had made an indelible impression on her, and Mary was grateful for the kindness and advice that her old friend had given her over the months she'd cared for her. She recalled one of the last times they'd spoken. They'd been talking about Jeffrey's climb up Ben Macdhui, and Agnes had told her how happy she was that he was going.

Agnes had then asked her to help her into bed, and Mary was tucking her in when Agnes had grabbed her hand.

"You know there's mare tae him than meets the eye."

Mary had stopped her task and focused on the wrinkled face.

"He's a good man, a clever man. You'll no' meet a kinder one, either." Agnes's blue eyes had been rheumy, and Mary thought she'd seen tears looming.

"I know he's a good man. He's *your* son, after all." Mary had smiled and patted the stick-thin thigh lying under the blanket.

"You'll need tae be patient, though. It'll be worth it, I promise. But he is'nae a fast worker." At that, Agnes had broken into her customary cackle, sending her false teeth shooting out onto the bedspread and herself into a violent coughing fit.

"Just breathe, Mrs. Mere. Slowly, now." Mary had patted her back and handed her a glass of water to sip.

"After all this time, you'll still no' call me Agnes?" Agnes had stared at her as she spoke.

Mary recalled feeling a little odd about it, but she had agreed to call her Agnes if she promised not to tell the home's manager, who insisted on the use of surnames as a mark of respect to the residents. Agnes had tutted and rolled her eyes as she nodded her consent. It had remained a tiny and yet significant secret between them until the day Agnes had died, and Mary had treasured the cloaked intimacy of using her Christian name when no one else was around.

Mary knew Jeffrey was a good man. No one could have cared more for his mother or been more patient, kind, and gentle. But the question Mary asked herself was, did she *want* a nice man, or at least one as nice as that? There were many things she liked about Jeffrey, but she had to admit, the snail-like progress they were making as a couple was driving her up the wall. As she watched the checkout girl scanning her groceries, Mary wondered if she'd have the patience to wait for him, to take a leap of faith.

"That'll be twenty-six pounds thirty, please." The checkout girl smiled expectantly.

"Oh, right. Hang on." Mary rummaged in her handbag for her purse and then pressed her credit card into the outstretched young hand. It was shocking, the price of food these days. She scanned the meager pile of goods and proceeded to stack it in the two plastic bags the girl slid towards her on the conveyor belt.

The walk home was relatively short, and as the winter evening drew in around her, Mary breathed in the air of her town. As she turned into Willow Street, the adorable Subramanian twins were out on their bikes, wrapped up in thick jackets they turned small circles in the road. Their mum watched them closely from the living room window. Mary raised a bag in greeting as she passed, and the pretty woman waved back and smiled her startling, pearly smile.

Willow Street was a place Mary had always dreamed of living. Not this Willow Street particularly, but she'd imagined living in a street where she would wave to her neighbors, attend street parties, make new friends, and most of all not feel afraid, either outside or inside her own walls. She loved her little cottage and could honestly say that she'd never felt vulnerable since moving in a few months before.

Agnes had told her about the death of the old man who had lived there, and Mary had been first to call the estate agent and inquire about the house, before it had even gone on the market. The moment she'd walked inside, she'd known this was her home. She'd put an offer on it within the week, and two days later knew it was hers. It was the first home she'd owned by herself, and that made it all the more precious. As a longtime tenant in both Glasgow and Edinburgh, the idea that these hearty stones belonged to her still hadn't lost its novelty.

She glanced over at Jeffrey's house as she passed. He'd told her he'd be up at the allotment, so she knew he wasn't in. The climbing roses were resplendent around the door, and if she wasn't mistaken, there was a casserole sitting on his front step. She giggled to herself, as she figured Matilda had been up to her tricks again. More stew, no doubt. Poor Jeffrey would explode rather than upset his neighbor by saying no to her offerings. She was looking forward to seeing him that evening and hoped that he'd enjoy the film she'd picked.

The cinema was busy, and it took them a few minutes to find one another. The film was one she'd wanted to see for a while. Anything with George Clooney in it was worth seeing, and this one, involving a bank heist, would also amuse Jeffrey, she hoped.

"Hello, there." Jeffrey lunged towards her, his hands full of Maltesers and licorice allsorts.

"I got your favorites." He smiled and held the packet of allsorts out to her.

"Great, thanks. Shall we go in, then?" Mary took the offering and fell into step beside him. To her surprise, he reached for her hand and, taking it in his, led her through the small crowd into the dark theater.

Mary felt her heart patter and, enjoying this new momentum, allowed herself to be guided to a seat.

"Is this OK?" Jeffrey indicated a row in the middle of the little theater. He leaned in towards her ear as he spoke, and she could smell his peppermint breath.

"Perfect." She nodded and pressed her fingers into his cool palm. "Great spot."

As her eyes adjusted to the dim light, she saw him smiling. He had a lovely smile. His teeth were good and white, and all just about where they should be. His cheeks were pink and taut, belying his 64 years, and when he laughed, his eyes closed ever so slightly, as if being squeezed shut by the mirth oozing out.

"Can you come back to my place after? I'd like to talk to you about something." Jeffrey looked at her over his shoulder.

She nodded, curious and hopeful at the same time. "OK. For a wee while."

Was this it? Was he finally going to go for it? At the very thought, she felt both excited and nervous. Was Jeffrey Mere finally going to kiss her?

CHAPTER 22

❖

"Rome?" Mary sounded incredulous as Ralf, splayed out territorially on her lap, licked his paw.

"Yes. I know it's a bit rash, but there it is." Jeffrey shrugged and blew on his own steaming mug. He preferred drinking-chocolate to cocoa, as a rule, but had run out.

"So when did you come up with this idea?" Mary sipped carefully.

"Today." He grinned.

Jeffrey didn't generally grin — well, not often, anyway, but this felt like an appropriate moment to do so. He was overcome with the deep sense of rightness about his decision, and now all he wanted was to get organized and go. Spending Christmas in Rome seemed like the most natural thing in the world to him today.

Mary watched his face. He was grinning. Despite her shock at his announcement, she couldn't help but think that the more she saw this expression on him, the more she liked it.

"Well, Jeffrey, I'm sure you've thought it through." She stroked Ralf's back as he purred loudly.

"No. Not really." Jeffrey chuckled. The sound was vaguely familiar to her, and as she stared at him, Mary realized that it resembled her old friend Agnes's throaty laugh. It was a deeper version but carried the same dusting of amusement that the old lady could liberally apply to the oddest of situations.

Suddenly, Mary found herself laughing too, but despite her pleasure at his obvious excitement, inside she felt a pebble of disappointment forming. He'd chosen to go away now, at Christmas. Had he given no thought to her and what she might do?

He chatted on and she found herself only half listening. To mitigate the overwhelming feeling of being unconsidered, left behind, she tried to remind herself that Jeffrey had been dreading this Christmas, his first without Agnes. This spontaneous trip would certainly be a departure from the norm. It would mean that he didn't have to endure any form of customary celebration that had a newly gaping hole in it. She nodded to herself imperceptibly. She supposed he had to do what he had to do, with or without her, but the without her part hurt.

Finished with his toilette, the cat stretched theatrically, then jumped down onto the fireside rug. Flames licked greedily around the logs as tendrils of pale smoke wound up into the chimney.

"I know it's a bit sudden, but..." Jeffrey's voice faded. He looked at Mary's sweet face, her cheeks glowing from the heat of the fire and the hot drink. Her red hair curled over the back of her collar the way he loved. He suddenly wanted to touch those glorious curls, press his fingers onto her neck, pull her close, and inhale her cinnamon breath. If he kissed her rosy mouth, would she taste of cinnamon, or perhaps cocoa? Jeffrey cleared his throat awkwardly, embarrassed by his train of thought.

Mary squeezed out a smile.

"Well, it is sudden, but I get it, Jeffrey." She nodded and took another sip of cocoa. "I think it's a good idea."

"Really?"

"Really."

Jeffrey rose and padded into the kitchen. A few moments later, he returned with a colorful brochure.

"Look at this place." He placed the brochure on her knee and sat down next to her on the couch. "It's called the Grand Plaza."

Mary scanned the pictures of a shimmering hotel lobby littered with gold leaf and marble, frescoes, and statues, things she'd read about but never seen for herself.

"Goodness. It's gorgeous." She nodded approvingly, the unpleasant pebble shifting in her stomach.

"They have a special Christmas deal on. Seven nights, full board, including a cocktail reception on Christmas Eve and a banquet on the twenty-fifth with an orchestra and dancing in the ballroom." He leaned over and turned the page.

Mary looked at a scene plucked straight from one of her favorite period dramas. Elegant couples in tailcoats and ball gowns twirled in a fantastical room, the domed ceiling high above them covered from edge to edge with painting, the likes of which she'd never seen. Huge candelabras stood around the perimeter of the room, and an orchestra, also in tailcoats, sat at one end. She could almost hear the music, feel the flicker of the candlelight, as she stared down at the page. This was agony.

"Jeepers."

"I know. Terrific, isn't it?" Oblivious, Jeffrey turned another page to a picture of the Spanish Steps and several cafés with wrought-iron tables on the pavement.

"Everyone looks so glamorous." Mary glanced at Jeffrey's profile as he stared at the brochure on her lap. How could he flash this brochure in her face, then not ask if she wanted to go too? As she looked back at the stylish couple, Mary guiltily allowed herself to enjoy a moment of spite, thinking that Jeffrey would not fit into this scene, with his Scottish-ness worn so blatantly on his sleeve.

As if reading her mind, Jeffrey chuckled again.

"Well, I'll be a big dose of doon hame reality, won't I?" He nudged her arm playfully. "Do you think I could get away with my tweed, or will I need to get a monkey-suit, like that?" He pointed to a stylish man walking down the steps in a sleek black suit. The woman on his arm wore a hat and a dress with broad stripes that reminded Mary of one Audrey Hepburn wore in *Breakfast at Tiffany's*.

Despite her pain, Mary saw the joy in Jeffrey's face and giggled.

"I don't think the tweed will do, somehow."

"Perhaps I can rent a suit?" Jeffrey rose and put another log on the fire.

Mary watched him poking at the logs. He was running away from Christmas, which she understood, but was he also running away from her?

Jeffrey's back was hunched over his task. His Argyle sweater had ridden up his back, revealing the loose tail of his flannel shirt, and underneath, she caught a glimpse of a white vest. The sight of his rumpled clothing, simple and yet so intimate, made her feel crushingly alone. It had been so long since she'd been held, caressed, cared for, that the absence of that level of human contact threatened to choke her. Why would he not just kiss her? She was sure he'd wanted to on several occasions, but he always backed away. She really didn't know how much longer she could wait.

Jeffrey turned and saw her watching him. As their eyes met, he knew in his heart that she wanted to be asked to go to Rome. However, slightly deeper in his heart, he also knew that he wasn't ready to ask her.

"Well, I'd better be going." Mary rose abruptly and placed her half-empty cup on the coffee table.

"I'll walk you home."

"It's eight doors down the street, Jeffrey. I'm quite fine on my own."

He heard something in her voice. Could it be disappointment? Frustration? He recognized it as a caution but, as he helped her on with her coat, Jeffrey Mere felt incapable of giving her what she wanted.

Everyone told him that he was a nice man, a good man, but Jeffrey knew that sometimes even a nice man could be selfish or even hurtful.

Mary thanked him for the evening, accepted his circumspect peck on the cheek, and set off down the road. As she passed Fred and Matilda's, their TV glimmered blue through a crack in the curtains. Glancing in, she saw them sitting close together on their new couch. Their heads were inclined towards one another, and Fred's arm was around Matilda's shoulder. The couple sat, warm and companionable, oblivious to the lonely world hovering right outside their newly painted window.

Mary felt the prickle of tears and, annoyed at her own self-pity, rubbed at her eyes with a gloved hand. So what if Jeffrey Mere couldn't get his finger out. She'd show him. She'd get on with her life, and too bad if he came back to her too late. There were other fish in the damn sea.

She sniffed loudly and picked up her pace. The cold was making her nose run. She caught the smell of fragrant curry as she passed the Subramanians' house, and wood smoke hung in the air the rest of the way down the street.

Letting herself into her cottage, she hung her coat on the rack and slipped her shoes off in the vestibule. Her sheepskin slippers were soft and welcoming, and as she walked into the kitchen to turn on the lights, her feet were already warming up.

CHAPTER 23

Jeffrey stood in the arrivals hall of Leonardo da Vinci Airport, still somewhat awestruck by his first-ever flight. His suitcase had yet to show up on the conveyor belt, but rather than feeling panicked by the delay, he was focused on the people around him.

Everyone looked like they'd stepped out of a magazine or film set. Many of the women were wearing dresses and high heels. Even those in jeans and casual jackets had an elegance about them. With colorful scarves draped around their shoulders and huge leather handbags draped over their arms, they all looked indifferent, relaxed, as if they flew every single day of their lives. The men were wearing bright-colored trousers and jackets with such an air of confidence. Some, to Jeffrey's surprise, even wore pink, and many also carried big satchels.

Looking down at his tweed trousers and heavy brogues, Jeffrey felt suddenly conspicuous. His hand hovered over his cap. Should he take it off? His head was cold, so he decided to leave it where it was. Besides, no point in gilding the lily, as Agnes had often told him. He was who he was, and that was that. You'd certainly never see a Pitlochry man wearing pink trousers or carrying a satchel, unless it was to the annual fancy dress party at the town hall.

After another twenty minutes of people-watching, Jeffrey's dark green suitcase, bought especially for the trip, finally appeared on the belt. Having tugged it off and carefully checked the large label he'd attached to it in Edinburgh Airport, he headed through customs and out onto the main concourse. As he stared around, mesmerized by the huge skylights, the expanses of intricate scaffolding above his head, and the smell of freshly ground coffee, Jeffrey failed to notice the young man leaning down over his suitcase. Turning abruptly, he jumped at the intrusion.

"Excuse me. What are you doing?" Jeffrey asked, alarmed.

"You are Mr. Mere?" The voice was like molten chocolate as the young man raised his dark brown eyes to Jeffrey's and smiled a movie star smile.

"Yes, that's me." Jeffrey swallowed.

The young man had thick wavy hair, wore a dark gray suit, and carried a clipboard. He laughed and stepped back, extending a hand towards Jeffrey. "Welcome to Roma."

"Thanks." Jeffrey shook his hand and blushed.

"I am from Air Italia, we are choosing you as special guest, for free tour of Roma. Congratulations!" The young man beamed over the clipboard, which he now held close to his chest.

Jeffrey stared, uncomprehending.

"I didn't enter any competitions."

"Is no competition. Air Italia choose, from passenger list, one name, you, Mr. Mere. No competition." The man wiggled the clipboard at him and grinned even more widely.

Jeffrey gasped. He'd never won anything in his life. Was it possible he'd been picked from the entire planeload of people? Perhaps his luck was changing for the better?

"Well, I never." Jeffrey returned the young man's smile.

"My name Paolo. You come with me now."

"Now? I don't think I want to go on a tour *now*." Jeffrey frowned.

"No no, sorry, sir. I take you to your hotel now. Then, tomorrow I come — take you on tour. Is OK?"

Jeffrey's shoulders relaxed and he nodded. "Aye, that'll be better. I'll get settled in first."

He hitched his camera strap up onto his shoulder and, pulling his suitcase behind him, followed the young man out the wide sliding doors. The sky was clear and the air chilly. As Paolo pointed out a silver-gray minibus parked opposite the terminal and they walked towards it, Jeffrey shivered. He was glad he'd brought the heavy jacket he'd bought for climbing Ben Macdhui. He'd read that it could get damn cold in Rome in December.

In the driver's seat sat a hulk of a man who watched them approach, unsmiling. Paolo indicated towards the back of the vehicle, and the man got out and walked around to meet them. His scuffed leather jacket stood out in sharp contrast to Paolo's smart suit. Jeffrey watched as the big man pulled off his gloves and shoved them nervously in and out of the pockets of his faded jeans. He then dropped his burning cigarette to the ground, crushing it under his boot. Jeffrey nodded at him as, with thick-fingered hands, the man swung the suitcase into the back.

Getting no response, Jeffrey turned back to Paolo.

"Where you stay?" Paolo asked, as he opened the back passenger door with a flourish.

"Grand Hotel Plaza." Jeffrey replied and slid into the seat. He was feeling a little tired, truth be told. He wondered if they made a decent cup of tea at the hotel. If not, he had a box of PG Tips in his case. One should never compromise on tea.

"Excellente." Paolo tossed the clipboard onto the front seat and then climbed in. "Andiamo."

Jeffrey watched as the busy streets slipped by the window. Traffic gradually increased as they neared what he guessed was the city center. Tiny Lego-like cars buzzed past, and a sea of mopeds seethed around the van, slowing their progress. Soon enough, however, he caught sight of the towering walls of the Coliseum. He craned his neck as they passed, staring up at the breathtaking height of the remaining structure. He tried to imagine it in its heyday, full to the brim with Romans baying for Christian blood. They'd been a bloodthirsty lot, these Romans.

Paolo chatted as they drove, but Jeffrey was too distracted to respond, especially as Paolo didn't seem to require him to. The traffic around them was pressing in, making it difficult to maneuver the van down the ever-narrowing lanes they were entering. Jeffrey thanked his lucky stars that he didn't have to deal with this kind of thing back home. Even though his Mini was the perfect size for these streets, he'd be a nervous wreck.

As he shifted in the back seat, Jeffrey felt something against his foot. Looking down, he was surprised to see some crumpled food wrappers, a plastic bag, and an empty drinking cup rolling around. Not a very good impression for Air Italia, to have rubbish lying around inside their vans. Now that he thought about it, he couldn't recall seeing an airline insignia or logo on the outside. How odd. As he looked down at the seat, he noticed that the upholstery was torn in several places and then, turning behind him, saw that one of the side windows was cracked, held together by large strips of wrapping tape. At the sight of the broken window, Jeffrey felt a twinge of anxiety for the first time since meeting Paolo. His throat tightened slightly, so he took a deep breath and tried to reassure himself. *It's OK. Everything is fine. These men work for the airline, so it must be OK.*

Suddenly, the van took a sharp turn to the left, and the paper cup rolled over his foot. The alleys were now impossibly narrow, and Jeffrey glanced at the buildings on either side, noticing that the doors could do with a coat of paint and some windows were missing glass here and there. There were large groups of youngsters wandering around with hunched shoulders under their hooded sweatshirts. This was not feeling good. It was time he spoke up.

Clearing his throat, he placed a hand on the back of Paolo's seat.

"So, Paolo, how much farther to the hotel? I'm pretty tired, you know."

Paolo, without turning around, said, "Almost there."

Jeffrey swallowed over his rising anxiety.

"The guidebook said it was only seventeen minutes from the airport. It seems like we've been driving for a lot longer than that."

At this Paolo turned to the driver and spoke in Italian. The big man nodded silently and then, pressing his heavy elbow along the edge of his window, knocked the central lock button down. The thunk of the locks made Jeffrey's stomach jump. OK, he was in trouble now.

"Paolo?" Jeffrey tried again. "I don't think Air Italia would be very impressed by this behavior. Can you take me to the Grand Hotel Plaza right away, please?" Jeffrey's voice was firmer than his insides felt. The formerly chatty Paolo was now silent.

The van turned again, and the height of the closely packed buildings looming on either side of the vehicle cut out much of the light, making the interior as dim as any dank December evening in the Highlands. Jeffrey squinted out of the window, his intuition telling him that he needed to make note of some landmarks, distinctive buildings, or road signs that he could recount later, when he told the police what had happened. He'd definitely be speaking to the police about this as soon as he got to the hotel.

After they crossed a river, the buildings gradually began to spread out again. Larger and larger gaps appeared between them, and the tarmac road underneath the wheels gradually turned into a rough track. The van bounced along until Jeffrey thought he saw the Olympic Stadium to his left and then, after a few more minutes, there was a junkyard to his right. Old cars littered the side of the road, abandoned and lifeless.

Jeffrey began to pant softly as beads of sweat ran down his neck and under his collar. He tried his best to be quiet, as he didn't want either of these men to know how scared he was. If only he'd paid more attention at the airport, asked more questions of this smart young man before trusting him so blindly. He wondered what this pair had in store for him. Would they rob him? Steal his case and his credit card, then leave him by the side of the road? Worse still, would they hurt him when they realized he had virtually no cash, just a book of traveler's checks?

At the prospect of a beating, Jeffrey quivered, his throat

closing a tiny bit tighter against the bile that was rising. He had never been a fighter, not in school and not in adulthood. He had his own way of fighting, right enough, but it had never involved his fists.

Both men had ignored his attempts to question them, but perhaps he could still persuade them that this course of action was ill-advised?

"Paolo. I can give you my credit card, if that's what you want? It won't get you far, but you can have it all the same."

The young man stared ahead without answering, and Jeffrey, deflated, sat back in his seat, preparing for the worst. He should have told Mary how much he admired her. He should have asked someone to check on the bees. He should have paid the gas bill before he left. He should have had that dram with his old land-lord, Frank Duff. So many should haves crowded his mind that his head felt fit to burst.

Turning his attention back to the road, ahead he saw a few scattered homes with loosely hung doors, corrugated iron over the windows, and lengths of rough chains forming makeshift fences. The houses, if you could call them that, had messy numbers painted on the doors, and some had names written on them.

The people they passed had become a mixture of what appeared to be South Americans, Asians, and some that Agnes would have called Gypsies, with swarthy skin and darkly shadowed eyes. Their clothing was tattered, and a couple of them had no shoes on. Jeffrey supposed these could be the Romany people his guidebook had mentioned.

As the van continued along the track, dark-eyed people looked on uninterestedly. Jeffrey wondered whether, if he banged on the window or shouted for help, any of these poor souls would have the energy to take notice, never mind lend a hand? He doubted it. This was supposed to be the City of Joy, but as far as he could see, there was no joy in the faces they were passing.

Paolo said something to the driver in Italian, and the man abruptly turned the van into a driveway and halted in front of a tall wooden gate. Paolo jumped out and opened it, and the van pulled forward slowly into a courtyard with several shanty buildings crouching around the perimeter. Jeffrey felt his heart clattering under his shirt as he searched the area for any other visible exits, only to be disappointed.

The van drew to a stop and Paolo, if that was even his name, ran around to the side and opened Jeffrey's door.

"You get out now, Mr. Mere." The formality of hearing his surname threw Jeffrey slightly. A tiny surge of optimism crept into his chest. Could this all be some awful misunderstanding? Perhaps Paolo was just making an unscheduled stop before taking him to the hotel?

Paolo took Jeffrey roughly by the arm, dispelling his last shred of hope, and led him towards one of the shanties.

"Where are we going?" Jeffrey spoke to the side of the young face that was turned away from him. "I won't tell anyone, you know, son. If you let me go now, I'll not tell a soul."

Paolo laughed harshly and shouted something to the driver, who followed closely behind them, dragging Jeffrey's suitcase. The impulse to tell the big thug to be careful with the brand-new case was strong, so Jeffrey bit down on his tongue to keep his thoughts to himself. Young people had no sense of the value of anything anymore, and it infuriated him. Such disrespect.

Paolo opened a makeshift door and pushed Jeffrey inside the dark structure.

"Sit," he barked.

There was a three-legged stool in the corner. As it was the only piece of furniture in the place, Jeffrey walked over on shaky legs and sat down. The floor was a mixture of gravel and dust, and apart from one small window behind him, the room was devoid of openings. It was airless and close, and Jeffrey could smell something sour, like old cabbage or dirty socks, which threatened to turn his already queasy stomach.

"Your pockets, empty them." Paolo stood over him, holding open a plastic bag as Jeffrey, with quaking hands, reached into his pockets and pulled out his wallet, his passport, a piece of paper with the hotel's address on it, his airline ticket, the door keys to the cottage, and a packet of spearmint gum.

"That's it?" Paolo growled. Jeffrey nodded.

As Paolo rummaged through the bag, discarding the keys, ticket and gum, the other man had opened the suitcase and was dumping Jeffrey's belongings out onto the dirty floor.

"Watch that," Jeffrey blurted on an impulse when his best Harris tweed jacket sent up a cloud of dust as it hit the ground. The big man, startled at the sound of Jeffrey's voice, stopped what he was doing and looked up at Paolo.

"Shut up." Paolo turned quickly and grabbed Jeffrey by the collar. "You don't speak. OK?"

Jeffrey nodded as his collar was slowly released, and he felt his heart flip-flop.

Jeffrey watched silently as his shirts, underwear, trousers, and toilet bag were emptied unceremoniously onto the ground. It stung to see his possessions being treated this way, but then, when he saw the days-of-the-week socks being thrown into the dust, something in his mind snapped. If there was one thing he could not stand, it was that.

Before he could stop himself, Jeffrey was up on his feet. He stood a full head and shoulders taller than Paolo, which he had not noticed before this moment.

"NO. Not the socks. That's enough," he shouted.

As he lurched towards the bigger man, to his surprise, the great hulk raised his hands, as if to cover his head from an attack. Ignoring this, Jeffrey crouched down and quickly picked up several of the pairs of socks.

Standing up, he saw the big man cowering away from him and Jeffrey, feeling oddly empowered, stood looking down on the crouching giant, taking in the bizarre reaction of the man.

Suddenly, he felt Paolo come up behind him. The young man launched himself at Jeffrey, piggy-backing on him, his wiry arms wrapped around Jeffrey's neck. The sharp toes of his shiny shoes dug into Jeffrey's thighs, pummeling him with kicks. Thin fingers sought Jeffrey's eyes, which were mercifully protected behind his glasses. Paolo clung on like a limpet as Jeffrey spun around and around, trying to dislodge his unwelcome passenger.

He felt the grip of the thin legs loosen and then, eventually, as Jeffrey continued to spin, Paolo released his grip and fell to the ground with a yelp. Jeffrey turned on him, wielding the socks like a handful of grenades.

Paolo sat on the ground, bemused, and looked up at Jeffrey. Shouting something sharply to the other man, he pulled a thin-bladed knife from his sock.

"You leave my brother alone. You hear?"

Jeffrey, spotting the blade, was struck by the rash stupidity of his actions. What was he thinking? For a few pairs of socks, he had lost his grip on the seriousness of the situation. But these were not just any socks, these were his Mon-Day to Sun-Day and two Any-Day pairs. Every stitch, every letter, was a connection to Agnes that no one was entitled to sever. No, no one would ever muck around with these socks.

Paolo was up on his feet again, and before Jeffrey could gather himself, he felt the sharp blade being pressed up under his rib.

"Sit down. I no want to hurt you, Mr. Mere." Again the ludicrous formality of his name hung heavy in the atmosphere of the smelly room.

Jeffrey raised his hands, still gripping the socks, and sat back down on the rickety stool.

So this monster of a man was Paolo's brother? Having not heard him utter a single word since the airport, Jeffrey wondered if he was disabled in some way, deaf perhaps, or maybe just slow? Hamish Taft, the blacksmith in Pitlochry, had a slow son. He'd kept him close, at the forge, and eventually the boy had learned to work the bellows. The town knew him well, and he was valued as a member of the community, having his own beer mug at the pub.

Jeffrey glanced over at the big man, still crouching down with his hands over his head. He wondered if this poor soul had been accepted in the same way. What kind of life did he lead, being dragged into this kind of shenanigans by his brother? It was a damn shame, so it was.

"You know, you need to take better care of your brother." Jeffrey, heart still pounding, spoke quietly as Paolo walked over and gently pushed his brother's arms back down to his sides. He spoke quietly to him, and Jeffrey saw the fear in the bigger man's wide brown eyes subside as the smaller man's voice permeated.

"You're lucky to have a brother, son. It's a gift, and some of us weren't so lucky." Jeffrey shook his head slowly as he spoke and Paolo, standing up, replaced the knife in his sock before walking back to the low stool.

"You shut up. Stay, sit. I don't hurt you. OK?" Paolo's eyes, now cold, searched Jeffrey's face.

Jeffrey nodded slowly and replied, "If you say so, then I believe you."

"Where is the money?" Paolo was again rummaging in the plastic bag.

"I don't have much cash. My credit card and traveler's checks are in my wallet. That's all I have."

Paolo lifted the leather wallet and pulled out a Bank of Scotland twenty-pound note and a small wad of checks.

"What is this?" He flapped the unfamiliar paper at Jeffrey, a frown creasing his smooth brow. "No cash?"

"No. Those are instead of cash." Jeffrey squinted at the young man. Had he never seen traveler's checks before?

"What I do with these?" Paolo looked questioningly at Jeffrey.

"You spend them, in the shops. Just like cash. I sign them and they become valid." As the words were out, Jeffrey felt a tiny glimmer of hope. "I can sign them for you and then you can spend the money. If you let me go, I'll sign them for you. OK?"

Paolo shuffled through the pile, shaking his head. The big man was back up on his feet and now stood with his back pressed up against the wall of the room. Jeffrey's belongings lay scattered across the floor, and time seemed to stand painfully still as Paolo pondered his options.

Finally, his captor spoke. "OK. You sign, we let you go."

Jeffrey watched the young face scanning his own. As he nodded his assent, he wondered again how young folk got themselves into these scrapes nowadays. If Agnes had been here, she'd have grabbed the two of them by the ears and read them the riot act, that was for sure. One word from her, and they'd have toed the line.

Paolo located a pen in his inside pocket and shoved it at Jeffrey. Jeffrey's wits were now about him. Perhaps it was the rush of adrenaline, but for once he felt his power. He would sign nothing until they agreed to take him somewhere safe.

Shaking his head, he explained to Paolo that they needed to take him back into the city. He would agree to sign the checks when he saw a safe street where they could drop him off. Paolo considered; then, after a few moments of silence, he nodded. He barked some instructions at his brother and took the van keys from his quivering hand. Jeffrey gathered that he and Paolo were leaving without the brother. The idea of being alone with Paolo made him more nervous.

Jeffrey bent as if to retrieve his belongings and Paolo, seeing what he was doing, shouted. "No. You leave it."

Jeffrey recoiled as if burned, but mutinously shoved a few of the pairs of socks he held into his pockets, his ominous look enough to silence the young man's protests.

Paolo gestured towards the door and Jeffrey walked ahead of him, but just as he was leaving the rank room he turned and looked at the brother.

"You take care, big man. OK?" The man stared at him wordlessly as Jeffrey nodded and walked out the door.

Having driven back along the dirt track, Jeffrey could once again see the Olympic Stadium ahead.

"You can leave me here." He looked over at Paolo, who was driving faster than his brother had, kicking up big clouds of dust that followed them from the shantytown.

Paolo slowed the van down then pulled over into a gap between two parked cars.

"You sign now." He shoved the wad of checks towards Jeffrey and flashed the menacing knife for good measure.

"There's no need for that." Jeffrey tutted and, taking the pen, began to sign each check.

As he passed them back to Paolo, one at a time, Jeffrey mentally calculated the amount of money he was handing over. Agnes had left him almost two thousand pounds. After paying for his plane ticket and hotel, he had decided to bring the remaining five hundred euros with him to spend. Each check served as a painful reminder of his naivety and stupidity as it left his hand and settled on the open palm of this young criminal.

With six pairs of socks crammed into his pockets, minus his passport, ticket, credit card, suitcase full of clothes, and his spearmint gum, Jeffrey Mere stepped out into the street. The van screeched away, leaving him standing in the road. As he watched the back of the vehicle disappear, his legs finally gave way underneath him and he slumped into a heap of tweed and wool.

CHAPTER 24

———◆———

Mary opened the door to Jeffrey's cottage. She'd agreed to feed Ralf and keep an eye on things for him while he was away. He had turned the heating down when he'd left, and the air was frigid as she walked into the vestibule.

Deciding to keep her coat on, Mary called up the stairs.

"Ralf. Here, kitty kit."

She walked through to the kitchen and opened the larder door. It felt both odd and somewhat thrilling to be in Jeffrey's house without him. He hadn't done a bad job of decorating it, for a man. There were definitely things she'd change, however, but then, it wasn't her place. The frayed rocking chair at the fireside would go, if she had her druthers.

Momentarily, the cat was at her feet, and she spooned fishy-smelling meat into the porcelain dish.

"Here you go, lovely boy." She stroked the fluffy back as the cat dived its nose into the food.

On the wall, pinned to the corkboard behind the table, was the brochure for the Grand Hotel Plaza and a sticky note written in Jeffrey's hand with instructions for the cat. On a separate piece of paper was the location of the main water stopcock in case, for some reason, a pipe should burst. Heaven knew why he thought a pipe might burst but if it did, she knew just where to go under the kitchen sink to turn off the water. The number of the local plumber was also attached to the board.

She giggled at Jeffrey's odd plumbing precautions. What a strange man. There was so much about him that she liked, but he was an odd duck at times, there was no denying it.

Mary pulled out a chair and sat at the table while Ralf ate his meal. The hotel brochure glowed on the board, so she pulled it off to have one more look. She wondered if Jeffrey was sitting in that golden lobby, drinking tea from a china cup. Or perhaps he was in the restaurant, having a nice meal? The thought of him sitting at one of those grand tables all by himself made her a little sad. But then, in the same instant, she was irritated. He had chosen to go alone, so he'd have to lump it if he felt lonely. Turning back to the brochure, she wondered if it would be possible to feel lonely in such a beautiful setting. She'd love to see Rome, too, someday.

Pinning the brochure back on the board, Mary picked up the empty dish and washed it in the sink. She lifted the cat, who was winding himself in between her ankles.

"Are you lonely, boy?" She walked into the living room, wondering momentarily if she needed to check upstairs for anything amiss. Deciding it wasn't necessary, she flopped down on the couch with the cat on her lap.

As she began to feel the warmth of the feline gradually

permeate her coat, the phone rang. Its shrill tone, cutting through the silence of the house, made her jump. Should she answer it? Jeffrey had no answering machine, as he'd told her that they were a daft invention, serving solely to alert potential burglars to the fact that the house was empty. Mary had laughed at him and asked him how many burglars he knew who had his phone number? Jeffrey had harrumphed at her mockery, and the subject had been closed. He certainly was an odd duck.

The phone continued to ring, jangling her nerves. Whoever it was was pretty insistent, as it went on and on until she could take it no longer. She gently placed Ralf on the cushion next to her and stood up, trying to figure out who would be calling. What if something was wrong? Or what if it was Jeffrey, checking whether she was there to feed the cat at precisely the right time? At that, she was annoyed, so she grabbed the phone. She'd give him a piece of her mind if he *was* checking on her that way.

"Hello?" She spoke firmly.

"Ah, hello. Is Mr. Mere there, please?" The heavily accented voice took her aback.

"Um, no. I'm a neighbor. A friend. Mr. Mere isn't here at the moment. Can I take a message?" Mary scanned the room for a pen and something she could write on.

"I'm calling from the Grand Plaza Hotel, in Roma. Mr. Mere has not checked in yet, and we cannot hold his room after five pm today. Is the conditions of the reservation, madam. So sorry."

Mary let the words sink in. He had not checked in yet? She looked at her watch, and by her quick calculation, he should have been at the hotel hours ago.

"Was his plane delayed, maybe?" She asked hopefully.

"No, madam. We check with the airline. It was on time." The caller waited for her response.

Mary felt her heart begin to clatter under her coat. What was going on? Where was he? Trying not to let her mind run away with her, she took a deep breath. While somewhat naïve, Jeffrey was not a fool. Perhaps he'd decided to take a tour or do some exploring before going to the hotel? As she thought about it, she knew that was highly unlikely, as he'd have his suitcase with him, and the Jeffrey *she* knew would want to unpack, have a cup of tea, and relax before venturing out anywhere. Besides, Rome was an hour ahead, and it was already five in Scotland, so Jeffrey would be hungry for his dinner by now. Rome or no Rome, there'd be no exploring for him on an empty stomach.

What if he'd missed the plane in Edinburgh? She'd told him not to risk it by taking the train, but he'd insisted that he'd have plenty of time to make his connection in Perth and still get to the airport in time for departure.

"Is there any way to check if he was on the flight?" Mary was getting increasingly worried.

"No, madam. They will not release that information to the hotel."

She didn't know what else to suggest. Mary raked her hand through her hair and stared out the window to Willow Street.

"Perhaps if I called the airline, they'd tell *me*?" She was grasping at straws, but it seemed better than doing nothing at all.

"You can try, madam, but we cannot hold his room after five pm today. Thank you."

"Wait a minute, don't hang up." Mary heard the click at the other end, and the line went silent.

"Well, thanks for nothing." She spoke out loud, noticing the tiny spiral of breath winding into the cold room as it left her mouth.

Replacing the receiver, she felt a knot of fear under her ribs. What kind of mess had Jeffrey Mere got himself into?

CHAPTER 25

———— ◆ ————

Jeffrey sat on the pavement, his stomach somersaulting and his legs shaking. The Olympic Stadium behind him, he could see a large park a couple of streets away. A sign said "Parco D. Stadio" and a slew of cars slid by between him and the green space, reminding him that he was in a public place, surrounded by people, so he should be safe.

He had no idea how long he'd been sitting here, but he didn't trust his legs to hold him up just yet. A few passersby had looked at him, but no one had spoken or asked if he was OK, which he found odd. In Pitlochry, if you saw someone sitting on the ground, you'd not pass them by without asking if they were OK.

He looked around, realizing that he still held two pairs of days-of-the-week socks in his hand. He tried to shove them into his pockets along with the other pairs he'd retrieved from the dirt floor of the shack. It was no good; he'd have to stand up. Pulling his legs underneath himself, he pushed up on his hands and raised himself from the ground. As he stood to his full height, he felt dizzy and reached for the metal road sign next to him. Steadying himself, he took a few deep breaths and began looking around to assess the position he was in. He had no money, no passport, no plane ticket, no credit card, no traveler's checks, no clothes, the list went on and on. However, what he *did* have was a tongue in his head and the name of his hotel, so there was nothing else for it. If no help was forthcoming, he'd just have to ask for some.

He felt suddenly cold and pulled the collar of his jacket up close under his chin. Stepping backwards, he moved into the center of the pavement and straightened his cap. He needed to be presentable before he spoke to anyone. He didn't want them thinking he was a vagrant or anything equally alarming.

A middle-aged couple was walking towards him. They wore heavy coats and had their arms linked and their heads close together as they studiously avoided meeting his eyes.

"Excuse me." Jeffrey spoke to their averted faces. "Excuse me, I wonder if you can help me?"

The man shook his head, holding his hand out flat, as if to push Jeffrey away. The lady turned her face into her husband's shoulder, and to Jeffrey's amazement, they walked past him, hurrying on their way.

"Well, blow me down." Jeffrey exclaimed.

Behind the couple was a group of young lads. They wore football jerseys and were laughing loudly. Having just had the experience he'd had with a very respectable-looking youngster, Jeffrey thought it best not to approach this group for help, so he turned his back on them as they passed.

After a few minutes, a woman appeared, pushing a baby in

a buggy. She looked at Jeffrey, protectively tucked the blanket tighter around her child's legs, and then steered the buggy away from him, towards the stadium. Heavens, did she think he wanted to steal her baby?

This was not going well. What was he to do? As several other people passed him, and Jeffrey asked politely if they could help, to no avail, he began to feel desperate. He supposed it was time to start walking. He knew that the stadium and the river had been on his right when the brothers had driven him out this way, so as long as he kept them on his left, he should be heading back into the city. He needed to find his way to the hotel, then to a police station.

Stuffing the remaining socks he held into his jacket pockets, he set off. Within a few minutes, Jeffrey felt his heart rate slow, and as he breathed rhythmically in time with his steps, he began to feel slightly better. It was good to be moving, and he needed to focus on getting somewhere safe before dark. It was around five, and he didn't have much time before night fell.

There were various groups of people on the streets — couples with children, a woman with several heavy shopping bags, two men in long dark coats — but Jeffrey walked on and avoided their eyes. As he followed the line of the river, keeping it on his left, ahead of him he saw the bridge they'd driven across in the van. A rush of relief made him pick up his pace.

Suddenly, the sense of a presence behind him made him glance over his shoulder. There was no one there. His nerves were still raw, so he was probably imagining things. He walked on, focusing on the bridge ahead. There it was again, the feeling that he was being followed. Taking a deep breath, he swung around to confront his tormentor. He swiveled his head from side to side but saw nothing. Then, hearing a snuffling noise, he lowered his eyes to the pavement. There was the large shaggy head and familiar twisted dreadlocks of the dog. The dark eyes glistened from behind the matted hair, and its massive paws were incongruously spread on the Roman concrete, like great hairy anchors.

Jeffrey took a moment or two to gather himself. How was this possible? Could it be the same dog as up on Ben Macdhui and in the hospital after the fire? Bending down, he extended a hand to the creature, and instantly it was up on its feet, pushing its huge head into his palm. The long tail swished dangerously as Jeffrey leaned down and wrapped his quivering arms around the massive body, squeezing the dog into a hug.

"Hello, girl. How did you get here?" Jeffrey felt his eyes water as the dog leaned in, seemingly returning his embrace.

He could feel the animal's heart beating through the shaggy coat. The dog seemed real enough, despite his tendency to think this could be a dream, or an hallucination brought on by his desperation to see a friendly face. The creature made no attempt to move or shake him off, and as his legs gave way again, Jeffrey's knees touched the pavement. The dog's head was heavy on his shoulder, and he could smell the musty scent he remembered from inside the tent on Ben Macdhui.

Eventually, Jeffrey released the dog and stood up, glancing around self-consciously to see if anyone had seen him cuddling this ratty street urchin. The dog stood and looked up at him expectantly.

"I'm a bit lost, girl." Jeffrey sniffed and continued to look around him. At this, the dog raised its head and licked his hand. Blowing a noisy snort from its nostrils, the animal walked behind him and headed down the road. After a few paces, it turned back to look at Jeffrey.

"Where are you going?" Jeffrey pulled his collar closed against the cold evening air and walked the few paces to close the gap between them.

The dog snorted again and continued to walk ahead of him. Jeffrey shivered and followed close behind. The big mutt appeared to be heading along the river, in the general direction Jeffrey was taking, so he went with it and let himself be led.

This was like being in a Lassie film. The dog seemed to know where it was going, and as long as Jeffrey kept walking, the dog kept moving. If Jeffrey stopped, the dog seemed to sense it and stopped too. If he had not been so tired, hungry, and cold, Jeffrey might have found this quite comical.

The two companions continued on their way, crossing back over the river, and after a while, the surrounding buildings grew taller and more majestic. On their left, Jeffrey could see a square with a huge church, and just as he was admiring the tall columns and stone curlicues around the impressive portico, the dog made a hard right turn and walked decisively away from him. Nervous he'd lose sight of her, Jeffrey turned and hurried after his guide.

On either side of the street stood rows of smart boutiques. Although they were closed now, Jeffrey could see an array of well-lit, sleekly cut winter coats, leather handbags, shiny shoes, woolen scarves, and hats. There were a couple of electronics shops selling wafer-thin phones, and even a store with Disney toys and clothing in the window. All these establishments were housed under elegant arched facades with what appeared to be high-ceilinged apartments above them. Wrought-iron balconies protruded from the upper floors and hovered over their heads, and the people they passed in the darkening evening were dressed elegantly, carrying large bags or briefcases.

As they passed a café with some patrons sipping hot drinks, Jeffrey's mouth watered as he tried to remember how long it had been since he'd had the slightly dry ham sandwich and cup of tepid tea on the plane. Just as he was aware of his stomach rumbling, ahead of him he saw several sets of broad stone steps separated by low, square balustrades. At the top of them stood a tall structure with two bell towers and in front of it a needle-like obelisk with a cross at the top. Several people wandered up and down the steps as he looked on. Staring at the floodlit scene, Jeffrey remembered that he'd seen it somewhere before. Of course — these were the Spanish Steps he'd read about in the brochure. As he recalled, the Grand Hotel Plaza must be very close.

Having been distracted by his surroundings, Jeffrey turned around and realized he could no longer see the dog. Feeling panic rising again, he scanned the street for the familiar form. A little ahead of him it sat, looking over a shaggy shoulder, waiting patiently for him to catch up. He trotted over and patted the messy head.

"Sorry, girl. Got a bit distracted there." The dog shook itself vigorously and walked on.

Within a few moments, Jeffrey could see a tall building with the same high arches as the shops they'd just passed and tall windows stacked on the upper floors. The stone of the frontage was floodlit from below and glowed a soft pink. Several colored flags mounted over the entrance fluttered in the cold wind. The Grand Hotel Plaza was a sight for sore eyes indeed. He couldn't remember being this pleased to be anywhere in a very long time.

As he approached the doors, the dog sat its heavy back end down and then slowly lay on its stomach, its legs stretched out in front of it like a scrappy sphinx. Jeffrey halted and squatted down to pet the huge head.

"I don't think they'll let you inside, girl. I wish they would."

Jeffrey let his hand stay on the dog's head. Its dark eyes glistened behind the dirty dreadlocks and Jeffrey, for an instant, was reminded of Agnes's beady stare. He caught his breath. The dog lifted its nose and snuffled at Jeffrey's pocket.

"What is it?" he asked, as the pressure from the big damp nose increased. "I've not got any food in there, you know."

The dog continued to nose his pocket and then, opening its large mouth, it started to nibble delicately at the side of his jacket.

"Hey, don't do that, girl, you'll snag it." Jeffrey, despite his tired and desperate state, chuckled. "Thank you for bringing me here. I'd have been lost without you."

At this, the dog shoved its muzzle farther into his hip with such a force that Jeffrey lost his balance and fell backwards onto his bottom.

"Whoa!" As he fumbled on the step to push himself up, he noticed that a pair of socks had fallen out of his pocket. Picking them up, he turned them over and could see the "TUES" in yellow woolen letters. Smiling, he shoved the woolly ball back into his coat pocket before glancing down at the dog who was staring up at him intently. Those eyes, they were so familiar.

"You'll run off again now, I suppose?" Jeffrey spoke to the eyes. To his amusement, the dog vigorously shook its head, apparently denying his accusation, and Jeffrey laughed again.

"Well, stay here then, OK? I'll get myself sorted out, then come and find you. Perhaps we can get you something to eat, at least?" He looked at the large hipbones protruding through the

161

shaggy coat.

"You're a bit skinny, girl."

CHAPTER 26

The hotel lobby was as big as a football field and bathed in red and gold. The walls were paneled and opulent, with cleverly concealed lighting highlighting the richly patterned paper. The ceiling, towering high above his head and painted with a magnificent fresco from one edge to the other, was held up by a series of golden columns standing around the room in close pairs.

The biggest rug he'd ever seen lay on top of the shiny marble floor, and tall, elegant palms stood in between the columns, creating a corridor around the edge of the space.

A few upholstered armchairs and small tables had been artfully placed in the middle of the room, but Jeffrey noted that no one sat at them. Perhaps they were just for show? He could imagine seeing a "Keep off the furniture" sign if he got up close.

A few guests sauntered around silently, and Jeffrey could smell the aroma of freshly ground coffee. He began to salivate, reminded of his thirst and mounting hunger.

He scanned the perimeter of the space, looking for the reception desk. Where would you put it in this stylish room without it sticking out like a modern-day sore thumb? As he turned around, he spied a marble platform, much like an altar, and behind it a chic-looking woman in a red suit. Her dark hair was pulled tightly back from her face, and she wore a careful smile on crimson lips.

Jeffrey nodded and walked tentatively over to the platform.

"Posso aiutarti, signore?" Her eyes scanned Jeffrey's face, and at his lack of response, she switched to English. "Can I help you, sir?" Her voice was low, as if reverent to her surroundings, the way someone might speak inside a cathedral.

"Um, yes. I hope so." Jeffrey coughed and mimicked her half whisper. Suddenly concerned with his appearance, he glanced down at his feet. His trousers and shoes were dusty, but aside from that he hoped he passed for a respectable type of guest. Grabbing his cap off his head, Jeffrey smoothed his fluffy earmuffs of hair.

"I have a reservation. The name's Mere."

The woman nodded and turned her attention to a computer monitor that Jeffrey noticed was cleverly suspended beneath the glass top of the table. After a few moments she looked up at him.

"The name again, sir?"

"Mere, Jeffrey Mere. I reserved the room from Scotland." Jeffrey felt his recently controlled panic begin to resurface.

"Ah, Mr. Mere. You did not have a late check-in requested, correct?" The smile was gone, and the woman looked coldly at Jeffrey.

"Well no, but I reserved my room and board for the whole

164

week. The Christmas package…" His voice faded as the woman stared down at the screen again, her head shaking almost imperceptibly.

"We cannot hold rooms after five pm unless late check-in is requested. I'm afraid we have released your room, sir." The smile was back but this time it was cold, and, Jeffrey thought, somewhat self-satisfied.

"I beg your pardon?" Jeffrey felt his face flush hot. This was not happening. "I reserved the room for a week and paid in advance with my credit card. Can you please just give me my key?"

Her glossy red nails tapped aggressively on the keyboard, and the woman continued to stare at the screen below the glass. Watching her, Jeffrey twisted his cap angrily and stood his ground.

"I'm sorry, sir. The room is no longer available. I can direct you to another hotel where —"

Before she could finish her sentence, Jeffrey felt something in his temple pop. This was just too damn much. After everything he'd been through, there was simply no more patience to be had. He slammed his hand onto the counter, and his cap shot across the surface, falling dully at the woman's feet.

"I want to speak to the manager, now." The previous dulcet tone gone from his voice, he stared at her dangerously. "Now, please."

The self-satisfied smile wiped from her face, the woman handed him his cap, nodded curtly, and walked away across the cavernous lobby.

Jeffrey felt his heart clattering in his chest and realized he needed to sit down. The only chairs in the vicinity were the posh ones in the center of the room. To hell with it. He was entitled to sit in them. With a determined air, Jeffrey paced across the massive rug and plonked himself down in an armchair. As he stared around rebelliously, daring anyone to challenge his occupation of the seat, he saw the woman returning with a small, dark-haired man in tow.

Jeffrey made to get up and then changed his mind. *Let them come to me. I've been through enough today at the hands of these Italians.*

The man spoke quietly to the woman, who then slipped back behind the counter. Then he turned and approached Jeffrey in the center of the room.

"Mr. Mere? I am Giovanni Giacomo, General Manager of Grand Hotel Plaza. There has been some misunderstanding, I believe?" The man held his hand out towards Jeffrey and smiled at him from behind narrow, metal-framed glasses.

"No, no misunderstanding. I just want my room key and the number of the local police station, please." Jeffrey rose unsteadily and reluctantly accepted the extended hand.

"Mr. Mere, there is no need to be so upset. Hotel policy is that we cannot hold rooms after five pm if the guest does not check in as expected. This is stated clearly on our website and reservation materials. If you'd like to come with me, I am sure we can find you alternate accommodation." The man's voice faded at the sight of Jeffrey's face.

"I don't want alternate accommodation! I want the bloody room I paid for with my bloody credit card a bloody fortnight ago! That's what I want!" Jeffrey was shouting. As the words left his mouth, so did several small beads of saliva, one of which landed smack on the lenses of the manager's sleek metal-framed glasses.

"Mr. Mere, please. There is no need..." The man backed away as he spoke and removed his glasses. Taking a red silk hanky from his lapel pocket, he wiped the lenses and replaced them, along with his practiced smile.

"No need? I'll tell you what. You take me to your office and I'll tell you exactly what I need. How about that?" Jeffrey's voice shook. "I've been abducted, robbed, abused, abandoned, and insulted since landing in this god-forsaken country, and all because I wanted to spend Christmas in Rome. God knows what I was thinking. I could be at home now with Mary and Ralf, watching *White Christmas* and having a dram, but no, I'm here, in Rome being told what I bloody well need."

The uncharacteristic outburst left Jeffrey drained, and he flopped back in the chair. The manager's eyebrows shot up at Jeffrey's words, and he lowered himself into a chair opposite.

"Mr. Mere. You say you were abducted, robbed?" The silvery smile was gone. Jeffrey scanned the younger man's face and thought he saw a flicker of genuine concern.

"Aye, I did say that. That's why I want the number of the local police station." Jeffrey ran a hand over his thinning hair and nodded as he spoke, his voice returning to its usual controlled tone.

"Please, come with me, sir. We will talk in my office." The manager rose and extended a hand to Jeffrey. Jeffrey accepted the hand and pulled himself up, noticing the firm, cool grasp of this Mr. Giacomo. Agnes always said you could tell a world about someone from their handshake.

The two men walked across the lobby and through a door concealed in one of the papered wall panels. With a few quick steps, Jeffrey found himself inside the inner workings of the building. The walls, still thick, were now plainly painted, and there were no windows in the long corridor they passed down. After a few minutes inside the dull tunnel, they emerged into a bright central space with several desks located around the semi-circular walls. Mr. Giacomo indicated another tall glass door and stood back to allow Jeffrey to go in ahead of him.

"Please, go ahead." The hotel manager pulled out a leather chair from the desk and directed Jeffrey towards it. "Can I get you some coffee, a glass of water, perhaps?"

"I could take a coffee, and some water, thanks. I haven't eaten since the flight, and that left plenty to be desired." Jeffrey's voice faded.

Mr. Giacomo picked up the telephone on his desk and spoke quickly in Italian. Jeffrey couldn't make out much, except for the word *espresso*, which he knew to be coffee, and then *grazie*, which he knew to be thank you.

"So, Mr. Mere. Please tell me what happened to you." The manager sat back in his chair and clasped his hands together in a steeple of long fingers.

"Will I be getting my room, though?" Jeffrey smoothed his cap out on the desk and looked at the man opposite him.

"Of course, of course. We will arrange it for you immediately."

Jeffrey felt a surge of relief as the younger man nodded and patted the air, dismissing his concern. Perhaps these Italians weren't all bad?

As he told his story, a young woman appeared in the office with a tray. There was a small silver pot and a doll-sized cup and saucer. Next to that was a plate with long narrow biscuits on it and a bowl of figs and red grapes. Mr. Giacomo leaned forward and poured thick dark liquid into the tiny cup. Jeffrey could smell the rich coffee as a small spiral of steam wound up from the spout of the pot.

Accepting the full cup, Jeffrey sat back and sipped tentatively. It was very strong, and normally he liked milk in his coffee, but this was an extraordinary taste, and he found he liked this espresso just the way it was.

"Biscotti?" Mr. Giacomo indicated the long biscuits on the tray. "These are excellent with espresso." The man smiled as Jeffrey picked up a biscuit and bit hungrily into it, momentarily surprised by the hardness of it. This certainly wasn't anything like a HobNob, but it tasted of almonds and was delicious.

"You can dip it in the espresso. It's very good." Mr. Giacomo mimed the motion, dipping his one hand into the other cupped one, and nodding encouragingly. Jeffrey complied and then continued with his story.

His words, as he heard them, sounded outlandish, removed from reality, as if he was talking about a film plot rather than the events of his day. Mr. Giacomo was silent, but wrote some notes down with a slim golden pen on a piece of paper.

Lifting his eyes to Jeffrey's as Jeffrey explained about the dog leading him to the hotel, Mr. Giacomo listened intently.

"But you are not hurt?"

"I'm not hurt, just angry and upset." Jeffrey shrugged and swallowed the last of the biscotti. "They took everything — wallet, credit card, plane ticket, traveler's checks, passport, everything."

Mr. Giacomo nodded and lifted the telephone receiver once again. Another spurt of Italian followed while Jeffrey picked up a second biscuit, refilled the tiny cup, and sat back in the chair.

"OK Mr. Mere. I have called the *polizia*. They will be here in a while. Now, we can take you to your room, where you can rest. When the *investigatore* arrives, I will call you. *Bene?*"

Jeffrey knew that *bene* meant good.

"Aye, that's fine." Jeffrey stood and brushed a thin layer of crumbs from his trousers. The figs and grapes looked good, and he wished he'd eaten some of those, too.

Seeing his glance, Mr. Giacomo smiled.

"I will have these fruits sent up to your room. Perhaps you would also like a *panino* or some pasta?"

Jeffrey blushed.

"Well, I'd appreciate it. Yes, I am famished."

After a few moments, a young man in a black jacket with large gold buttons appeared in the doorway, and Mr. Giacomo spoke to him in a low voice.

"This is Umberto. He will take you to your room and then we will talk more when the *investigatore* arrives. Tomorrow we will show you the British Embassy and you can request new passport. Airplane ticket is also simple. We call Air Italia and request a new return ticket."

Satisfied that they had thought of everything, Mr. Giacomo glanced at his watch.

"I must leave you now, Mr. Mere. I am so sorry for your bad experience in Roma. Tomorrow we fix everything. OK?"

Jeffrey nodded and smiled. This man was decent and was definitely doing his best to help.

Just as he was turning to follow the bellman, Jeffrey remembered the dog. He swung around and addressed the manager's back as he headed back into his office.

"Oh, Mr. Giacomo. What about my dog?" Jeffrey called after

him.

The man stopped, turned and again glanced at his watch. Jeffrey sensed he was pushing his luck, but it was worth a try.

"You have a dog?" The manager looked puzzled.

Jeffrey realized this must be odd, a tourist with an animal in tow, but he went on undeterred.

"Yes. Remember that I told you earlier? I found her, here in Rome."

"Well, we do not allow animals in the Grand Plaza, Mr. Mere." The Manager hesitated. "But, I suppose. Just for tonight, you understand, just one night?"

Jeffrey nodded enthusiastically and waved his thanks. He hoped the big mutt was still outside. The poor lass deserved a good meal out of all this, at the very least.

After pocketing the room key and dismissing the somewhat puzzled Umberto, Jeffrey circled the outside of the hotel twice before he spotted the dog in one of the back alleys, sniffing at some rubbish bags. He beckoned to her and she padded over to him, tail swishing.

"Come on, lass. We're going inside now."

The two companions rode up in the heavy-doored elevator, both staring straight ahead at their reflection in the brass panels. The door slid open on a brightly lit hallway. The room doors were of dark glossy wood and widely spaced on each side, and the carpet felt soft and bouncy underfoot. Jeffrey could smell coffee again.

Finding the number he was looking for at the end of the long hall, he opened the door with the key card.

"Prego." He smiled and stepped back, letting the dog walk in ahead of him.

Jeffrey stood inside the entrance and scanned the room. This was just like in the brochure. The high ceiling and tall window arches, the plush carpet and rich red bedspread were luxurious. The bed itself was huge, with four fat pillows, and was draped with gauzy fabric from its tall, four-poster frame. Two gold-colored regency chairs sat at a round marble table, behind which French windows led out to a small balcony.

Jeffrey walked over and opened the French doors, catching his breath at the sight below. It was dark, and at his feet, Rome sparkled against the night sky. Domes and towers, row upon row of lights and reflections, glittered in the night. To his right, Jeffrey could see the two towers he'd seen earlier, at the top of the Spanish Steps. If he still had his camera, he'd have snapped a few shots of this to show Mary.

This scene was exactly how he'd imagined Rome, not being driven through the back streets of a ramshackle shantytown by well-dressed thugs who rifled through his belongings and left him on the streets with nothing but a few pairs of socks. That had not been how he'd imagined spending his first day in the City of Joy.

An hour later, after polishing off a large plate of veal escalope smothered in a tomato sauce like none he'd ever tasted, as well as a large glass of red wine, Jeffrey lay in the bath. He'd used the bubble bath from a fancy bottle on the shelf and now floated in a cloud of lemon-scented foam, his toes protruding from the water near the big gold taps.

After inhaling a bowl of thick stew from a porcelain plate, the dog lay snoring on the plush white bath mat. Jeffrey had taken a second glass of wine into the bathroom with him, and as he lay, letting the hot water soak away his woes, he spied an elaborate phone on the dressing table in the corner. Perhaps he should call Mary and let her know he'd made it OK? What a story he'd have to tell her when he got home.

At the thought of Mary, Jeffrey felt his blood quicken. He could picture her red curls, her bright green eyes, and the spattering of freckles across the bridge of her nose. The desire to kiss those freckles was growing every time he saw her. As he took a deep swallow of wine, he made himself a promise. Having made it through today, surely he could afford to be a little bolder? He'd take the bull by the horns. He'd tell her how he felt and then, what would be would be. Jeffrey was hopeful that Mary was interested in him, more than just as a friend. He felt sure he'd seen something that looked like affection in her eyes on more than one occasion. All he had to do was stick his neck out and find out if that affection extended anywhere towards romance. It was time he took the leap.

The dog snorted loudly and woke with a start. Jeffrey drained his glass and then laughed out loud just as the phone rang shrilly, causing him to drop the empty glass into the sea of bubbles.

Having dressed again in his dirty clothes, and pulling on the clean Thurs-Day socks he'd had in his pocket, Jeffrey left the dog in the room and headed down to the lobby to meet Mr. Giacomo and the police inspector. He was surprised that the man talking to the hotel manager was so tall. From what he understood, most Italian men were shorter than your average Scot. However, as Jeffrey approached them, he stood a head and shoulders above the general manager and yet looked the elderly police inspector directly in the eye.

After half an hour of questions in Mr. Giacomo's office, the inspector, whose English was impressive, told Jeffrey he could go back to his room. He said he'd be back in the morning, at which time they'd take Jeffrey to the station so he could make an official statement and then look at some mug shots of known criminals who operated the type of scam that Jeffrey had fallen for. Jeffrey agreed readily. He was far too tired to go anywhere that night. Besides, now that he had a full stomach and clean skin, if not clothes, he could almost feel that big bed up there underneath his sore bones, soothing him to sleep.

"We will help you to the police station tomorrow, and also to the British Embassy. Your room is paid for on your credit card, but you will need to cancel that one, as it has been stolen." Mr. Giacomo frowned as he waved goodbye to the departing policeman.

"Ah. I didn't think of that." Jeffrey felt his heart sink.

"But we will fix it all in the morning." Giacomo smiled once again and extended a hand to Jeffrey.

"If you need anything else, call the concierge. Also, we have an excellent laundry." The smaller man winked at Jeffrey, and he looked down at his grubby trousers.

"Right. I'll use it, then." Jeffrey returned the smile and shook the man's hand. "Thank you, Mr. Giacomo, for all your help. For the food and for sorting out my room."

"*Prego, prego. Buonanotte.*"

Back in the room, Jeffrey stripped off his dirty clothes and stuffed them into the laundry bag he found in the wardrobe. He pulled on the fluffy white robe that hung on a hook in the bathroom and slipped his feet into a pair of oversized terry-toweling slippers. Hotels were great, really. You could survive with very few of your own things, if the need arose.

Having called room service to take away the empty dishes and the laundry to pick up his clothes for cleaning, Jeffrey circled the room, switching off the lights, then settled into the large bed. Within a few minutes, he felt the mattress sinking on one side as the dog stepped heavily and carefully up onto the edge of the bed.

"Well, I'm sure that's not allowed." He chuckled as the big matted body circled around precisely three times before settling in a tight ball on the bedspread next to him. He reached over and patted the massive head.

"Night-night then, lass."

That night, he dreamed of Agnes. She stood at the end of the bed, her hands in her apron pockets and her tartan slippers on her feet. Her thick glasses glinted and her teeth clacked as she talked, scolding him for his naivety in accepting the ride from the young man.

"What were ye thinkin', Jeffrey? He wasn'y in uniform, it was an unmarked van, you didn'y ask for any identification, you just followed him like a Highland lamb to the slaughter, you big nungie."

Jeffrey had the familiar sinking feeling of being scolded by his mother that he had had many times when she was alive. He woke with a film of sweat on his upper lip, and forcing his leg out to the side, he searched for the comfort of the warm dog. To his disappointment, she was gone. He reached over and flipped on the bedside lamp, scanning the room, but the big creature was nowhere to be seen. Jeffrey slid out from under the covers and tiptoed across the floor to the bathroom. The warmth had gone out of the room, and the marble floor was cold under his bare feet. He could see by the light of the moon sliding in the window that the mutt wasn't in here either.

Puzzled, he returned to the bedroom and checked the French doors and the door to the hallway, which were all still locked securely. Feeling the chill against his naked skin, Jeffrey shivered and jumped back under the covers. As he settled his head back onto the soft pillow, it finally dawned on him. Every time he'd seen the dog, he'd been in a risky or awkward situation. Just when he felt panic rising, there she was, turning up like a lucky penny, helping him out in one way or another. Then, as quickly as she'd appeared, she'd be gone again. No rhyme or reason — just gone.

Now here he was in a hotel room in Rome that he might not have found his way to without the dog's help. Sure enough, a few hours later she was gone again, and with no discernible way out of the room other than the door they'd come in, which was still locked from the inside.

He sat up abruptly and turned the light back on.

"Are you there?" His voice hung in the quiet room.

Silence wrapped itself around his heart as he lay back down and turned off the light again.

CHAPTER 27

———◆———

Mary paced along Willow Street. She hadn't slept well, with worrying about Jeffrey. She'd tried calling Air Italia from his house the night before, but, as the hotel clerk had predicted, the airline wouldn't share any information with her about a passenger. Frustrated, she had switched off all the lights, said goodnight to Ralf, and walked home. If Jeffrey needed her, he knew her phone number; he could call her.

Now, as she passed the Subramanians' house again, the twins waved to her from the living room window. They were lying along the back of the couch, head to head like two lithe cats, watching the street through the gap in the curtains. Mary smiled and mouthed "hello" as she passed. The children giggled, and then one pushed the other off the back and onto the cushions. They really were adorable little things.

Jeffrey's cottage was still, and as cold as she'd left it. She wasn't sure what she'd expected, but the atmosphere inside was almost eerie this morning as she padded through to the chilly kitchen. The Grand Hotel Plaza brochure hung on the pin board, and Mary leaned over and pulled it off. Perhaps she should call them, just to check if he was there?

She began to shrug off her coat, then, shivering, thought better of it. Lifting the phone from the wall cradle, she sat at the table and dialed the number. As she waited for a connection, Ralf appeared in the doorway. The cat hopped up onto her lap and began his morning toilette, starting at the shoulder and working his pink tongue down each front leg, licking meticulously as he went.

Mary listened to the odd single rings at the other end of the phone until finally, she heard a voice.

"Buongiorno, Grand Hotel Plaza Roma."

"Em, hello. I'm calling from Scotland. I'd like to check on one of your guests, a Mr. Mere."

"Yes, madam. What room number?" the woman asked in a musical voice.

"I don't know. He was supposed to arrive last night." Mary hesitated.

"One moment. You say Mere?"

"Yes, Jeffrey Mere." Mary felt her voice catch in her throat.

"Ah yes, Mr. Mere. Shall I connect you?"

Mary felt relief flood over her, then, to her surprise, anger. Whatever nonsense he'd got up to, Jeffrey had arrived safely after all. If he'd been in trouble, she felt sure he'd have called her, which he clearly hadn't, so why was she so worried about him? The last thing she wanted was to be connected to his room and have him answer. Then what would she say? She didn't want him to think she was checking up on him. She'd better get off the line as soon as possible.

"No, thanks. That's fine. As long as he's there safely." Her voice faded.

"Yes, madam."

"OK, thanks. Bye, then." Mary sniffed and hung up the phone. He really was an infuriating man at times.

She fed Ralf his breakfast and checked briefly over the living room before letting herself out of the cottage. She needed to get to work, but perhaps she'd stop at the bakers and pick up one of Mrs. Barnes's famous sausage rolls, just as a wee treat to herself.

She had planned a half-day at work so that she could finish her Christmas shopping, and she intended on going into Perth for a change. There were only four days to go, and while she rarely went overboard buying gifts, this year she had enjoyed picking out small presents for her colleagues at the home. She wanted to get a minding for the Subramanian children and, of course, something nice for Jeffrey.

At home, her little tree glittered at the side of the fireplace, and she'd placed the few cards she'd received on the mantelpiece. With the holly wreath on the front door, the house looked Christmassy, and for the first time in years, Mary was in her own place, feeling safe and settled. So why was she letting Jeffrey get under her skin this way? He was the tiny particle of grit in the oyster of her new contentment. Perhaps one day he'd evolve into the pearl she hoped for, but for now, he was infuriating.

Later that day, as she wandered through the cobbled streets of Perth, Mary finally felt better. Her shift had gone smoothly at work, and she'd made it to Perth in good time. She'd stopped for a bite of lunch in a little brasserie that smelled of garlic and freshly baked bread, and now she was looking for Jeffrey's gift. She'd thought about getting him something to do with hill climbing but, when browsing in a hiking shop, she'd felt overwhelmed. She had no idea what the equipment was for or whether Jeffrey would even have need of it. The shopkeeper, smiling at her apologetically, had been busy helping a group of young foreigners with obvious money to spend, so she'd given up and left.

Mary loved Perth. There had been a time when she'd considered moving here, before the job at the home in Piltlochry had come up. However, she was glad she'd made the decision to take the position, as she loved her life in the little town. Perhaps Perth would have been too big a place to make friends and start over again at this stage in her life.

The sun was sitting low over the surrounding flinty buildings, and having walked around for almost two hours, Mary began to feel tired. She'd had success with her shopping, finding matching woolly hats and gloves and a large-piece jigsaw puzzle of Edinburgh Castle for the twins. She'd even bought herself a gift, a soft cashmere scarf from the Woolen Mill. She'd never owned anything cashmere, and it felt incredibly self-indulgent, but the baby pink color and the clever salesman had both helped to close the deal.

All that was left was to find Jeffrey something. As she glanced at her watch, Mary saw that it was 4:45, so it was probably time to head home. She still had a few days to shop, and if she was thinking of something hill walking or hiking related, she could always go in to the mountain sports shop in Pitlochry and ask Joe MacFarlane for some advice. That might work better, after all.

By 5:20, happy with her spoils, Mary drove home though the Perthshire countryside. The darkening landscape swept alongside her little Ford as the night drew in around her. The utter darkness of night in this part of Scotland never failed to amaze her. Unlike Glasgow, where the streets were perpetually lit with harsh orange streetlamps and the glow of row upon row of shops, flats, and businesses, out here there were hundreds of miles of country roads with virtually no lighting whatsoever. Apart from the car's stalwart little headlights reaching bravely out into the heavy darkness ahead, she was all but blind to the surrounding scenery.

A Celtic station played on the radio, and Mary sang along to an old favorite. Today had been a good day, and all things considered, this was going to be a good Christmas, too.

The car bumped along the A9, leaving Perth and then Dunkeld behind, when Mary felt sleep pulling at her eyelids. Turning up the volume of the radio, she shifted in her seat. Perhaps some cool air on her face would wake her up? Mary reached for the vent and tipped it towards her cheek. She instantly felt the blast of cold air and shook her hair out of her eyes, focusing on the road ahead. But the car was warm inside, and as she drove on, her eyes felt heavy again.

The clock on the dashboard wasn't working, so she checked her watch but couldn't see the face clearly in the dim light. She needed to turn on the interior light to see what time it was, so she reached up above her head, feeling along the header for the switch. After a few moments of fumbling around to no avail, Mary raised her head and looked up.

Suddenly the steering wheel lurched to the left. The crunching sound and several shattering jolts came simultaneously. There was the sound of breaking glass, and she felt cold air on her face. Mary's head bounced off the headrest and then ricocheted forward into the blooming white firmness of the airbag. What was happening? The engine had shuddered to a halt as soon as her foot had left the clutch, and as the car finally jarred to a stop, all she could hear was her own shallow breathing.

After a few moments, she tried to lift her head from the deflating airbag but felt something sharp against her cheek. Turning her eyes to the left, she saw a long tree limb coming in through the windscreen, passing her ear and piercing the driver's seat above her shoulder. At the sight of it, Mary felt nauseated. It had missed her head by a matter of inches. As she tried to move, she realized that her left arm was trapped between her chest and the steering wheel, and her left leg felt heavy and numb. There was a pain in her left side — a dull throbbing that worsened as she took a deep breath — and now she was aware of a warm trickle making its way down the left side of her face. What in god's name had she done?

As she sat still, trying to assimilate the situation, Mary's first worry was whether she'd hit another car. Her concern for having possibly hurt someone else moved her to shift again in the seat. This time, she leaned away from the vicious branch and was able to carefully sit back. Releasing her left arm, she reached down and felt her leg. It was tacky under her fingertips, but to her relief, she was aware of her own probing fingers investigating the wound, and she almost cried with relief at the shock of pain she caused herself by doing so. So, no paralysis, then. Thank heavens.

Wiggling her left hand and fingers, she felt no particular pain, so it was safe to assume she had no breakages there. Her handbag had been on the passenger seat, where she always sat it when driving. Of course, now it was on the floor, and from what she could see, the contents were strewn all over the mat. All she needed was her mobile phone, so she struggled to focus her eyes on the items she could see, searching for the familiar rectangular shape with the blue-and-white Saltire cover. As her eyes adjusted to the darkness, she spotted the phone. Thank god. Now she needed to see if she could get out of the car and walk around to the other side to get it.

Being careful not to snag her face on the tree limb, Mary reached over and released her seatbelt. She pulled on the handle to her right and pushed her shoulder against the door, but it was jammed fast. As she looked out into the darkness, trying to focus on what was around her, she saw the bark of another tree pressed up close to the car. She was obviously wedged against the trunk, so there was no way she could get out that way. Turning back to the inside of the car, Mary slowly slid down in her seat as far as she could go, hoping that she'd be able to lean over and reach the phone from the driver's side. The pain in her side was getting worse with the movement, and her leg throbbed badly as she shifted. She felt a fresh wave of wetness trickle over her ankle and so stopped wriggling. The tree limb, lying low over her right shoulder, and the central console, rising up on her left, left very little room for her arm; and despite numerous tries, she soon realized that she couldn't reach the phone. After a few minutes, she gave up and pushed herself back up in the seat with her good leg. This was useless. She was trapped.

The car began to feel cold, and Mary realized that she was shivering. It was probably shock, although the outside temperature was also dropping quickly as the Highland night closed in. She knew she must stay awake. If she fell asleep, she could fall into a coma, and then who knew what would happen? At the thought of losing consciousness, Mary felt her heart rate increase. She needed to stay alert. Reaching down, she turned the key in the ignition, hoping that the engine would catch. There was a metallic churning sound, as if unlubricated cogs were tearing against each other, but the engine didn't start. To her relief, however, the left headlight flickered on, showing a bank of trees ahead. The dashboard lights and radio also sparked into life, and she heard the Celtic DJ, still speaking in low, melodic tones as if nothing untoward had happened. The voice was comforting, and while she knew she needed to stay focused, the blast of warm air from the vent on her face was pleasantly soothing. As she closed her eyes and let it wash over her face, the air quickly turned to cold, making her catch her breath. Of course, there would be no more heat if the engine wasn't running. Closing the air vent, she sighed as the first prick of tears burned the backs of her eyes.

Mary knew that she needed to be careful. If she had the power on this way for too long, the battery would quickly die. She hurt badly now, and the state of her leg was worrying her. She really should try to see if she could assess how badly she was injured, and maybe try to wrap her leg in order to stem the bleeding. But the branch was preventing her from bending down low enough to see her own feet. At the very least, she thought, she could pack something down there to immobilize the painful limb.

With careful movements, she shrugged her coat down over each shoulder, then with small tugs as she rocked her weight forwards and backwards, was able to pull it off and drag it to the right side of her body. She bunched the coat up into a ball and then, taking a deep breath, shoved it down between her left leg and the side of the console. Scalding pain rushed up her leg, and a wave of nausea made her close her eyes as a scream slashed across the night. For a moment, Mary didn't understand that the raw sound had come from her. The dashboard lights grew fuzzy and then, as she tried vainly to keep them in view, darkness engulfed her.

Mary's eyes opened with a start. Her whole body was freezing, and the windows of the car were coated in a layer of condensation. The radio still warbled softly inside her dark prison, and the dashboard lights reminded her that she had less than a quarter of a tank of petrol. Squinting at her watch, she could see it was 8:50 pm. She coughed abruptly, sending an excruciating wave of pain through her side. Once she was able to stop shaking and catch her breath, Mary calculated that she had been unconscious for about two hours.

As she looked around, the familiar little car took on a sinister atmosphere. Was this the place she'd draw her last breath? Was this how it all ended, on a dark country road outside Dunkeld — now, when she was finally getting her life together; now, when she could smell the happiness that had eluded her for so long; now, when she had so much unfinished business?

As hot tears made their way down her cold cheeks, Mary shook her head. This wasn't how she was going to take her leave, damn it.

She lifted her hand and wiped the condensation away from the driver's side window. Just as she did so, she thought she saw a light. She caught her breath and peered out of the window into the darkness. There it was again. She hadn't imagined it, a quick flash of light in the wing mirror. Thinking quickly, Mary slammed her hand onto the horn, and a high-pitched beep crept out from under the bonnet. Please God, let whoever it was out there hear it.

Pressing on the window button, Mary was disappointed when it didn't open but, as she continued to pump her hand on the horn, the light in the mirror got brighter, bobbing up and down oddly as it drew closer. It didn't look like car headlights, and as she strained against the glass of the side window, she could see that it was a single beam, small, like a torch. Sure enough, as the light came up on the side of the car, she could just make out a tall figure behind it.

"Hello? Are you all right? Hello?" A man's voice seeped in through the window.

"I'm here. In here." Mary's own voice sounded foreign to her as she reached down and turned off the radio, then tapped her ring hard against the glass to confirm her presence.

"Oh, my god. You poor thing. Are you hurt?" The man shouted once again as Mary watched the torch light move around behind the car and then flash in from the passenger side.

"My leg, and my side. I can't move the branch. My head is bleeding, too." Her voice faded as the effort of shouting sent the rippling pain back through her ribs.

"Stay still, hen. I'll call an ambulance. Just stay still."

Mary nodded into the blackness and then, as she felt relief flood her insides, she slipped back into sleep.

CHAPTER 28

She was moving, but was lying down. How was this possible? Mary opened her eyes to see a ruddy face looking down at her. The man's cheeks were wide, with tiny broken capillaries across them, and the eyes above them were bright blue and warm. He smiled.

"Well, hello there. Decided to join us, did you?"

Mary made to sit up, but the man pushed her gently back onto the bed with his big paddle of a hand.

"No, you don't. Not yet. You're in an ambulance. We'll be at the hospital in a few minutes. Just you rest, now."

She reached across her body to touch her cheek and felt the tug of an IV line at the crook of her arm.

"You needed some fluids. You lost quite a bit of blood, pet." The man pressed his three fingers onto her wrist to check her pulse, then plugged his ears with a stethoscope and lay it flatly on her chest.

Twisting her head on the pillow, Mary looked down at her leg. It was wrapped in an open splinted boot, and the blanket that was draped over her hips was covered in blood. She felt faint, so she straightened out her head against the flat pillow.

"The firemen had to cut you out of the car. You'll no' be driving that one again." The man smiled and patted her arm gently through the blanket. "You were lucky, and that's a fact. A local farmer was driving by and saw your taillights in the trees. He called the police."

Mary nodded, silent.

"How's the pain?"

As if in response to his words, she felt pain rip up through her leg and into her groin. Her ribs ached, and her heart thumped loudly in her ears.

"Bad." Her voice was rough and quiet. Even speaking hurt her side.

"I canny give you anything th' now, not until we get to A&E. Just hold my hand, pet. It'll no' be long."

Mary gripped the big man's hand and kept her eyes focused on his round face. He asked her questions about herself, what she did for work, where she lived, but Mary couldn't speak. Her teeth chattered, and the effort of keeping her jaws clamped shut in order to stop it happening was exhausting.

The man chatted to her about his daughter, who was away at university in Edinburgh, and told her about his two hounds that he took up into the Highlands every Saturday to chase grouse in the wilds. If his voice stopped for any reason, she'd squeeze his hand even harder, and sensing her need for distraction, he'd start on a new tale.

"What's your name?" She finally asked him through gritted teeth.

"Oh, mine? It's Duncan. What's yours?" The man blushed slightly.

"Mary. Mary Ferguson." Mary coughed, the pain making her grab her side. She felt dizzy and reached back for Duncan's hand.

"Thank you." She smiled up at him, then slipped back into darkness.

Some time later, Mary woke in a hospital bed. Her leg was bandaged and in a large hammock suspended from the ceiling above the bed. She couldn't feel it much, but wiggled her toes just to check for movement. She saw her toes move, but the leg itself was mercifully numb. Her left arm had a large Elastoplast on it, and around her rib cage was a tight bandage, like a vice, making it hard to breathe. She lifted her right hand to her head and felt another bandage around her forehead. Each tiny movement she made sent shivers of pain throughout her body.

The room was silent and the bed next to hers lay vacant, the sheets and blankets tucked tightly around the thin mattress in readiness for the next occupant. It was dark outside the long window on her right, and as she turned her head, she spotted her watch and handbag on the bedside table. She wondered what time it was. It felt late, she was disoriented, and her head thumped annoyingly. There was a faint smell of toast mixed with bleach, and as she shifted her good leg in the bed, she felt the renewed coldness of the sheet under her heel. The light blanket on top of her wasn't enough to keep her from shivering against the chill of the room.

Lying next to her was the call button, so she pushed it to summon the nurse. She lay back, afraid to move too much in case she set off a chain reaction of hurt across her battered body. The screen on the little TV that sat on a bracket high on the wall flickered, but the sound was muted. *Antiques Roadshow* was on, and an expert was handling an art deco brooch, turning it over and pointing out the clasp to both the owner and the camera. Last time she'd watched this program had been at Jeffrey's, right before he left for Rome. They'd gotten fish and chips from the place in town and had drunk a bottle of Spanish wine while watching two episodes back-to-back.

At the thought of Jeffrey, she felt a pang of loss. She missed him. She wondered how he was enjoying Rome and whether or not he'd found himself a nice Italian lady to take to dinner and enjoy Christmas with. She hoped not. Suddenly annoyed at her own maudlin thoughts, she shook her head slightly, sending a needle of pain through her eyeball. She really needed to stay as still as possible. Where was the nurse?

After a few minutes, a nurse came in, carrying a jug of water and a plastic glass. She was as wide as she was tall and had a broad smile.

"Hallo, darlin'. You back in the land of the livin'?" Mary tried to guess at her accent, Jamaican maybe?

"I think so," Mary whispered. "I'm afraid to move." She watched the nurse lean over her bed and place the jug on the side table.

"Best if you stay still, my love, for a while anyway. You took quite a beatin'."

Mary could see the nametag glistening against the dark blue uniform.

"Esmé. What a lovely name." Mary smiled as the nurse re-tucked her already tight blanket under the mattress.

"Well, thanks. After my grandmother, rest her soul."

Esmé circled the bed, adjusted the IV drip, took Mary's pulse, listened to her chest, and checked her blood pressure. Noting everything down on the chart, she hung the metal clipboard back at the end of the bed.

"How's your pain, darlin'? You need somethin'?"

Mary nodded with as little movement as she could manage. She had questions she wanted answered before she slid back into blissful sleep.

"I'd appreciate an extra blanket too, if it's not too much trouble." Mary closed her eyes, just to rest them momentarily while Esmé left the room and then came back with another light blanket. She laid it carefully over Mary and began tucking the edges in under the corners of the bed.

Mary let her thoughts wander back to the car. She was still unsure exactly what had happened. Perhaps Esmé could fill in some of the blanks?

"What happened? Did I hit anyone else? How long was I in the car before they got me out?" The questions tripped off her tongue, and Esmé let her ask them in quick succession. After a few moments, the nurse picked her chart back up and flipped the page over.

"Well, Duncan, the EMT, he said you'd driven off the road into a stand of trees. Some local farmer who was passing spotted your taillights off to the side of the road, and he called the police. The ambulance arrived first, but they had to call the fire brigade, 'cuz they couldn't get you out of the car."

Mary listened, nodding carefully.

"Anyway, Duncan, he stabilized you in the ambulance. Gave

you fluids and some blood. When you got here, the doctors operated and set your leg. It was a nasty break. You have a pin in the tibia and twenty-eight stitches along your shin, eleven stitches in your head, two cracked ribs, a mild concussion, a laceration on your forearm, and dehydration. I think that's about it." Esmé winked at her.

"Gosh." Mary swallowed carefully. "That's enough to be going on with."

Esmé chuckled. "Well, at least you haven't bruised your sense of humor, darlin'."

Mary smiled faintly and nodded.

"So, the pain. Where is it on a scale of one to ten?"

"About a seven," Mary replied.

"OK, I'll get you a lil' morphine and then the doctor will be here in half an hour to check on you. OK?"

Mary nodded and once again felt her eyelids heavy as suitcases. She wondered if anyone had picked up her shopping from the back seat of her car. She wondered if she'd need to get something else for the twins, if the jigsaw and the hats and scarves had been left behind. She hoped she'd have time to find them something before Christmas, if that was the case, bless their little hearts.

Esmé was back with a syringe within a few moments, and Mary felt the coldness of the fluid trickling through her IV portal. As the blessed painkiller crept through her veins, she let herself relax and felt the muscles in her back release their tension. She was floating, the bed rippling underneath her, as she closed her eyes and let sleep wrap her up in its arms once again.

CHAPTER 29

Jeffrey woke to the sound of the telephone. It had an odd single ring. It was a shrill alarm to wake up to, and as he sat up in the huge bed, it took him a few moments to remember exactly where he was.

The French windows must've been open a crack, as the long net curtain billowed inwards and he felt the light breeze of morning against his face. Scanning the room, he saw there was still no sign of the dog. Disappointed, Jeffrey threw back the covers and reached for the phone.

"Hello?"

"Mr. Mere. Buongiorno. This is Giovanni Giacomo."

Jeffrey nodded into the quiet room.

"Good morning."

"Today the British Embassy is open from ten until noon only. I arrange for a car to take you there, if you can come downstairs now."

Jeffrey leaned over and looked at the clock on the bedside table. 10:29 am, so he'd slept a long time, much longer than he would have at home. It was scandalously late, really, and Agnes would have called him a lazybones.

Tucking the phone under his jaw, Jeffrey pulled on the fluffy bathrobe and padded into the bathroom.

"I can be ready in a few minutes, yes."

Looking in the mirror, he assessed himself. The robe was plush and ankle length, even on his tall frame. Tied in the middle, it made him look like a comically chubby version of himself, and the too-large slippers didn't help either. A smirk crept onto his face, but the sudden realization that he had no clothes wiped it away in an instant.

"Oh, Mr. Giacomo. My clothes. I sent them to the laundry last night." Jeffrey ran a hand over the matching patches of fluffy hair above each ear.

"Laundry is on the way up now."

"Well, that was fast."

Jeffrey thanked Mr. Giacomo, replaced the phone, and walked back into the bedroom. Just as he reached the door, there was a single sharp knock. A young woman in the corridor smiled and handed Jeffrey his clothes, hanging neatly on a heavy wooden hanger and sealed inside clear cellophane.

"Grazie." He smiled back and accepted the hanger. Feeling bad that he had no cash to tip her with, he blushed and patted the flat pocket of his robe theatrically.

"No cash. No money at all, actually. Sorry about that." He shrugged and the young woman's brow crinkled as she tried to understand his attempt at mime.

As he stood there, holding the clean laundry and fumbling in his empty pockets, she quickly got the message, nodded curtly, turned, and walked away. Jeffrey called another thank you after her, by way of apology, as she headed down the hall.

Twenty minutes later, he was standing in the grand lobby, his cap and coat on, having swallowed an espresso that the manager had offered him while he waited for the car. The driver was a middle-aged man with a thick accent. Jeffrey guessed he was Polish, or maybe Russian, but he certainly knew his way around Rome. Within what seemed like just a few minutes, they pulled up opposite an impressive building with a Union Jack fluttering outside its tall wrought-iron gates. There were two long pools with fountains of water splashing into them on either side of a narrow paved walkway leading to the doors.

The man nodded silently towards the big gates and reached across the seat to open the door for Jeffrey.

"Thanks. I can manage." Jeffrey pushed on the door and stepped out into the street.

Realizing that he could soon be abandoned, once again lost in this city he knew so little of, Jeffrey panicked and spun back around.

"Will you wait for me?" He leaned into the car, waiting for a reply.

The driver nodded, mumbled something in his gravelly baritone voice, and pointed to the opposite side of the street, where Jeffrey saw a small sign for parking. Relieved, he nodded, closed the door, and headed through the gate towards a small hut that looked like a security checkpoint.

Jeffrey guessed the attaché, a Mr. Sutton, was in his mid-thirties. A slim young man with piercing blue eyes, sandy hair, and exceptionally long, thin fingers, he sat behind a large mahogany desk. He was polite and helpful, dispelling the preconception Jeffrey had formed about diplomats and government employees. Agnes had called them leeches, a bunch of public school boys who couldn't hold down jobs in the private sector. She resented paying their wages with her taxes and said so loudly and often whenever the opportunity arose.

As he sipped the tea he'd been offered and listened to the calming sound of a polished English accent as Mr. Sutton gave him instructions, Jeffrey began to feel reassured. It was at times like this that he was glad he was British. Brits really knew how to manage a crisis. With a pot of strong tea, a little sympathy, and a good plan, all could be set right, given time.

Apparently he could apply for a temporary passport while his old one was officially reported stolen.

"We will help you contact your bank at home and arrange for some funds to be transferred to a local bank here in Rome. We'll also assist you with the credit card company and the airline, to have a replacement return ticket issued." As he spoke, Mr. Sutton wrote on a thick pad with a gold pen.

Jeffrey nodded mutely.

"We'll call you at the hotel when the temporary passport is available."

Apparently, it might all take a day or so to arrange, but the young man assured him that he'd be safely on his way home within the week.

Jeffrey finished his tea and the last bite of his second digestive biscuit, then stood and thanked the attaché profusely.

"So, in the meantime, I can stay at the hotel?"

"Yes, Mr. Mere. The manager has agreed to let you stay, and once your new credit card arrives, you can transfer any outstanding payments accordingly."

"That's wonderful." Jeffrey nodded and gathered up his coat and cap.

"In the meantime, perhaps you can try to see a little of Rome. You might even enjoy some of your time here?" The young man eyed Jeffrey as he carefully adjusted the brim of his cap.

"I suppose so." Jeffrey was uncertain but nodded his agreement all the same.

"Mr. Giacomo will arrange for you to make your statement to the police this afternoon, and then we will coordinate with the inspector on any developments." Mr. Sutton rose and extended his hand to Jeffrey. "All the best, Mr. Mere."

"Thank you again. You've been so helpful." Jeffrey shook the cool hand vigorously and walked back outside into the brightness of the day.

The police station was apparently close to the hotel so, after Jeffrey had a light lunch at the bar in the restaurant, the driver came back to take him to see the inspector.

The same tall policeman whom he'd met in the hotel led Jeffrey to a windowless room and then sat down opposite him. He opened up a laptop computer and swung it around towards him.

"You look at these photographs. Tell me if you know any faces."

Jeffrey turned his attention to the screen. The inspector showed him how to scroll through the pages and asked if he'd like water or espresso.

"Yes, espresso, please." Jeffrey nodded, feeling quite cosmopolitan with his request. He shrugged his coat off and began to go through the mug shots. There were some faces in here that only a mother could love, that was for sure. Impossibly wide jaws, ears and noses with multiple piercings, tattoos, and shaved heads that made Jeffrey squirm. Part of him wanted to see Paolo's handsome face staring up at him from one of these pages, but another part of him dreaded it, too. The brother, now he was a different kettle of fish. At the thought of the bigger man cowering on the dirt floor, Jeffrey's heart softened. What a life he must lead, the poor soul.

After an hour of combing through the pictures, Jeffrey had failed to recognize anyone.

"You are sure?" The inspector tried one more time.

"Sure. Sorry." Jeffrey shrugged apologetically.

He had shown the inspector, on a map, where he'd been taken, to the best of his memory. To his relief, the policeman appeared to know exactly the industrial area he was referring to. It seemed they did not need Jeffrey to go there with them, which was such a relief that Jeffrey could feel some of the pent-up tension in his back release. He had to admit that he'd been dreading going back there, even with police protection.

By 4:30, he was back in the hotel lobby and heading for his room. A nice bath sounded good about now, then perhaps some dinner from room service and an early night. He'd certainly not get his usual Thursday fare here in Rome, but he felt sure he could find something good to eat on the menu.

As he rode up in the lift, Jeffrey wondered if there were any English-language TV stations here.

The room was silent, and the bed had been made. The French windows were still slightly ajar, and as a frigid breeze blew in,

Jeffrey pushed them closed and locked them tightly. Opening the drawer under the large TV, he saw his remaining socks lined up neatly, the days of the week in perfect order, from left to right, minus the pair he was wearing. He'd squeeze the Thurs-Day socks through in the sink tonight and dry them on the radiator. They were too precious to be sent to the laundry.

CHAPTER 30

Jeffrey woke in the middle of the big bed. This time, he knew exactly where he was, and as he lay looking at the drapery above him, he stretched out each arm and leg, reaching for the four corners of the mattress. The sheet was cool under his legs and the pillow soft beneath his head. He had slept surprisingly well, and turning his head towards the window, he glanced at the clock. It was 9:05 am.

He could hear the low rumble of activity outside in the street, the hum of voices, and even some distant music. A church bell chimed, underlying it all, and as he tried to focus on the various layers of ambient noise, his stomach gave an almighty rumble, shattering the serenity of the moment. He slapped his hand across his middle and pushed down. Something in Rome was making him very hungry. He'd eaten a huge plate of pasta the night before, followed by tiramisu. He'd also been delighted to find several English-language channels on the TV and had fallen asleep, his empty dessert plate lying on the bed, with old episodes of *Dr. Who* flickering light around the darkened room. Despite having eaten all that just a few hours ago, he was starving again. Perhaps he'd picked up a worm on the plane? It wouldn't surprise him, as the plane food had been really revolting.

Shaking the notion from his mind, he threw off the covers and reached for the robe. The room service menu was on the dressing table, so he grabbed it on his way to the bathroom. Using the small travel toothbrush that the concierge had given him, he cleaned his teeth while reading the list of breakfast fare. There were many things he did not recognize, but there were also various types of eggs, omelets, and fresh fruit that sounded good and comfortingly familiar. As he skimmed over the list, he saw oatmeal listed in the "Healthy Options" section. The idea of being in Rome and eating porridge was suddenly ridiculous, and he let out a guffaw, spraying toothpaste over the mirror like a coating of peppermint snow.

He decided on toast, an omelet with bacon, and then some yogurt. Yes, that sounded healthy and satisfying. Having called room service to order his breakfast, he stood at the French windows and pushed back the net curtains. Outside, in the Roman morning, people were going about their day. Down below was a café with several small tables outside on the cobbled footpath. He was surprised to see a few people sitting outdoors, drinking from tiny cups. In this cold, it was amazing. These Italians were a funny bunch.

He knew that until the money transfer from home arrived, he was limited in what he could do. Once he got his funds through, he'd go out and buy himself some alternate clothes. Perhaps then he could take a tour of the city, but one organized by the hotel. No more of those dodgy outings with spurious young men in shiny suits. He'd learned his lesson there.

As his mind replayed the nerve-wracking episode with his abductors, he realized that he was rather proud of having been able to regain some semblance of control in the dirty little shack. He'd negotiated his way back to safety, even if at the cost of his belongings and money. He had handled that as best he could.

As the tiny nugget of unaccustomed pride swelled, he thought about the past few months. Had he not, in fact, climbed a mountain, saved Matilda's life, spent time getting to know the lovely Mary, and then taken a flight to Rome? Had he not taken more strides towards a broader life than ever before? Deciding he needed to give himself more credit, Jeffrey nodded decisively.

A little while later Jeffrey wandered back out onto the small balcony. The top of the Spanish Steps was visible from where he stood, and as this Friday morning played out in front of him, Jeffrey spotted two nuns. They had extremely large, stiff white headdresses with great white ski slopes swooping dramatically out over each ear. Each nun had a long, dangling rosary at her waist, and they walked in sync, their steps perfectly aligned and timed, as if they were performing a well-choreographed duet.

Jeffrey sighed. He really didn't know how he felt about religion these days. He'd gone to church in Pitlochry with his parents when he was a child, but after his father had died, Agnes had had her faith shaken somewhat and had taken a leave of absence from attending. As he thought about her sitting in the small Episcopal church, Jeffrey remembered her funeral. There had been such a sense of finality, peace, and sadness all wrapped up in one package that day. The image of Agnes's coffin, so small and vulnerable, would not leave him, he suspected, ever.

Jeffrey shivered both at the memory and at the brisk breeze.

Just as he was about to close the doors against the chill, he caught sight of a dark shape in his peripheral vision. The dog was crouched down outside the café, licking its front paws purposefully. Before he could stop himself, he threw the French doors wide and stepped out onto the small balcony.

"Hey there, pup. I'm up here. Hey, girl." He waved his arms manically above his head, and as he did so, was aware of a shock of cold creeping up underneath the bathrobe. Some faces turned up towards him. He felt the curious stares, but the slight discomfort that afforded wasn't enough to deter him. He wanted to get the dog's attention. He and she had unfinished business.

After a few moments, the animal raised its massive head and sniffed the air, as if trying to locate the scent of his voice.

"Up here, lass." He bounced from foot to foot.

The dog scanned its surroundings, then raised its eyes to the balcony and, appearing to spot him, let out a sharp bark.

Jeffrey laughed out loud.

"Good girl. Stay there. I'm coming to get you." He patted the air, indicating that the hound should sit, stay. He'd seen the gesture on TV, on one of those dog agility contests. He wasn't sure if this particular dog would get it, but it was worth a try.

He grabbed his room key, pulled the door behind him, and scuttled down the corridor. As the heavy doors opened, he caught sight of himself in the gold-framed mirror at the back of the lift. He was a ridiculous sight in the bathrobe, but for the first time in as long as he could remember, he really didn't care.

The lift quickly settled on the ground floor, and as the doors slid open, Jeffrey scanned the lobby to see how many people were around, assessing which was the clearest path to take to the front doors. To his relief, the place was fairly quiet. One couple sat on the posh chairs in the center of the room and there were a few staff members coasting around the edges of the space. A small man in a dark suit stood next to the reception desk, but his back was turned towards Jeffrey, presenting the perfect opportunity for him to make a dash for it.

He shot out of the lift and took off running. The overly large slippers skidded across the marble floor, and he felt himself lose purchase a couple of times. The momentary fear that he might fall, skittering across this grand floor with the robe flying open, thoroughly embarrassing himself, buried itself in his excitement.

Having made it across the lobby, Jeffrey pushed hard against the great glass door, and as he emerged into the day, the intensity of the cold caught him by surprise. The street outside the hotel was bustling with activity. Smartly dressed couples turned to stare as the man in the bathrobe trotted along the pavement, heading towards the bottom of the Spanish Steps.

A young woman he passed called out to him and laughed. He couldn't make out what she said and didn't have time to stop and figure it out, so he just waved over his shoulder as he kept on moving.

As he reached the café, he could see the dog crouched down where he'd last seen it. A large man in a long coat was sitting at one of the outside tables and appeared not to notice the massive hound at his feet.

Jeffrey rushed over and, bending down, ruffled the dog's head.

"Here you are, girl. Good stay." The dog leaned into his caress and raised its big back end up off the ground.

"Let's go back now." Jeffrey found, to his surprise, that his eyes were blurred with tears. Tightening the bathrobe around his middle, he reached down and gently wound his hand into the ruff of matted fur at the back of the dog's neck.

"Let's go, lass."

The man at the table next to him looked startled as Jeffrey, bowing slightly in apology at the interruption, touched his forelock comically.

"Buongiorno. Mi scusi." That phrase book Mary had given him had really come in handy.

The man sniffed, slid his coffee cup closer to himself, and shook his head disapprovingly.

Jeffrey shrugged and, with the dog pressing tight to his thigh, began walking back to the hotel. A few paces down the road, a car horn beeped at him and then a young man on a moped shouted something in Italian. Whatever it was, he was sure it wasn't complimentary, but he was nearly back to the hotel, and it made no difference to the price of eggs what anyone thought of him, anyway.

As the two unlikely companions walked across the lobby, Jeffrey spotted the hotel manager standing close to the lift. Now this could be problematic, as he'd been quite clear about dogs not being permitted in the hotel under normal circumstances. The closer the pair got to the lift, the more Jeffrey began to panic. Mr. Giacomo's face was scarlet. He was talking animatedly to a young woman in a red uniform, but his eyes never left Jeffrey.

"Mr. Mere?" The younger man wrung his hands and looked around the lobby, as if assessing the damage this odd Scotsman may have done to the other guests' equilibrium with his ill-advised foray outside in his bathrobe and slippers.

"I know. I'm sorry. But there's nothing I can do — she needs to be with me, for today at least." Jeffrey held on tight to the matted neck and searched the man's face for a sign of his intentions.

Mr. Giacomo sighed, clearly deciding that there was little advantage in trying to understand this strange Scottish man and that the best thing for everyone would be to get him out of sight, fast.

"Please, go back to your room, Mr. Mere. I think it's best." The younger man let his eyes flick down over the bathrobe as he spoke.

Jeffrey extended his free hand and shook the manager's smaller one. Surprised that Mr. Giacomo was not protesting at the presence of the dog, Jeffrey nodded.

"Agreed."

Back up in the room, Jeffrey was glad to see his breakfast had arrived. A tray was set on the small table in front of the window and he could smell the espresso, the aroma lingering in the air.

"Come on, lass. Let's get some food into you."

Jeffrey picked up the bacon and a slice of toast and placed them on the floor at the dog's feet.

"Go on, then. That's for you."

As Jeffrey settled himself down to eat the omelet and drink his coffee, the dog nosed the food, quickly gobbled it up, then lay down on its side, stretching its legs out towards the window.

His breakfast done, Jeffrey looked down at the shaggy body and wiped his mouth with the heavy cotton napkin.

"You and I need to talk."

The dog lay still and waited patiently as Jeffrey moved over to perch on the end of the bed.

"You've a canny knack of appearing just when I need you, lass. How's that, then?" He watched the big animal blink.

The dog rolled up onto his haunches, and its brown eyes seemed to bore holes into Jeffrey's face as he spoke. The intense scrutiny of the animal brought his mum to mind once again. Was it ridiculous to think this dog was somehow connected to Agnes?

As this thought occurred to him, not for the first time, the dog shook its head violently, sending a trail of drool flying across the floor. Jeffrey jumped and moved his foot out of the way of the airborne dribble, startled by the animal's sudden movement but also by the feeling that it was responding to his unspoken thoughts. He looked down at the big face, and before he could think himself out of it again, he spoke.

"Mum?"

At the word, the dog lifted its head from the carpet. It sat motionless as Jeffrey slid off the end of the bed and gently shuffled over to sit next to the big animal on the floor. His head was now on a level with the dog's as he reached out and stroked the matted head. The dog accepted his caresses; then, pushing itself up on its back legs, it rose to its full height, towering over Jeffrey's shoulders.

Silence followed as the two stayed in this position, the dog looking down at Jeffrey and Jeffrey looking up into the beady brown eyes. There was no need for words, no need for questions or explanations. For the first time since Agnes had died, Jeffrey felt a lifting of the heavy boulder of sadness that he'd been carrying in his solar plexus.

He didn't know how much time passed, but eventually Jeffrey's backside grew numb from sitting on the floor. He shifted his weight, breaking the silent tension of the exchange that was taking place between them. The dog shook its head and sneezed loudly, causing Jeffrey to laugh out loud as he pushed himself up and sat back on the bed.

As he watched the animal circle around precisely three times, then curl up into a small ball at the foot of the bed, Jeffrey knew what he had to do.

"I'm going to be OK, you know?" Jeffrey felt the words thick in his throat. While he didn't want this to be the last time he saw the dog, he knew that as long as she felt he needed her, she'd never leave him.

He watched as the dog's nose twitched. It raised its head, then tilted it quizzically to the side, as if trying to interpret his words. The big animal rose and padded over to him. He held out his hand, the dog pressed its muzzle into it, and he felt the rough tongue across his palm.

"Thank you for taking care of me." Hot tears welled up in his eyes as the dog continued to bathe his fingers. "You are the best."

Jeffrey felt overwhelmingly tired. He rose and walked to the bathroom, washed his hands, then turned on the tap over the claw foot bathtub. A nice hot shower would set him to rights. Then, hopefully, he'd get his clothes back from the laundry once again, and perhaps would venture out for a walk before dinner.

Feeling clean and refreshed, he wandered back into the bedroom. The dog lay curled up on the bed, snoring loudly. Smiling to himself, Jeffrey lay down carefully next to it. Perhaps he'd just take a wee nap, then see what the rest of the day had in store. As he closed his eyes, he could picture Agnes, her knitting needles clacking, along with her false teeth, as she sat in the big wing-backed chair in the home. Yes, she really had been a good

CHAPTER 31

M ary lay and looked out the window. The sun had risen, and the sky was a pearly pink. She loved mornings like this one. Even if she was stuck in the hospital, she could still enjoy the Perthshire light.

Esmé had left her with a breakfast tray and a cup of tepid tea that Mary had drunk out of pure desperation. Hospital tea left much to be desired, but beggars couldn't be choosers.

It had been two days since her accident, and she was already antsy to get home. The doctor had said two more days and then he'd assess her ability to get around, manage the wheelchair, and care for herself before making his decision to discharge her. Mary knew that this was the correct procedure in cases such as hers, but the idea of spending Christmas in hospital brought a lump to her throat. Could fate be so cruel as to deprive her of her little home on the very first Christmas she lived there? It really would be sod's law.

She knew she'd need assistance when she got home. There was only so much she could do for herself, even as a nurse. Health visitors would come to her house and help her with bathing, dressing, and changing her wound dressings. It would be a few weeks before she could put any weight on her leg, so she'd have to get used to the idea of people invading her space. Not her favorite state of being, but she had no choice.

As she shifted in the bed, the *Woman's Realm* magazine she'd been reading slipped onto the floor. It was no great loss. She'd read it cover to cover twice now, and she'd practically committed the recipe for chocolate-dipped shortbread to memory, determined to try it when she got home. She suspected Jeffrey would enjoy it, with his sweet tooth.

Her leg thrummed with every pulse of blood through the veins and blood vessels. She wondered how long she'd need the heavy-duty painkillers she was taking. The doctor had taken her off the morphine the day before and put her on codeine. While not as woozy as she had been on the morphine, she still felt somewhat disconnected from reality on the new pills. She kept seeing her old history teacher fussing with her bedding or Agnes knitting in the chair in the corner. Once, she even thought she'd seen her ex-husband Jimmy standing at the end of her bed. That time, she'd pressed the call button. Her heart racing, she'd hoped to see Esmé's warm smile coming around the doorway. Instead, a different nurse had come in, and had been less than impressed when Mary, embarrassed, said she was fine, really, but just needed another pillow.

Her head and arm were feeling better, but her ribs were still problematic. Every time she moved, she was stabbed in the side. She breathed shallow, tiny breaths and was terrified of sneezing, the pain of which she felt sure would send her into a faint. She must not sneeze under any circumstances.

As she watched the sky change color from pink to lemon and then to pale blue, Mary slipped in and out of sleep. She did not hear the soft footsteps of the visitor as he entered her room.

She woke to the smell of beef stew and turned her head to the side to see a large ruddy face she didn't recognize hovering close.

"Hello, there. How are you feeling?" The man was huge, leaning in towards her, grasping a bunch of yellow flowers in his mammoth hands.

Mary felt a surge of panic and tried to push herself up in the bed, causing such a wave of agony through her side that she let out a yelp.

"Oh, stay still, hen. Don't move." The big man lurched backwards as if stung. Jumping up from the chair, he retreated to the far side of the room.

"It's just me, Duncan, the medic from the ambulance. Remember?"

As the pain abated, Mary slowly regained her equilibrium, and as her breathing returned to normal, the moon-face across the room gradually clarified itself to her. Of course, the kind man in the ambulance.

"Sorry. I didn't recognize you." Seeing his stricken face, she regretted her overreaction.

"S'OK. I should have waited a wee bit longer before coming in, but I was in the area today." His voice faded as a shy smile crept back across his wide cheeks.

Mary, now feeling back in control of herself, beckoned to him.

"It's fine. Please, sit down." She indicated the spindle-backed chair he had previously occupied. As she watched him lower his big frame into the seat, she worried about its frail construction and, despite herself, suddenly pictured the narrow wooden legs giving way under his bulk. She had an image of his legs flailing in the air as he flipped over backwards, leaving a pile of kindling in place of the chair. She suppressed a giggle that, rightly so for her wickedness, sent a ripple of pain through her torso. *That'll teach you, Mary Ferguson*, she scolded herself.

What was his name again? Mary adjusted her glasses, and on a reflex, her hand went up to her hair. What must she look like?

The yellow flowers hung awkwardly from his meaty fist. Mary nodded at the side table.

"There's a vase somewhere." She smiled. "It's very kind of you." Duncan, his name was Duncan.

Duncan rose and awkwardly lifted an empty vase from the shelf over the radiator. He walked into the bathroom and she heard the sink running. He returned, sticking the flowers in the vase unceremoniously.

"They're lovely." Mary smiled at the vase as he placed it on the bedside table.

"So, how are you?" He scanned her leg, still suspended in the hammock.

"I'm all right, thanks to you."

"Well, no, it's thanks to the farmer, really." Duncan blushed and sat back on the chair that was too small for him, overflowing its edges.

Mary watched him wringing his hands between his open knees and felt sorry for him. She wasn't sure what more to say to him, and the awkwardness of the silence crept over her skin like

212

a colony of ants on the move.

It was obvious he was here because he liked her, was interested in her for some reason. This man had gone out of his way to visit her, and she a perfect stranger. At the irony of his interest despite her injured state, rather than being flattered, Mary felt a new wave of irritation at Jeffrey. There he was, lording it up in Rome, while she lay here like a beached whale. He had no idea that she was hurt, that she'd nearly been killed, and yet, as Duncan sat and stared mutely out the window, nodding at her and smiling shyly, all she could think about was Jeffrey and how long it'd be until he'd be home in Willow Street.

At the thought of Jeffrey's cottage, Mary caught her breath.

"Oh, god. The cat."

"Pardon?" Duncan frowned as he leaned in again, towards her.

"Someone needs to feed the cat." Mary stared at him.

"Your cat?" Duncan eyed her closely.

"No. Jeffrey's cat." Mary's eyes swiveled back to the window.

"Ah." Seeming to understand, Duncan sat back against the chair and the thin spindles creaked against his bulk.

Mary stared at the sky. Here was a perfectly nice man, showing concern, bringing her flowers. While flattered, she wasn't particularly happy about it. Had she mentioned Jeffrey deliberately?

Duncan stayed for another ten minutes. They talked about his dogs, and he told her about his home in Perth. He spoke quietly, almost reverently, and apologized again for scaring her. Mary told him about her job at the home and then, to her surprise, she talked about Agnes. The old lady's loss had taken a deeper cut at her than she'd realized. She still missed their chats and the laughs they had together.

After Duncan left, she lay looking up at the blistered ceiling tiles, counting the seams from one edge of the room to the other. Mary closed her eyes and inhaled deeply, realizing that she was lonely. It wasn't something she'd allowed herself to acknowledge while she'd been fleeing Glasgow and getting her life back together after her divorce. But now that she had nothing else to focus on, the thought snuck up on her, nibbling away at her subconscious.

Having been in the hospital for two days, Mary had been visited by two of her fellow nurses at the home, who'd stayed for fifteen minutes, then made their excuses. Matilda had popped in twice already and brought her some scones, which the nurses had eaten as Mary had no appetite, and then Duncan had come by. While she was very touched at them all making the effort, the one face she wanted to see more than any other was absent. She sighed. *Mary Ferguson, you need to make more friends.*

She finally felt safe here in Pitlochry, having her little house and her wonderful job. Thankfully, she'd heard nothing from Jimmy in almost four years, so perhaps it was time to let her walls down? It was times like this that made someone sit up and take stock of their life, and when she did so, Mary Ferguson wasn't altogether happy with what she saw.

CHAPTER 32

Jeffrey sat in the café opposite the Spanish Steps in his newly laundered clothes. He swirled the last of an espresso in the cup and watched the activity around him. The hotel had sent him in a car to a local bank, where he'd picked up the funds that had been transferred from home, and then he'd gone on to the embassy to collect his temporary passport.

He'd bought a few things at a department store along the street from the hotel. A large white bag sat next to his feet containing a small digital camera, some new underwear, two long-sleeved shirts, a V-necked sweater, and a pair of dark green cords. The color would not have been his first choice, but this was the only pair of trousers in his size in the entire shop, it seemed. He needed a change of clothes, so green it was.

All he had to do now was wait for the replacement air ticket to be delivered to the hotel and he was all but ready to go home.

Home. For the first time since the terrifying diversion from his intended holiday, Jeffrey thought about his cottage. He wondered if the plumbing was OK; if there was a really cold snap, pipes did have a tendency to freeze. He hoped Ralf was fine, but of course Mary was taking care of him, so there were no concerns there.

Mary. He watched various women circulating the steps, sitting in the café, and passing by on the street. While they generally looked nice, even elegant, there was nothing that particularly drew him to them. Now, if they'd had red hair, or perhaps some freckles, that would be a different story.

He finished the last of his coffee and laid some euros down on the table. It was 12:45 pm, and he had the rest of the day to fill. His initial instinct had been to go straight back to his room once he'd returned from the embassy, but instead he'd chosen to find a clothes shop he could afford and then go to the café near the Spanish Steps, sit for an hour, and just observe Roman life. As long as he kept a close eye on the crisp new euro notes and the thin, bendy passport that occupied his pocket, surely no harm could come to him here?

While it was a cold day, the sun was shining bravely, and there was a hint of new optimism in Jeffrey. What if he did a little sightseeing? It would be a shame to have come all this way only to see the hotel and the café. He had three more days until his return to Scotland, and as that thought dawned on him, he realized that this must be Christmas Eve. Tomorrow was the dinner dance at the hotel, then he'd have Boxing Day to fill, and then he'd fly home on the twenty-seventh of December.

He'd planned on being home in time for Hogmanay, and he and Mary were going to spend the evening together. He liked to watch the New Year's celebrations on Celtic TV, and Mary had offered to cook him a dinner of steak pie and rhubarb crumble. At the thought of the familiar food, Jeffrey felt a spurt of saliva in his mouth.

New Year's Day was the annual Pitlochry Street party and ceilidh. Each year, Atholl Road was closed off so that locals and visitors could join in the fun — eating, dancing, and sharing wee nips of whisky from each other's flasks. The Vale of Atholl pipe band played as people danced Strip the Willow and the Dashing White Sergeant, and then the crowd would form an enormous circle, clasping hands, to sing "Auld Lang Syne."

Jeffrey loved the event and never missed it. When Agnes had been well enough, she'd especially enjoyed the dancing. He remembered her "yeuching" and "wheeching" loudly as she turned in circles under his arm while the pipes wailed her favorite Military Two-Step. It would be strange and sad not to have her around this year, but then everything had changed now. He must accept that.

As he leaned down to pick up the shopping bag from under the table, he noticed two red, pointy-toed shoes standing next to him. Lifting his head, he saw a woman, tall and slim, in a red suit, a black coat, and an extravagant wide-brimmed hat.

"Mi scusi." She smiled and scanned Jeffrey's face. "English?"

Her brown eyes were warm and softly wrinkled at the edges. Jeffrey swallowed and nodded mutely.

"You visit, on holiday?" Her smile was still there.

"Um, yes." Jeffrey pulled the bag closer to his leg and sat back in the chair. Was it so obvious that he was a tourist?

"First time in Roma?" The woman took a step closer, took off her hat and ran a hand through her dark wavy hair. There were flashes of silver at her temples and as she moved, Jeffrey caught a whiff of a marvelous scent, reminding him of the jasmine that climbed up the side of his cottage.

"Yes. First time." Jeffrey nodded and gave her a tentative smile.

"Lucia. Nice to meet you." She removed a glove and extended an elegant hand.

"Mere. Jeffrey Mere." Jeffrey half raised himself from the chair and took her hand, which felt cool and smooth in his rougher one.

"May I join you?" She eyed the empty chair across from him.

"I was just leaving, actually." Jeffrey sounded more brusque than he'd intended. However, once bitten, twice shy. This woman, while looking very classy, just as Paolo had before he robbed him, was very forward for a total stranger.

"Leaving? That's a shame." Lucia shrugged and pulled a chair out from the table. "If you are going, may I have your table?"

Jeffrey looked around him and realized that while he'd been daydreaming, the café had filled up. He and his empty cup were now holding a table for two to ransom. He felt his face flush. She wasn't being over-familiar. She just needed a place to eat her lunch.

"Yes, of course. I'm sorry." Jeffrey made to rise.

"No need to go. Why not join me?" Lucia settled herself in the seat and reached for the long narrow menu.

"Well, I wasn't really planning on having lunch here." Jeffrey watched her as she slipped some half-lensed glasses onto her thin nose and scanned the menu.

"But it is lunch time?" She lifted her gaze to his and smiled again.

"Well, I suppose it is." Jeffrey shrugged and felt his shoulders release a little of the tension they'd been holding.

"It is always better to have company, to eat. Yes?" Lucia raised a hand and waved the waiter over.

In a split second, surprising himself, Jeffrey decided he'd stay.

"I *could* eat a little something." He settled back into the seat and shoved the shopping bag under the table with his feet.

"*Meraviglioso.*" Lucia placed the menu back on the table and spoke quietly to the waiter.

Jeffrey scanned the menu and quickly ordered a panini with prosciutto, basil, and mozzarella. He knew that this was a fancy ham and cheese sandwich, and now, the idea of food was suddenly attractive. He was actually hungry again.

Lucia pulled a mobile phone from her handbag and ran a long finger over the screen, checking her messages. Jeffrey cleared his throat, suddenly awkward again in the company of this striking woman. As he watched her, he wondered if this was perhaps not unusual for Roman women, to accost strangers and invite themselves to join them for lunch. The thought made him smirk as he fiddled nervously with the salt and pepper shakers in front of him, twirling them around each other in a dance.

"So. How long you are in Roma?" Lucia was looking at his hands as he played with the condiments.

"I've been here three days now. I have three left."

"Back to England?"

"To Scotland, actually." Jeffrey pushed the salt and pepper back together and left them in the middle of the table.

"Ah, Scotland. I love Edinburgh. I was there for the festival, many years ago. So wonderful." Lucia smiled and, taking her glasses off, placed them on the table.

She really did have lovely eyes. So dark they were almost black, and yet friendly. At another time in his life he could easily see himself being attracted to Lucia. Her easy nature and stylish curves made it difficult not to stare. Why, then, was he thinking about Mary?

"So you've been to Scotland? That's wonderful." Surprised, Jeffrey felt himself relax a little more. She had been to his homeland. She couldn't be all bad, then?

"Yes. I went with my husband and daughter. We had a beautiful time. We stayed in Princes Street and ate haggis." Lucia giggled.

Jeffrey felt a few more of his closely held reservations break down.

"Have you been back since then?" He watched as the waiter laid a plate of cheese and cold meats and a glass of red wine in front of Lucia, and the toasted panini and another espresso in front of him.

"No. It was a long time ago." Lucia looked wistful, pulled the plate towards her, and lifted the glass to her lips.

Jeffrey tried hard not to show any reaction to her drinking wine at lunchtime. There was something rather scandalous about it, and yet, he found it oddly exciting. Italians were truly hedonistic, but perhaps they had it right?

From the distant look on her face, Jeffrey wondered if he should perhaps not ask any more questions, but something compelled him to. He was curious about this woman.

"So, do you and your husband travel a lot?" He took a sip of his coffee.

"We did, before he passed." Lucia's eyes were glassy, and she took a long draft of wine. She wiped her mouth on the crisp white napkin and then shook her head slightly, as if dismissing a painful memory.

"Oh, I'm sorry. I didn't mean to upset you." Jeffrey once again felt the ground shift underneath him. He'd put his foot in it, up to the knee, obviously.

"S'all right. He passed away, two years ago, but every day I think of him." She shrugged and smiled sadly. "My daughter is gone to live in Zurich, with her new husband, so now I am just me. Da sola." She took a piece of wafer-thin meat and a slice of cheese and popped them into her mouth.

Jeffrey felt a lump in his throat. The poor thing was lonely, and that was something he could certainly relate to.

They ate and talked, sharing stories of their homes and the people they cared about. They finished their lunch, then ordered more wine and coffee. The more Jeffrey relaxed, the more he told her of Pitlochry, his retirement, his bees, climbing Ben Macdhui, and of course his sadness at losing Agnes. He also told her about his encounter with Paolo, the hotel, the police, and the embassy, and Lucia expressed her shock and sympathy. She apologized for the bad first impression of Rome, seeming to feel personally responsible for the city's shortcomings.

At Lucia's encouragement, he joined her in a glass of wine, which loosened his tongue even more, and before he knew it, he was telling her how much he admired Mary.

"You must act." Lucia was animated, and as she spoke, her elegant fingers spread wide and reached towards the ceiling. "Don't wait, Jeffrey. This life is short and love is, how do you say, love is everything, no?" She sat back, and he noticed a slight flush to her cheeks.

"Yes, you're right. I'm just afraid to do it wrong." Jeffrey surprised himself with his candor.

"How can you do love wrong? You tell her you love her. What can be wrong about that?" Lucia searched his face, a small frown of non-comprehension wrinkling her brow.

"I suppose you're right. But what if she doesn't feel the same?" Jeffrey, hearing the words out loud, realized that this was what had been holding him back. "What if I declare my love and she laughs, or I embarrass her?" He felt prickly under his collar, so he ran a finger between his shirt and the skin of his neck.

"If you feel it, it is real. You will know if she feels it too. And if not, then you have lost nothing." Lucia placed her palms down decisively on the table. "There is nothing else you can do. You must tell her."

Jeffrey drained his wine and beckoned the waiter over to ask for another.

"Do you have to rush off?" He asked Lucia as she checked her lipstick in a small compact mirror.

"No. I have time." She snapped the compact closed and crossed one long leg over the other, as if settling into the chair for the long haul.

CHAPTER 33

———◆———

Jeffrey had dropped his shopping and passport off at the hotel and grabbed his camera, and now he and Lucia were walking towards the Trevi Fountain. She had told him over lunch that if he were to see only one thing in Rome, it should be the fountain, and as it was so close to the hotel, they could walk there in ten minutes.

He looked at the tall stone buildings on either side of them along Via Della Mercede. The white, pale pink, and caramel-colored facades seemed to lean in on them. Each was two or three stories tall, and many supported elegant balconies. At the ground level, scores of tiny cars were parked, nosed in towards the buildings at an angle like multi-colored fish scales.

They passed several cafés with large umbrellas outside, most of which were bound tightly against the breeze. They walked and talked easily, Lucia pointing out things of interest along the way. On Via Poli, the street spilled out into a small square, and seeing the sky open up above him, Jeffrey realized how much he'd felt enclosed by the height of the buildings. For the first time since landing here, he was actually enjoying himself, but he still missed the open air and clean spaces of home.

They passed several kiosks selling coffee and small stores with displays of religious icons and souvenirs. Lucia pointed out the National Central Library and a stunning building he couldn't remember the name of, with ominous iron grids over all the windows that marred the beautiful marble construction. They stopped for a few minutes at the Column of Marcus Aurelius so Jeffrey could snap some pictures. He knew Mary would want to see that. He was careful not to take any with Lucia in them. There shouldn't be any of those.

When they eventually walked into the Piazza Di Trevi, once again the sky opened up and Jeffrey gasped. The midafternoon light struck the huge fountain ahead of them, which seemed to dwarf the small and otherwise insignificant square.

"So. Bernini's fountain." Lucia swept a hand across their view. Jeffrey nodded mutely.

"You see the center figure, the man in the shell chariot? He is Neptune, or Poseidon. The two sea horses pull him, you see?" Lucia turned to Jeffrey, who stood mesmerized.

"One horse is, how you say, excited, and the other one is pacifica — um, calm?" Lucia shrugged, seeking confirmation that she'd found the correct words. Jeffrey nodded his understanding.

"Gives balance, no?" She smiled again.

"Yes, I see." Jeffrey swallowed. "This is really extraordinary."

"Come." Lucia took Jeffrey's hand and led him to the stone steps. "We have to throw a coin."

Jeffrey allowed her to guide him gently down the steps to the smooth rim at the edge of the fountain. Two stone maidens looked down on them, one holding what looked like fruit and the other a vessel of some kind that a snake was drinking out of. Jeffrey stared, feeling very small.

On the bottom of the fountain he could see the glint of a layer of coins of various sizes and colors, peaceful, lying in wait. He'd read that the coins were collected daily and donated to charity, which he thought a very good idea. From the guidebook, he also knew that the coins represented wishes. As he watched them all glinting in the watery light, he wondered what the people who'd thrown them in there had wished for.

As if reading his mind, Lucia went on.

"You know the legend? You throw a coin in and it means you will return to Rome." Lucia watched him as he nodded. He reached into his pocket, jingling some loose change.

"Some say that if you throw two coins, you will find new romance. Three will bring a marriage." She scanned his face.

Jeffrey felt himself blush. Based on this new information, he knew exactly how many he wanted to throw in, he just wasn't sure he wanted Lucia to see.

"Go on." She nudged his arm. "Three, I think. No?" She laughed.

Jeffrey smiled and, releasing his arm from her grasp, pulled out a handful of coins. Selecting three, and feeling suddenly spontaneous, he lifted them to his lips and kissed them.

"For luck." He chuckled and threw the coins in.

"Bravo," Lucia said warmly.

They walked back towards the hotel, Lucia's arm linked loosely in his. Jeffrey wasn't sure if it was the wine, the Roman attitude, or the fact that he had been able to verbalize his feelings about Mary, but he felt as if he were floating. In the space of a few hours, this woman, a total stranger to him, had been the catalyst for what felt like a momentous step forward. As he listened to her melodic voice giving information about each street and small square they passed through, as well as several impressive statues, Jeffrey's mind was racing. He needed to get home. He needed to go 'round to Mary's house and just tell her how he felt. What was he waiting for? Love was, as Lucia so aptly put it, everything.

As the two new friends approached the hotel, Jeffrey felt oddly reluctant to let Lucia leave. The sun was going down and the chill picking up, and as he watched her adjust her hat, he decided to ask her to have dinner with him. No sooner had the thought entered his head than he second-guessed himself. Surely she'd have plans? It was Christmas Eve, after all. But nothing ventured, nothing gained.

"Lucia. I don't suppose. I mean, it's Christmas Eve and, well, would you like to have dinner with me tonight?"

Lucia slipped her hands into her soft black leather gloves as she eyed him. The next few seconds that passed tore painfully at Jeffrey's diaphragm as he imagined her laughing kindly, telling him she was grateful for the invitation but had a room full of good friends waiting for her. Eventually, she put a gloved hand on each of his shoulders and looked him in the eye.

"Well, Jeffrey. I would love to."

He exhaled loudly, and then the pair laughed in unison.

"You see? It's not so difficult, is it?"

Jeffrey nodded, feeling elated.

"I know a wonderful place. You like fish?"

"I do, actually."

"*Perfetto.*"

At that, Lucia linked her arm through his, and the new friends turned their backs on the hotel and walked out into the cold evening.

CHAPTER 34

⎯⎯◆⎯⎯

The wheelchair bumped over the door jam, the central bolt of one wheel cutting a sizeable chunk from the paint of the frame. Mary huffed loudly and lowered her shoulders carefully, trying to turn the wheels without bending too low and hurting her ribs.

Matilda, her neighbor, had volunteered to help her come home. While she'd never been particularly close to Matilda and Fred, Mary had been touched when the little woman had shown up at the hospital the day after her accident, asking if she needed anything. She'd been in every day to see Mary, and had brought her magazines, homemade scones, and some fresh fruit. Mary wasn't quite sure how she'd ever be able to repay her kindness. Matilda had also offered to take over the task of feeding Ralf, before Mary had even remembered to ask.

Mary had initially asked Matilda to wait and let her try to get inside herself, to no avail. Eventually, between the two of them, they'd maneuvered the unaccustomed bulk of the chair up over the doorstep with the help of a wooden ramp the occupational therapist had lent them.

"Phew. That was harder than I imagined." Matilda laughed nervously. As Mary nodded, she noticed a frown cut across her neighbor's forehead. "I'm not sure how you'll cope, Mary, on your own. This is probably no' a good idea, you know?"

Mary pushed gently at the wheels, trying to move the chair towards the living room.

"Here, let me do that." Matilda stepped over and, taking the handles, pushed the chair into the room.

"I'll be fine. I just need you to make up a bed for me down here, and then the health visitor will be over in the morning to help me get up and dressed."

The doctor had been reluctant to discharge Mary so soon, but she had insisted that she could cope. With her medical training and her agreement that she'd accept the help of health visitors and nurses for the first few days, until she was more adept with the chair and could get around inside the cottage, he had finally given in. He said he'd drop in himself in a day or so to check on her. Mary had agreed and thanked him for understanding that she simply couldn't bear to spend Christmas in hospital.

As she turned the chair around, the small tree at the side of the fire caught her eye.

"Matilda. Would you turn on the tree lights?"

Matilda grinned and, leaning her babushka body behind the armchair, flipped the lights on.

"That's better. Thanks." Mary smiled.

"So, where's your thermostat? It's freezing in here." Matilda slipped her trademark macintosh off and turned on the lights as she walked through to the kitchen.

"It's in the pantry," Mary called after her. She could hear the tap running and guessed Matilda was putting the kettle on. Thank goodness. The first decent cup of tea she'd have had in four days.

Mary heard the boiler kicking on and shivered. Matilda had been round to her cottage once since the accident to pick up clean nightdresses and underwear for her, but she hadn't thought to ask her to turn the heating up. The weather had turned a lot colder over the past three days. Mary looked out of the window at the darkening sky over Willow Street. It was only four, but it already felt like night was close.

"You'll need to be getting away. Fred will be waiting for you, and so will Ralf." Mary called into the kitchen.

As she waited for her friend to respond, Mary was surprised by a tiny pinprick of jealousy that Matilda currently had possession of Jeffrey's house keys.

"Aye. I'll get you a wee something to eat first and make up your bed, then I'll be off. Fred is cooking tonight, lord help us, so there's no rush."

Matilda walked back into the room with two steaming mugs and a packet of ginger snaps under her arm.

"Found these. Hope you don't mind, but I'm a wee bit peckish." She laughed as Mary eased the biscuits out from her armpit and took a mug from her hand.

"Brilliant. I'm ravenous myself." Mary smiled. Matilda really was a good soul.

"So, I put a few things in the fridge the other day. I made some more scones and a tray of caramel shortbread, which are in the tin. I can whip you up something light now. It won't be very Christmassy, though." Matilda pulled her cherry mouth down into a theatrical grimace.

"Anything that's not hospital-generated will taste like Christmas to me." Mary laughed, then immediately grabbed at her ribs. "Oh, I must remember not to do that yet." She wiped a tear from her eye and sipped her tea.

"Not quite the Christmas Eve you'd imagined, I bet?" Matilda stood and headed up the stairs. "The sheets are in the hall cupboard, right?"

"Yep."

"I'll get the quilt from your bed, and your pillow." Matilda's solid little legs pounded up the stairs, her lilting voice floating back down into the living room.

"So have you let Jeffrey know about your accident?"

Surprised by the question, Mary snapped her head up towards the staircase, the movement causing a twinge of pain in her neck. She carefully forced her shoulders back and down and then circled her head slowly.

"No." she called back. "I haven't spoken to him since he left."

As she rolled her head up from her chest, she felt a pop between her shoulders, which seemed to release whatever had been causing her pain. Pushing the wheelchair was tiring, and she was unaccustomed to using her arms this way. The pain in her ribs, while improving, made it even more difficult, so she had to use small, metered movements and take her time with everything.

She breathed out carefully and turned the chair slowly to face the fireplace. Her TV stood dark at the left-hand side, and her favorite armchair sat empty across the room to the right. As she looked around, she was strangely disappointed to see that everything was exactly as she'd left it when she'd gone to Perth. The newspaper was folded on the footstool. Her half-finished crocheted blanket lay neatly furled in the basket next to the chair. The curtains were slightly open, the bottoms tucked behind the radiator under the window. Her boots stood in the hallway under the coatrack, and a small pile of mail, which Matilda had obviously picked up for her from the doormat, sat on the hall table.

Mary pushed herself gingerly over to the table. Reaching for the mail caused her to gasp, so she sat back extra carefully. The stack of envelopes resting in her lap, she flipped through them. A bill, another bill, a circular, a letter from her insurance company, a flyer from a new pizza restaurant in town, and a white envelope that looked like a card. She slid her finger under the flap and opened it. It was a get-well card from the manager of the home, which everyone there had signed. What a kind thought.

As Mary tossed the pile onto the coffee table, a wave of disappointment overwhelmed her. For the first time since being trapped in the car, she felt the prickle of tears. She wasn't one for self-pity, or for crying much, a lifetime's worth of tears having been shaken out of her during her years with her ex-husband, Jimmy. This was one of those moments, however, when she felt justified in being sorry for herself. It was Christmas Eve and here she was with a pin in her broken leg, cracked ribs, stitches in her head, and not even so much as a postcard from Jeffrey. Could he really have not thought about her for one instant, since he'd left? While she'd have said it wasn't possible, all evidence seemed to point to the contrary.

She remembered her old friend Agnes's words "he is'nae a fast worker." To Mary, at this moment, there was never a truer word spoken. A heavy thought settled on her. What if she had read all the signs wrong and Jeffrey was not interested in her? What if he was happy with their friendship just the way it was? Could she live with that?

Having made her an omelet, some toast, and a cup of cocoa, Matilda helped Mary to the bathroom to clean her teeth and got her into her nightie and settled on the couch. The heat had seeped into the room, and Mary was finally feeling both warm and sleepy.

"You've got the TV remote control, and there's a glass of water and your pills on the table. Keep your phone next to you so you can call me if you have any problems, all right?" Matilda was putting her coat on as she spoke.

"I'll do that. Thanks a million, really." Mary shifted painfully on the sofa and accepted the gentle, vanilla-scented hug that Matilda offered.

"Merry Christmas, Mary." Matilda smiled down at her. "I'll be round tomorrow with a Christmas dinner for you, probably around five o' clock."

"You don't have to bother, honestly. I'll be fine, now I'm home."

"Nonsense. You're not having toast on Christmas Day, not while I'm alive." Matilda winked playfully, patted Mary's good foot through the duvet, and left.

Mary switched on the TV. She had half an hour until she could take more painkillers, so she hoped there was something good on to distract her from the burn of pain that was creeping back into her leg. As she flicked through the channels, she caught snippets of the usual Christmas Eve programming: *It's a Wonder-*

ful Life, too depressing; *The Sound of Music*, a possibility; some yapping comedian from America with an inordinately big chin and silver hair, a definite no; and then finally — *Oliver*, yes, that was the one.

Pulling the duvet up under her chin, she felt her back relax into the cushions. The young boy on the screen was singing with his heartbreakingly beautiful voice, staring out of an undertaker's cellar window as snow fell on Dickensian London. It brought a lump to her throat.

"Whe-e-e-e-ere is love?" he sang. How apt, she thought.

CHAPTER 35

The hotel staff had decorated a beautiful tree, which stood in the lobby. Garlands of natural green, twisted with red ribbons, looped around the outer walls, and candles, like floating pebbles in a stream, twinkled in bowls of water on the tables and the reception desk. The scent of pine and cinnamon floated in the air, and in the corner opposite the front entrance, a harpist played dreamily.

Jeffrey sat in one of the chairs in the center of the space and nursed an oversized brandy glass holding an inch of amber-colored cognac. Now this felt really Christmassy, a truly fitting way to spend December the 25th.

He'd spent the morning at the Christmas market in Piazza Navona, looking for a gift for Mary. He'd bought her some local sweets, a beautifully boxed panettone, and a long silk scarf decorated with hand-painted wisteria blossoms. He thought the color, a soft lilac, would flatter her complexion and bring out the green of her eyes.

He'd stopped to buy roasted chestnuts from a street vendor and had then eaten a panini at a bakery that had smelled like heaven as he'd passed by on the street. The aroma of fresh-baked bread had been enough to seduce him, his feet taking him inside even before he'd decided whether he needed to eat again. If he lived in Rome he'd soon be the size of a house. He had little doubt about that.

Lucia had said she'd pick him up at the hotel at four pm and take him to see Saint Peter's Basilica. The Papal Mass would be over and everything cleared away, so they could take a walk around St. Peter's Square. Jeffrey had always been curious about the Vatican since Agnes had told him stories of Italy. He would take plenty of photos to share with Mary. Suddenly, he wondered if she was Catholic. Religion wasn't something they'd ever discussed, and now, within half an hour or so of seeing the Vatican, he was embarrassed that he hadn't thought to ask her about her beliefs. He really needed to pay more attention, be more interested, when he got home.

As Jeffrey sat watching the activity around him, his eyes wandered back to the sparkling tree. Despite Lucia telling him that trees were not traditionally part of the Romans' Christmas celebration, he wondered if they had one in the Vatican. Surely they must?

After St. Peter's Square, the plan was to go on to the Coliseum, where she'd assured him that they did indeed now put up a large tree. Having decided to skip the dinner dance at the hotel, as Jeffrey had no evening suit to wear, they planned on returning to the hotel for an early dinner before going to a concert at the Academy of Saint Cecilia. Vivaldi was another must-do, in

Lucia's book, and Jeffrey, who was fond of classical music, was happy to go along with her suggestion.

He couldn't remember when, if ever, he'd crammed so much into a single Christmas Day. It was definitely different from his usual celebrations, and while he was sure he'd enjoy the activities, and Lucia's company, immensely, he was increasingly thinking about home.

His cottage would be dark and cold this year. No tree, no fairy lights, no walnuts in the bowl by the TV, no bagpipes whining Christmas carols from his CD player. There'd be no customary dram with Matilda and Fred and, now that he'd left her behind, no Mary either. As he drained the last of his brandy, drinking before six being another new activity for him, Jeffrey felt a pang of homesickness. He savored the burn of the liquid sliding down his throat, and he swallowed over a newly forming lump.

Mr. Giacomo tapped him on the shoulder, and not having seen the hotel manager approach, Jeffrey jumped.

"Merry Christmas, Mr. Mere. How are you?" The younger man smiled broadly as Jeffrey shook his hand. Jeffrey imagined that Giacomo must be relieved that he was fully dressed today and not sitting here enjoying a brandy in his bathrobe.

"Merry Christmas to you, too, Mr. Giacomo."

"So you decided to stay a few days, maybe see a little of Rome?"

"I did. I've had a couple of lovely days." Jeffrey nodded and placed his empty glass on the table.

"Wonderful. I'm glad to hear it. Are you having dinner with us this evening?" Giacomo leaned over and adjusted the bowl with the floating candle, which sat next to Jeffrey's glass.

"I'm actually waiting for a friend. We're going out." Jeffrey blushed.

"Oh." The manager looked alarmed. "Not your, um, dog?" The young man's eyes were wide as they flicked to either side of Jeffrey's chair.

Jeffrey let out a laugh.

"No, not my dog. A new friend that I made here, actually."

"Ah, wonderful." Mr. Giacomo broke into a wide smile. "Well, have a good evening."

Jeffrey watched the gentle rhythm of people passing in and out of the lobby. A blast of cold accompanied each group as they swung through the main entrance. He saw several couples deposit their coats and be shown through the tall glass doors leading to the restaurant.

After a while, a family with three small children came in. The little ones, a girl and two boys, looked to be dressed in their Sunday best. The little girl, wearing frilled socks and a red velvet coat and hat, made Jeffrey smile. They all seemed so well-behaved, waiting patiently while their parents talked and then following them quietly into the restaurant. Jeffrey watched them go, and as the doors closed behind them, he wondered what it would have been like to be a parent.

He knew that while Agnes had struggled after his dad had died, she had done a good job of being his mother. As he contemplated a situation he'd never now find himself in, Jeffrey liked to believe that he'd have been a decent father.

A new blast of cold turned his attention back to the entrance. Lucia walked towards him, resplendent in a gold-colored coat with a thick fur collar and long brown boots that came up to her knees.

"Buongiorno." The jasmine scent surrounded him again, and Jeffrey accepted twin pecks on his cheeks, blushing only slightly this time. He was getting used to all this Italian *gioia di vita.*

"Ready to go?" She rubbed her hands together. "It's cold outside. You have gloves, no?"

"No. They were in my suitcase." Jeffrey shrugged. "I'll just put my hands in my pockets."

"Are you sure?" She pulled her own gloves out of her handbag.

"Sure. I'm used to the cold, you know." He grinned.

"OK. Andiamo."

St. Peter's Square was magnificent. Lucia parked her pocket-sized car and they walked into the square, which was not, in fact, square at all. To Jeffrey's surprise, it was shaped more like a huge key. They walked around the perimeter, staying close to the rows of massive Tuscan columns that lined it, then gradually made their way into the center.

Jeffrey stood under the ancient Egyptian obelisk, which he'd seen in his guidebook, and Lucia took his picture. To his surprise, as another couple approached, Lucia asked them to please take a photo of the two of them. Jeffrey, feeling oddly emboldened, agreed. He stood next to her, smiling, and pulled his shoulders down and back, just like his mum had told him to do in photos. There was nothing worse than slumping in a photo, the image of appearing slovenly being captured for all eternity.

Having thanked the couple, and handing Jeffrey back his camera, Lucia then pointed out the twin fountains. As they approached the second one, she stopped.

"Again, our friend Bernini. The other is Maderno." She

gestured toward the stone structure and smiled, expecting him to recognize both names. He frowned slightly, inclining his head to the side, much like an inquisitive puppy.

As they leaned over the delicate wrought-iron railing that protected the ancient stonework, Lucia slipped her hand through his arm. It felt good to have her light touch on his coat sleeve.

"No coins in this one, though."

Jeffrey nodded and stood up straight. Ahead of them, the floodlit basilica glowed gold and white, the columns and dome iridescent in the evening light.

"Travertine." Lucia looked at him as she swept a booted foot across the ground.

"Pardon?" Jeffrey was puzzled.

"The stone, on the ground. Is travertine."

"Right." Jeffrey nodded and, frowning, focused his attention on the tiles.

"What is wrong?"

Unaware that she'd been watching him that closely, Jeffrey looked startled.

"Nothing. Sorry. This is wonderful. Just wonderful." He nodded enthusiastically.

"You think of Mary?" Lucia's voice was warm.

As he looked into her dark eyes, he saw the depth of her understanding. This lady could read his mind. He knew that it wasn't polite to be so obviously distracted when Lucia had taken the time to bring him here, especially on Christmas Day, but he just couldn't help but think about Mary.

"I was just thinking that I should have asked her."

Lucia held on to his arm, her gloved hand light on his jacket.

"Asked her what?"

"To come to Rome with me." Jeffrey felt his voice falter and coughed to disguise the nugget of emotion that threatened to reveal itself.

"Well, you are going home soon, no? You can make amends then." Lucia squeezed his arm companionably and, running a hand through her hair, pulled her shoulders back purposefully.

"So, enough of the Vatican, I think. We go to the Coliseum now, OK?"

After snapping a few more photos, Jeffrey and Lucia made their way back to her little car. The ride to the Coliseum was one Jeffrey would never forget. The traffic in this city was intimidating, to say the least, but Lucia, having lived here most of her life, seemed immune to the colossal press of vehicles around them, all trying to navigate the too-narrow streets. She forced her way between large vans and mopeds, tour buses and cyclists, with aplomb. Despite trying to trust in her obvious skill behind the wheel, Jeffrey's neck and shoulders were tense, and he had rammed his foot onto a nonexistent brake pedal multiple times before she pulled up and parked in a tiny space behind the Coliseum. His stomach was quivering as he stepped out onto the blessedly stationary pavement.

It was impossible not to be impressed by the Coliseum. The elliptical amphitheater had stood here since 80 AD, and as Jeffrey tried to process that information, he felt incredibly humbled. Great gaping windows, like eyes in the stone façade, shone amber, the clever lighting creating a ghostly sense of heat emanating from within the arena.

"We go inside, if you want?" Lucia twisted the car key in the lock and tossed the tinkling bunch into her handbag.

CHAPTER 36

As he approached his hotel room, he saw the dog lying across the door. Jeffrey caught his breath and rushed along the corridor.

"Where have you been, lass?"

He knelt down and rubbed the matted head; the familiar dark eyes blinked at him. As he leaned over, his full stomach pressed on the waistband of his new trousers. He knew he shouldn't have had pudding. Lucia had insisted, so he'd gone against his better judgment to please her. The wonderful music from the concert was still resonating in his ears, and he felt content, if a little bloated with all this pleasure.

"Come inside before anyone sees you." He jumped up and slid the key through the electronic lock. Scanning the hallway in both directions, he pushed the heavy door open and stepped into the room.

The dog padded in after him, circled the bed, and then

settled itself on the Persian rug by the French windows. Its wooly eyebrows twitched as Jeffrey walked between the bedroom and bathroom, readying himself for bed. Nervous that the dog would disappear again, he came out of the bathroom, his toothbrush and a mouthful of foam between his lips. Seeing the big mutt sleeping peacefully on the rug, he went back in to finish the task.

His face was pink. It must've been the wine at dinner. He and Lucia had finished a bottle between them, then had brandy with their coffee. The conversation had been light and the subjects diverse, and he couldn't remember a more pleasant evening — other than with Mary, of course. As he'd watched Lucia's expressive hands, the way her eyes sparkled when she talked about her daughter, and the shadow that passed over them when she mentioned her husband, Jeffrey had felt their friendship shift to a deeper level. At another time in his life, he could have fallen hard for Lucia, but now she simply served to remind him of where his heart truly lay.

They'd agreed to meet the following day for a last lunch. Thinking about the prospect of more food made Jeffrey groan. He settled himself under the heavy covers and pulled the sheet up to his chin. His feet were cold, so he rubbed them together vigorously, waiting for the blood to recirculate. He could smell coffee again, as well as the now-familiar scent of the dog, which was difficult to altogether identify. It reminded him of home and of Ben Macdhui.

Reaching over to switch off the light, he heard a snore, low, soft, and reminiscent of his mother when she'd doze off in front of the TV. Smiling, Jeffrey relaxed his shoulders into the soft pillow and let sleep take him.

Mary was sitting at his kitchen table. She leaned over and poured tea into his mug as he chopped carrots at the sink. Her face was different, somehow. He couldn't put his finger on what had changed, but there was a touch of sadness around her mouth. Her eyes had lost their sparkle, and even her gorgeous red hair was not as lustrous. She was muted, her presence less than crystal clear. Jeffrey tried to focus on her face, but the more he stared, the fuzzier her image became. What was happening? He looked down at her hands and saw her fingers disappearing from around the handle of the cup. He felt panicked, but for some reason, he couldn't get his mouth to work, to say her name. As he watched, her forearms faded away, then her elbows, until her arms were gone all the way up to the biceps. He could see a light circling around her body, like a luminous eraser, smudging the lines of her form. She looked into his eyes and blinked as her left shoulder disappeared. Jeffrey needed to get to her, to grab hold of her before she was gone completely. He tried to move towards her, but his feet wouldn't move. He looked down to see thick tree roots wound around each ankle. Where had they come from? He opened his mouth to speak, but his lips were sealed closed. Mary's two shoulders were gone now, and her sternum was curling up towards her throat like a roller blind. As he watched, helpless, her eyes opened wide and he heard her voice.

"Where are you?"

He tried to tell her he was right here, but no sound would come out. He reached his hand out to her, but she had no hands to reach back. He was losing her. Mary's neck faded away until she was just a floating head hovering above the table. He needed to tell her to stay, to hang on, to try to wait. His tongue felt like a loofah, heavy and prickly in his useless mouth. He felt tears swim into his eyes as Mary's chin and mouth disintegrated. She stared at him and blinked twice, slowly and determinedly, and then her eyes were gone, too.

His mind screamed her name, and he swallowed against the loofah, which sucked all the sound out of him. Her forehead and fringe faded away, and as he watched, she was gone. Nothing was left except the tendril of steam rising from her still-full teacup.

Jeffrey closed his eyes. He couldn't bear the pain of seeing her gone. His heart was pounding, and he felt sweat trickle down his neck. As he tried to fill his lungs against a lead weight that lay on his chest, he heard a voice.

"Wake up, Jeffrey."

He lifted his leadened eyelids, blinking several times to orientate himself. Where was he? As his eyes adjusted to the dim light in the room, above him he saw the frame around the bed, the draping, and the canopy. The dog's head was heavy on his chest, its side rising and falling consistently with each breath in and out. Trapped under its weight, he turned his head and looked at the light coming in the French doors. He was trying to guess what time it was, when the image of Mary's disintegrating body refreshed itself in his mind. The flood of relief was overwhelming. He was in his hotel room in Rome. The dog was here, and there was no disappearing Mary. There was no ghostly version of her anywhere to be seen.

Jeffrey wriggled underneath the dog's massive head, trying to release himself. His heart felt like it would explode, and he needed a drink of water. The dog shifted lazily, its long legs stretching out against his hip as he slid off the bed.

In the bathroom, he turned on the light and leaned on the sink. His reflection was the same as earlier that night, his eyes deep-set and his cheeks ruddy. His hair stood out at an odd angle on one side, and his eyes were puffy. As he scanned his own face, Jeffrey breathed deeply, trying to slow down his racing heart. He was still drunk, or hung over, or both.

His dream had really shaken him, primarily the feeling of being powerless to stop what was happening to Mary. He didn't ever want to feel that way again. That'd teach him to mix the grape and the grain late at night.

He splashed cold water on his face and shook the droplets away before reaching for a towel. As he pressed the softness into his eyes, he sensed a presence behind him. Lowering the towel, he saw the dog sitting in the doorway. It licked its lips and then shook its head, sending a cloud of dust up into the atmosphere.

"Hi, lass. That was some dream."

The dog snorted and bobbed its head.

"It felt so real."

The dog stared at him, motionless.

"It feels like I should do something. I don't know what, though." Jeffrey looked at the dog in the mirror.

As he waited for a response, the big head drooped low between the broad shoulders, and the animal slowly slumped down onto the floor, its legs stretched out in front of itself.

"What do I do?" Jeffrey turned and sat down on the bath mat. He felt the coldness of the floor seeping through the mat and his pajamas, but the chill was soothing somehow.

The dog was nosing its leg, then began to lick its shin, working and working the big pink tongue over the same spot until it was wet and looked sore. The creature's eyes never left his, and as Jeffrey watched the oddly calming and repetitive motion, his heart rate gradually slowed back to normal. He could no longer hear it clattering in his ears, and the film of sweat that had covered his face had dried.

He pulled himself up off the floor and, stepping over the dog, made his way back to bed. Slipping under the covers, Jeffrey curled up on his side. There was something in that dream. It had felt like more than a dream. Perhaps Mary was in trouble and he needed to help her? Perhaps she was in some kind of danger?

Agnes had believed in the power of dreams and had often told him that she received messages from his dad while she slept. Was this one of those messages? Could Mary be trying to reach him?

As he stared at the clock on the bedside table, Jeffrey mentally calculated the time in Pitlochry. He'd not spoken to Mary since he'd left Scotland. He'd called her that morning, before heading out to the market, to wish her a happy Christmas. There had been no answer so he'd left a short and somewhat inadequate message on her machine.

As he figured out that it was now 3:00 am at home, and far too late to call again, a bubble of shame filled his throat. He hadn't even sent her a postcard. How could he have been so inconsiderate? It wouldn't have surprised him if she'd been home earlier, but had just chosen not to talk to him. If that was the case he deserved it for being such a worthless, selfish lump.

Turning over, Jeffrey resolved to call her again in the morning and make sure she was OK. That was what he'd do.

CHAPTER 37

E arlier that day, Mary had been in the bathroom when she'd heard the phone ringing. Looking around, she had realized, to her annoyance, that she'd left the receiver in the lounge. There was no way she could have moved quickly enough to answer it, so she'd taken a deep breath and, against her instincts, resolved not to try. Whoever it was could wait.

After a few moments, she'd heard the answering machine beep. A man's voice warbled a few sentences; then came the high-pitched tone indicating that the machine had stopped recording.

Two hours later, she was back in the bathroom when the phone rang again. Hearing the shrill sound cutting through the silence of her house made her jump and she realized that she had forgotten to listen to the message that had been left earlier. She shook her head in frustration. What was wrong with her memory? She was foggy and discombobulated due to the pills she was taking for pain.

The health visitor was due in fifteen minutes to check on her and change her dressings. Mary was pleased with herself for having managed to make some breakfast and have a wash in anticipation of her arrival.

Having hauled herself out of the wheelchair, she steadied herself against the sink and smoothed some moisturizer onto her cheeks. She glanced at her reflection in the mirror. Her eyes were sunken and her face flushed from the effort of simply washing herself with a flannel. Her skin was tingling from her brisk scrubbing, and while she felt cleaner on the whole, her hair badly needed to be washed. Perhaps the homecare visitor could help her do that when she came that evening?

As the cool cream sank quickly into her dry face, Mary closed her eyes and inhaled its almond scent. Holding on to the sink, she was careful not to put any weight on the injured leg. The large boot that surrounded her shin was pressing on the wound, and it had driven her mad during the night. She wanted badly to take it off, relieve the painful pressure, and access the accompanying itch.

She had had a difficult night, getting less than three hours of sleep. Her bottom had sunk, annoyingly, into the gap between the cushions on the couch. It wasn't ideal as a bed, but she had little choice for the moment. She'd been vigilant about the timing between doses of painkillers, so had slept fitfully for most of the night in the no-man's-land between dreams and wakefulness.

Mary reached up and gingerly lifted her fringe away from her forehead to inspect the damage. Peeling back the plaster, she could see several spidery black stitches, stark against her pale skin, the cut lurking angry and red beneath them. Esmé had reminded her, as she was leaving the hospital, that she must not get her wounds wet. So, as she stared at her lank hair, Mary reasoned, with disappointment, that she might have to wait a while longer before washing it. She replaced the plaster and let her fringe drop. Frustrated, she dragged a hairbrush through the lackluster red strands, then thumped the brush down on the counter.

She prided herself on empathizing with the elderly people she cared for at the home. She had always tried to be respectful of their dignity, taking time to ask about their lives, their families, frequently seeking their opinions on things happening in the news or in the town. She knew how important it was to make them feel visible, valued as human beings. Despite her understanding of their various levels of dependency on others, as she stared at her own face in the mirror, it was leveling to feel the frustration, firsthand, of not being able to fully take care of oneself.

After shrugging on a clean sweater and a loose skirt that Matilda had left hanging on the back of the bathroom door for her, Mary slid back into the chair and slowly wheeled herself out into the kitchen. Thank goodness for these old homes, having the bathroom on the ground floor. She didn't know what she'd have done if she'd had to go up the stairs. The truth was that the doctor would not have let her come home if that had been the case.

With some difficulty, she filled the kettle, put two tea bags in the pot, and dragged the biscuit tin towards her. As promised, Matilda had left it full, so she placed four slices of caramel shortbread on a tea plate, then readied two cups for when the nurse arrived. It was such an imposition to ask someone to leave his or her family on Christmas Day. The least she could do was offer whomever turned up a decent cup of tea and a biscuit.

The kettle chortled softly as the heating elements began to disturb the water. Rather than watch the pot boil, she pushed down on the wheels and went into the lounge to check the answering machine.

"Hello. Mary. This is Jeffrey Mere. I just wanted to say hello, see if you were doing all right. Sorry I missed you. Well, I hope you have a merry Christmas. I'll see you soon. Bye for now."

Mary stared out of the window. The little Christmas tree lights glinted in her peripheral vision, and she swallowed at the sound of Jeffrey's voice. A tiny smile pulled at her lips, and her heart pattered a little more quickly in her chest. He hadn't told her anything about what he was doing, about Rome, or his holiday, but at least he'd called. He was thinking about her.

She knew Jeffrey was due back in two days, so the fact that he'd called her at this late stage was slightly odd. However, she wouldn't sniff at it. He had called, and that was the most important thing.

She heard the kettle bubble loudly, then click itself off, just as the doorbell rang. Rousing herself, Mary pushed down on the wheels again and moved the chair into the hall. Tired and sore, she took longer to maneuver to the door than she'd hoped. She could see the reflection of the nurse through the glass panels in the door as she leaned down and peered through the letterbox.

"I'm coming. Sorry. Just coming," she called breathlessly as the chair moved slowly and heavily towards her destination.

By three o' clock, she had clean dressings on her arm, head, and leg. She'd eaten the sandwiches that Matilda had left in the fridge, made herself two cups of tea, enjoyed a slice of caramel shortbread, and taken all her allotted painkillers. She'd listened to

Jeffrey's message a further three times, then slept for two hours in her armchair while the hosts of a daytime TV program bantered and laughed over the day's headlines.

It was an odd way to spend Christmas Day but, all in all, it was still better than being in Pitlochry Community Hospital, faced with a sad turkey salad and the forced jollity of the short-straw nurses having to work over the Christmas period.

As she stared out at the heavy gray sky, Mary wondered if Esmé was working today. She'd appreciated the woman's warmth and straightforward manner. Esmé was someone she'd like to see again once she was better.

As her focus began to blur slightly with fatigue, a fat pigeon fluttered across her view and landed on the telegraph pole at the end of the driveway. Mary had always liked pigeons, despite their reputation as feathered pests. Some of the locals even called them flying rodents. As she watched the silvery bird stretch its wings, then puff out its metallic-blue chest, she remembered her father taking her to Trafalgar Square on her twelfth birthday. She'd been horrified at the prospect of those dirty-looking birds landing on her, pecking her hair and her clothes. Her father had laughed and said she just needed to hold her arms out still, like a tree, with a fistful of breadcrumbs in each hand. She had frowned at him, scared, but had done what he said and, after a few moments, had been giggling at the ticklish pecks in her palms as the birds grazed.

Her dad had taken a picture of her with several birds sitting along her outstretched arms and one perched on her head. She had been beaming, her cardigan flapping in the breeze, one sock slumped down to her ankle and the other up under her knee. That had been a great birthday. Where was that photo?

When Mary had fled Glasgow, escape from her ex-husband the priority, most of the remnants and reminders of her past had been left in the drawers, cupboards, and attic of the tenement flat. Her opportunity had come unexpectedly one day, when Jimmy was called for jury duty.

As she'd silently fried his eggs and bacon that morning, her mind had gone through each room of the flat, selecting the most important items that she'd take with her. By 10:00 am, Jimmy had left, without a word to her. By 11:45 am, the small dusty suitcase that lived in the cupboard under the stairs was full and standing in the hall. As she pulled the door closed behind her and posted the keys back through the letterbox, she was determined to leave all the pain and fear of the past few years on the other side of the door. Part of her was sad to leave so many memories behind, but another part of her wanted a clean slate, even from the majority of her childhood.

She recalled the lightness she'd felt as she'd walked through the rain to the bus stop with a few pounds in her pocket and no destination in mind. Unencumbered, she'd climbed on the number 47 bus on Dalgleish Street and had ridden it to the end of the line before her eyes had cleared and she'd finally known where she would go.

Outside the window, the big bird preened itself, its scrawny legs attaching it firmly to the wires that draped from the pole. Mary wondered at the strength of those pin-like legs, supporting the apparent bulk of the bird. Looking down at her own legs, she smiled. Now, with one disproportionately large one lying next to the other normal-sized limb, she must be an odd sight herself. Her dad would have teased her, saying she was off-kilter, and would have told her to be careful not to walk in circles.

She missed her dad. Nothing had been the same after he'd died. She'd been fourteen. And then, just a year or so later, her mum had taken up with that foul-mouthed butcher, William. Mary had learned to keep out of sight when William was in the house. Even her footsteps seemed to annoy him, giving him an excuse to deliver stinging slaps to her cheek. She remembered the smells of raw meat and sour blood on his big, bullying hands. The memory still made her shudder. By the time she was fifteen, it wasn't the slaps she was afraid of. William had a way of leering at her that made her skin crawl. A small voice inside Mary's head whispered that she needed to get away, and soon. Her mother retreated into a whisky-scented fog wherever William was concerned and was no longer the advocate or protector Mary needed. As Mary planned her escape, along came Jimmy. Little did she know that her rescuer, her heroic knight and soon-to-be husband, would also become her new tormentor.

Letting the shadows of bad memories leave her, Mary laid her head back in the chair and closed her eyes. It was all in the past now. She had a good life now, good people around her, and, best of all, some peace of mind.

At five o' clock on the dot, Matilda was at the door.

"Helloo. How are you, Mary? Merry Christmas, pet." The cheery voice preceded her rotund neighbor down the hall.

Matilda bent and hugged her, a dinner plate wrapped in tinfoil balanced precariously in one hand and a bowl wrapped in cling film in the other.

"Merry Christmas, Matilda." Mary smiled at the ruddy face and broad grin hovering above her.

"So, anything exciting happen since I left you?" Matilda padded into the kitchen and reached for the kettle.

"Oh, yes. I had a salsa dancing lesson, hung some new curtains in the lounge, and knitted a pullover." Mary chuckled, carefully pushing the fringe away from her forehead. Just the weight of her hair was irritating the wound on her brow.

"Well, I canny leave you for five minutes, but you're getting into mischief." Matilda giggled.

Having eaten the Christmas dinner, which Matilda warmed in the oven for her, Mary sat in her armchair, feeling full. Matilda had folded the duvet and sheet away and now sat on the sofa. A tiny glass of sherry shelved on her plump tummy, she leaned her head back on the cushion behind her.

"Christmas dinner is great, isn't it?" She eyed Mary. "It's not really anything special as ingredients go, but there's something awf'y special about them all together on the plate. Don't you think?"

Mary nodded and smiled at her friend.

"It was terrific, Matilda. You're some cook."

Matilda batted the air, dismissing the compliment, but Mary saw the flush of pleasure in the round face. It cost nothing to be nice to people, to make them feel valued. She wondered why it was so hard for some to do. As she watched the little woman, basking in the acknowledgement of her cooking prowess, Mary wanted to show her gratitude, to confide in her, make her feel special.

Before she could edit the thought, Mary blurted, "So, Jeffrey called."

Matilda started slightly, pushed herself upright against the back of the couch, and focused on Mary.

"Did he, now?" A little smile betrayed her pleasure and the

hint of mischief lurking behind it.

"Yes. Nothing special, just to say hello." Regretting her decision to share the information, Mary backtracked.

"Oh, sure. Nothing special, *my eye*." Matilda leaned forward and placed her glass on the coffee table. "I'm sure he called plenty of folk in town just to say hello." Matilda was now quivering as her smile turned into gentle laughter.

Mary frowned and shook her head.

"No. It's nothing, really."

Matilda was not going to be put off. She stood up and crossed the room until she stood in front of Mary's chair. Her apron was still tied tightly around her hourglass frame, and her stocky legs were anchored in the permanent fixture of her tartan slippers.

"Mary Ferguson. You tell me everything. I mean it." She leaned down, a hand on each arm of Mary's chair. "Spill."

Despite herself, Mary felt the tension in her face relax. She let out a laugh and gently pushed Matilda's shoulders away.

"For heaven's sake, sit down, woman."

"I'm going nowhere. Now wait, I'll make us another cuppa, and you can tell me all about it."

Mary giggled as the little woman trotted away into the kitchen, leaving a trail of cinnamon and apple scent in her wake.

"Don't you have to get back to Fred?" Mary called.

"Are you joking? This is much more interesting. He'll be snoring by now, anyway."

Mary listened to the hasty clattering of cups, the thunk of the fridge door, and the gurgle of the boiling kettle. There was no escaping it now. She'd have to tell Matilda what was going on with Jeffrey, whatever that was. Besides, it might be good to share her hopes with someone else. Perhaps sharing them would make this thing more real, more than just wistful words she whispered into her pillow at night.

CHAPTER 38

Jeffrey smoothed a hand over his hair, replaced his cap, and pulled the collar of his tweed coat up closer to his jaw. There was a bitter wind whistling across the square, and Lucia was late. The day had started well with a good breakfast in the hotel, and then he'd taken another walk around the market in Piazza Navona. He'd stopped for an espresso opposite the Spanish Steps and read a copy of the *Guardian*, which someone had left on the table next to him.

Now, as he stood outside the café, the sun was present, but weak in the sky, and scanning the street for the slim form of his new friend, he shivered.

As several people passed him, many carrying heavy bags and elaborately wrapped gifts, his mind went back to Mary and the message he'd left her the day before. The fact that she had not answered the phone lay heavy on his mind. If she was out, and not just ignoring his call, where would she be, on Christmas

Day? She had no family in town and, as far as he knew, had had no plans to go out. In fact, she'd told him that she intended to pop over to his house and feed Ralf, then go home, cook herself a nice meal, and watch a *Pride and Prejudice* marathon with her feet at the fire.

As he watched a group of youngsters bumping each other's shoulders and laughing as they climbed the famous steps, Jeffrey felt a wave of guilt. What right did he have to question Mary's actions? She could go wherever she wanted, with whomever she chose, and he could have nothing to say about it. Despite his logical reasoning, the thought of her out and about, perhaps laughing and having Christmas dinner with someone else, caused Jeffrey to experience an odd sensation in his chest. It might be ridiculous, but he was jealous. Having no official claim on her was one thing, but the thought of her with someone else was more than he could bear.

He wished he had not agreed to see Lucia for lunch. He should have said his goodbyes the night before, after the concert, and had done with it. As his irritation with himself prickled under his skin, he saw the now-familiar outline of Lucia coming towards him. Dressed from head to toe in cream, she was a picture. Jeffrey's irritation evaporated as she swooped up to him and planted the jasmine kisses he'd been hoping for on each cheek.

"Sorry. I could not find a parking." She glowed, and although she wore a frown as she spoke, her face was still angelic.

"*Nessun problema, il mio amico.*" Jeffrey stood and embraced the cream-colored shoulders, feeling her shapely frame through the soft cashmere coat.

"Wow. *Parli italiano ora?*" Lucia laughed warmly as she patted his shoulders. "Good for you, Jeffrey."

Jeffrey blushed. He'd been studying the phrase book in the bath that morning, and for some reason had come across the translation for "no problem." As if by design, Lucia had provided him with the perfect opportunity to show off his newly acquired language skills, so he'd taken it unabashedly.

"Pasta, I think, OK?" Lucia looped her arm through his and steered him away from the café. "A farewell farfalle con funghi and perhaps a little Chianti?" Her face shone, and Jeffrey was once again enchanted by the sheer joy she exuded at the prospect of more food.

"*Perfetto*." He attempted the sing-song pronunciation he'd heard Lucia use, as they headed off down a narrow cobbled lane.

The restaurant Lucia had chosen was tucked into the corner of a small, lively square. The door, dark wood, had large metal studs and a heavy brass knocker. As they pushed their way inside, Jeffrey's nose was assaulted by the rich smell of garlic. Lucia pointed upwards, and tipping his head back, Jeffrey gasped at the marvelous expanse of stained glass that formed the ceiling over their heads.

Their small table sat in a corner. Heavily carved screens encapsulated them, and Jeffrey and Lucia looked out at the lively square.

Having toured the Palazzo Barberini that morning, Jeffrey's mind was reeling, still processing the sight of the works of Caravaggio, El Greco, and Holbein. It was fantastic to imagine these great artists creating masterpieces, just to leave them behind for the likes of him to enjoy.

As he swallowed a mouthful of creamy pasta, Jeffrey wiped his mouth with the crisp white napkin.

"Do you ever think about it, Lucia? About what you'll leave behind?" He looked at her as she drained her glass.

"Leave where?" Her brow crinkled.

"I mean, when you go. You know, die?" Jeffrey was suddenly embarrassed both by her expression and by the seemingly maudlin question, so he turned his attention to his plate.

"No." Lucia's voice was clear and strong. "I don't." She shook her head. "I live the life, and when I no longer live, what does it matter?" She sounded irritated.

"Of course. I just meant whether you ever thought about what your legacy to the world might be. Tintoretto left his masterpieces, Bell left the telephone, Pythagoras his theorem." Jeffrey swallowed awkwardly. Why had he started this?

Lucia's face smoothed itself and she nodded, understanding him better.

"I see. Well, I leave my daughter. She is my masterpiece, no?" Lucia's smile was back.

"Well, of course." Jeffrey smiled again, relieved. "I sometimes wonder about what *I* will leave. The Jeffrey Mere mark will probably be a pretty insignificant one." He shrugged and lifted his glass to his lips.

"Not if you decide to change things." Lucia placed her cutlery across her empty plate and pushed it away from herself. After a few moments of silence, she spoke again. "You have time, Jeffrey Mere."

He looked into her dark brown eyes, trying to read the map to her thoughts. Did she think him a dullard, an obtuse Scotsman with no ability to dream or even make the most of the life he had?

The thought that Lucia might be disappointed in him made Jeffrey catch his breath. In the few days that they had spent together, he felt he had learned a great deal from this bright, stoic, and lively lady. She had survived the unexpected loss of her beloved husband, the departure of her daughter to another country, and the sudden and unwelcome alteration of a life she had planned on living for many more years to come. And yet here she was, telling him, in her own way, to grab life by the throat and shake every precious moment out of it. It wasn't too late for him. He just needed to believe it.

Jeffrey pushed his plate away and poured the remaining wine equally between their two glasses.

"You know, Lucia, you are a truly remarkable woman."

Lucia's eyes widened slightly, and he thought he saw a shadow of sadness cross their molten brown.

"Thank you, Jeffrey Mere. *Questo è un complimento.*"

She dipped her head, graciously accepting his kind words, and then reached into her handbag for a gauzy hanky that she dabbed at her nose. Raising her eyes to his again, Lucia swallowed. "Mary is a fortunate woman, to have your heart." She searched his face, her own a picture of honesty.

Moved, Jeffrey reached across the table and took her cool, slim hand in his.

"And I am fortunate to have met you." His thumb brushed across the smooth skin of her hand and then, they both knew, no more words were necessary. It was time to say goodbye.

CHAPTER 39

———— ❧ ————

Upstairs in his cottage once more, Jeffrey lay in the bath. Ralf had, to his surprise, greeted him at the bottom of the stairs when he'd arrived home, and the cat had been sitting on the toilet seat, bathing himself, since Jeffrey had sunk into the hot water fifteen minutes ago.

The flight back had been uneventful, and now that he was home, he wanted to soak in his own bathtub, read the newspaper, and launder the few clothes he'd brought home with him. The heating was kicking in, a load of dark clothes already rumbled around inside the dryer, and a cup of tea sat on the edge of the bath. It was good to be home.

Jeffrey planned on getting dressed, then popping over to surprise Mary with her presents. He'd debated calling first but had decided that everyone liked surprises, so he'd take a leaf out of Lucia's book and be spontaneous. The thought of Lucia made him smile. At another time, maybe he and she — well, who knew?

The newspaper lay on the bathmat, corrugated and soggy at the bottom, where he'd let it dip into the water by mistake. From what he could see from the quick scan he'd taken before discarding it on the floor, nothing much had changed while Jeffrey Mere had vacated his normal life for a few days. The government was still in disarray, the economy was still hovering on the precipice of disaster, and the same idiot was still hosting *Strictly Come Dancing*. Things had not changed for the better, and yet, despite all that, he had an undeniable sense of optimism.

His stomach felt fluttery, and as he lay in the warm water, he began mentally going through his shirts, deciding which one to wear to Mary's house. He hoped she'd like the scarf he'd brought her. He was especially pleased with that gift and could visualize it draped around her pretty neck. He needed to stop at the shop and get a few provisions, too. Perhaps he'd get Mary some flowers while he was at it?

Dressed in his good brown corduroys, a checked flannel shirt, and a dark brown sweater, Jeffrey inspected himself in the mirror. His Thursday socks winked out from under the hems of his trousers, and the sight of them made him smile. Raising his eyes to the mirror, he spoke out loud.

"Yes, Mum. I'm off to see Mary. You'll be happy about that." He nodded at his reflection and reached down to retrieve his brown brogues. He wanted to look smart but not overdone, casual but not slovenly. Why was what he wore suddenly so important?

Satisfied with his choices, Jeffrey bounded down the narrow staircase. He pulled on his woolen coat and put his cap on, adjusting the brim. He was walking into the lounge to pick up the parcel with Mary's gifts in it when the doorbell rang. No one knew he was home yet, so there were only two people this could be — either Mary or Matilda. As he approached the door, the outline of the rotund form behind it gave away the identity of his visitor, and he opened the door. Matilda was resplendent in a floral apron, a blue cardigan draped around her shoulders, and her broad feet firmly planted in the ubiquitous slippers. She was holding a biscuit tin and smiled broadly when she saw him.

"Welcome home." Her full-moon face split from side to side. "It's good to have you back. Here's some shortbread." She shoved the tin towards him. "I'll need the tin back."

"Thanks, Matilda." Jeffrey eased himself out of the door. Stepping onto the doorstep, he squeezed in next to her unyielding presence and accepted the gift.

"So much has happened. You'll have heard all about it, no doubt? Poor Mary. And her alone in the car all that time. It was a miracle, really. If it hadn't been for that farmer, and…"

Jeffrey's good mood splintered into a thousand pieces. He felt a weighted chill creep through his bones, and he could no longer hear Matilda, her voice fading into white noise as she wittered on and on about a miracle. What had happened? Where was Mary? Why had he left her behind? If anything bad had happened to her, he'd never forgive himself.

After what felt like an age, with him spiraling down a rabbit hole of regret, Matilda shook his shoulder.

"Jeffrey, are you listening to me? She's fine. Mary's fine. Just get yourself down there and see her, for heaven's sake. The poor love has been through the mill, and I know she's missed you."

At the very personal inference, Jeffrey snapped back to attention and stared at Matilda.

"What do you mean?"

"She told me that you phoned her, from Rome. Anyone can see that she's sweet on you. You must know that?" Matilda watched him, her blue eyes wide.

Jeffrey took a deep breath, turned, and walked back into the house. He lay the biscuit tin down on the stair and returned to the door.

"Where is she?" His voice was raw and sounded odd, floating outside his pounding head.

"She's at home, of course. She's not getting out, because of the wheelchair." Matilda's voice faltered as Jeffrey blanched, then reached for the doorframe to steady himself.

Wheelchair? What in god's name was going on? He needed to get to her. Matilda needed to stop talking, and he needed to run the length of Willow Street until he got to Mary.

"Matilda, I have to go." Jeffrey closed the door behind him and stepped into the drive. "Sorry, I don't mean to be rude." He was already walking away from her, so Matilda called after him.

"That's OK. Love's young dream won't be denied. Give her my love." He heard her chuckle, but didn't turn back to wave.

Jeffrey began running down the road, his brogues making a heavy thunk against the pavement with each lumbering step. Within a few moments, his heart was pattering alarmingly, and he could feel sweat gathering on his upper lip.

She was fine. Matilda had said she was fine. He needed to calm down and just get there so he could figure out what had gone on in his absence.

As he passed the Subramanians' house, the twins lay in their favorite spot, draped along the back of the sofa. They waved at him with perfect and graceful synchronicity. He raised a hand but didn't stop, hoping he wouldn't see anyone else he knew who might potentially divert him from his mission.

Up ahead, he could see Mary's front door, with the holly wreath hanging on the knocker. As he approached the house, he saw the glint of Christmas tree lights through the lounge window and thought he could smell wood smoke. His heart racing now, he stepped up to the door and rang the bell. After an interminable wait, he heard a voice. It was low, loud, and unfamiliar. A tall shadow approached the door, and as it opened, Jeffrey was faced with a giant of a man with a ruddy face and hands like meat plates.

"Can I help you?" the man asked, smiling but at the same time openly curious about this person on Mary's doorstep.

"Um. I." Jeffrey could hardly speak for panting, the sweat now trickling down his back and gathering at the waistband of his trousers. "Mary. Is Mary here?" He managed to squeeze out the words.

The man nodded and opened the door a little farther.

"Aye, she's here. May I say who's calling?"

Jeffrey coughed and slid a finger inside his collar. Taking a deep breath, he tried to slow his breathing down.

"Mere. Jeffrey Mere."

"Right. Just a minute." The voice was flat, and to Jeffrey's surprise, the big man closed the door and wandered back up Mary's hall, leaving him standing out on the doorstep. Who could this great brute be? He knew Mary didn't have any siblings, and he was sure if she'd been walking out with someone else, she'd have told him.

He felt shocked and humiliated standing out in the cold like a traveling salesman offering something the homeowner clearly didn't want. Jeffrey glanced around, checking to see if anyone was watching this bizarre scene unfold. To his relief, the street was quiet, and no neighboring curtains were twitching, as far as he could see.

After a few minutes, the door opened again. The big man looked sheepish as he stepped back and asked Jeffrey in. Jeffrey, relieved but also deeply unsettled, followed him down the hall and into the lounge.

Mary sat in a wheelchair. Her left leg was in a large boot supported by a metal platform with a cushion on it. She had a plaster on her forehead, and her left arm was heavily bandaged. Her normally vibrant hair lay flat to her head, her skin looked pallid, and her eyes were glassy.

Jeffrey felt his heart tear a little as he assessed the damage to her. He stood silently, scanning her up and down, as if afraid he'd miss something during his inspection.

"Hello, Jeffrey." The warm voice shook him out of his trance. "Welcome home."

She smiled at him and held out her right hand. Jeffrey, still dumbstruck, stepped awkwardly forward and shook her hand, as he might have a new client's. Mary's smile faded, and she retracted her hand from his. She glanced sideways, as if suddenly remembering that there was another presence in the room.

"Jeffrey, this is Duncan. Duncan, Jeffrey." The big man extended a massive paw and Jeffrey took it, but his eyes never left Mary's. As he shook the unwelcome stranger's hand, Jeffrey felt himself slipping back down the rabbit hole.

Was it possible that she'd met someone else in the seven days he'd been away? Could she have fallen for this man-mountain in such a short period of time? Had he lost her? Why had he gone to Rome? Why had he not asked her to go with him? Why had he decided to stay on after his abduction, and what if this was punishment for his spending time with Lucia? What if Mary knew? But how could she possibly know about Lucia? That made no sense at all. What would he tell her if she asked if he'd met someone?

As a million what ifs roiled around inside his head, Jeffrey felt nauseated. One question seemed to beat out all the others as he swam around inside his state of panic. How on earth was he going to fix this?

CHAPTER 40

Mary sat across the room from the two men. Jeffrey and Duncan looked oddly mismatched on the couch, and for a moment, she wanted to giggle. She knew it was nerves making her feel giddy, but the situation really was a little ridiculous. Mary's mum had often told her that men were like buses. She'd said that you could wait around for ages, never seeing the one you needed, and then two would turn up at the same time.

Here she was, Mary Ferguson, sitting at the bus stop with two shiny number 47s in front of her. The difference here was that she was only interested in one of them.

"Caramel shortbread?" Mary indicated the plate on the coffee table. Both men shook their heads, staring at her mutely.

She flicked her eyes from one man to the other, and then sniffed.

"I think I'd like a piece."

No sooner had she spoken than to her alarm, both men

jumped up from the couch and reached for the plate, sending it tumbling to the ground.

"Jesus." Duncan yelped.

"Sorry." Jeffrey choked out.

"It doesn't matter. Really." Mary felt remorse for her moment of wicked enjoyment at their predicament. "Just throw it away. Matilda will bring more tomorrow, anyway." She winked at Jeffrey, who stood by uncomfortably while Duncan scrabbled around on the carpet, picking up shortbread crumbs with his big, sausage-like fingers.

With the mess finally cleared away, the three sat in awkward silence once again. Mary knew by his face that she could torture Jeffrey no longer.

"So, Jeffrey, Duncan is the paramedic who saved my life after the accident." Mary smiled at the big man as she spoke. "If it hadn't been for him..." Her voice faded.

As Mary spoke, Jeffrey's eyes moved to Duncan's broad face.

"Och, no. It wasn'y like that." Duncan blushed, and for a moment, Jeffrey felt himself warm towards his adversary. "I was just in the right place at the right time. Just day'in ma job."

The big man seemed genuinely unassuming, even humble. Perhaps he wasn't that bad after all? No sooner had the thought entered his head than Jeffrey dismissed it. This hulk of a man was the enemy. He needed to stay focused.

Watching Mary shift in the chair, then wince in pain, made Jeffrey's hair stand on end. He couldn't bear to see her hurting. As his glance flickered between Mary and Duncan, Jeffrey realized that this was one of those moments he'd read about, a moment that could potentially define the rest of your life. Suddenly, the way forward was clear, and he found his voice.

"Mary, please tell me what happened." Jeffrey walked across the room and sat down on the carpet in front of the wheelchair. He reached up and took her hand in his and smiled deep into her gorgeous green eyes.

Duncan coughed and stood up abruptly.

"I think Mary needs to rest now." The man-mountain hovered close behind him, and Jeffrey felt his face grow hot.

"Mary can tell me if she's tired." Jeffrey spoke quietly, his eyes not leaving Mary's.

Mary blinked and slid her hand away. He thought he saw a cloud slide across her face, blocking him out like unwelcome sunlight. Her hand went up to her hair, patting it self-consciously. As he watched her, Jeffrey felt he could see some kind of inner conflict going on. She seemed to be passing through a mental agility course, her face twitching, her eyes flicking from side to side, and her lips pursing. Her silence felt like a great dumbbell in his chest. Each moment that passed added another twenty pounds to his heart. Had he miscalculated this all so badly? Was it too late?

At Mary's lack of response, Jeffrey felt he had his answer, so he stood up and smoothed his rumpled sweater.

"Well, I'll leave you to rest then, Mary. I'm very sorry about your accident. Please let me know if you need anything." His voice was formal, removed, and it sounded brittle in the silent room.

A pop from the fire made Mary jump, forcing her eyes to open wider and refocus.

"Thanks. I'm fine for the moment. You don't have to go, though." She smiled up at him, but he sensed little conviction or joy in her words, and saw no true invitation behind her expression.

Nodding in acknowledgment of his defeat, Jeffrey backed away and walked into the hall to retrieve his coat. Duncan followed him, the very presence of the man making Jeffrey feel as if he was indeed being ushered off the premises. He wanted to turn around and launch himself at the interloper. Who did this Duncan think he was, descending on Mary like a vulture the minute Jeffrey was out of sight?

Mary's front door clicked behind him and Jeffrey felt his feet moving, spiriting him along Willow Street. He wasn't sure why he kept moving forward when he was willing himself in the opposite direction, back to Mary. However, his feet persevered, and soon enough, he stood at his own front door.

The key wouldn't fit in the lock. He pushed at the unyielding lock, then realized that his hand was shaking so badly that he was trying to insert the key the wrong way up. He needed to breathe, just get a grip on himself.

A few minutes later, he hovered in his kitchen, listening to the kettle burbling. A solitary mug stood at the ready with a single teabag inside. Opening the fridge, he scanned the spartan contents. In his excitement to get to Mary's house, he hadn't gone to the shop as he'd intended. The sight of a tub of margarine, some jam, two eggs, and an empty space where the milk belonged brought his disappointment to an explosive head. Jeffrey slammed the fridge door closed, switched off the kettle, threw the mug in the sink and heard it break, then stomped up the staircase. He was bone tired, and bed was the only place he wanted to be right at this moment.

Tossing his clothes into a pile on the floor, Jeffrey yanked his pajamas from the drawer, put them on, then climbed under his duvet and pulled it over his head. He just needed to sleep. He'd figure out what to do in the morning.

He could hear a ticking sound, but not like the one his clock made. Jeffrey pulled the covers away from his head and looked around the dark room. There was an odd shadow in the chair in the corner. As he swallowed hard and screwed his eyes up to focus, he saw Agnes, her needles clacking as she knitted, her head lowered purposefully over her work.

"Mum, what're you doing?" he whispered.

"I could ask you the same thing, laddie." The little purple head tilted to the side, and his mother's dark eyes connected with his. "I don't understand ye, Jeffrey."

Jeffrey sat up in bed and turned on the bedside light. Meanwhile, Agnes carefully wrapped a long strand of wool around the bulk of what she was working on, stuck the needles through the bundle, and placed it behind her as she rose from the chair. He watched her familiar movements, afraid to move or breathe too deeply in case she wafted away.

When she sat on the edge of his bed, Jeffrey noted that she made no impression on the duvet, like a butterfly landing on a flower. He leaned back against his pillow and tried to focus on her face.

"What do you mean, you don't understand me?" He wanted to see her eyes to judge her intentions, but now the lamplight was bouncing off the thick lenses of her glasses. All he saw there was his own reflection.

"What the hell are you doing in bed?" Her voice was both soft and hard at the same time.

"I'm sleeping," he replied, knowing full well that his deliberately obtuse response would send her into an angry spin.

"Well, it's time you got your arse out of bed and back downstairs. You need a plan, son. No amount of sulkin' or hidin' will get her back."

Whatever modicum of patience she had been tapping was gone, and Agnes was shouting now. Her breathing was audible, rattly, sending a waft of ginger snaps and cabbage across his face. Jeffrey closed his eyes, rubbed them hard, and opened them again, expecting her to be gone.

Agnes was still very much there but, to his shock, she had begun to levitate, hovering above the mattress, her floral skirt hanging down from her tiny frame and her hair glowing purple in the dimly lit room. Translucent hands with thick, pumping veins gripped her narrow hips, and her pointed chin thrust out towards him in a classic Agnes expression.

"What are ye waiting for?" She looked down at him, furious, as her little feet, encased in her favorite checked slippers, dangled incongruously.

"OK, Mum. Take it easy." Jeffrey pushed himself up against the headboard. "Just sit back down, will you?" He patted the bed.

Agnes slowly lowered herself to the ground, and then settled next to him, laying a wizened hand over his.

"Jeffrey Mere. This is your life, no' a rehearsal. There's nae mare second chances, son. You need to make the things you want to happen, happen. Nae-b'dy else can dae that for you." Her voice sounded more like Agnes's again, raspy, but softer than before.

"I know, Mum. I'm just afraid it might be too late." He felt his throat tighten with the words.

"Well, lying here moping won't help. Put yer glad rags on, go over there, and stand up to the competition." She nodded decisively and patted his hand.

"I know. You're right. Sorry, Mum." Jeffrey felt her paper-light hand move away from his.

"Mum, don't go yet." He watched as the edges of her face began to fade into the shadows surrounding her.

"It's time, son." Her glasses glinted in the lamplight and she smiled. "You're ready."

Jeffrey woke with a start. The duvet was over his head, and he was breathing heavily. It took a few moments for him to register that he was in his own bed and that sharp morning light was filtering through the curtains. He threw the covers off and perched on the edge of the mattress, looking around the room, then squinted at the chair in the corner.

"OK, Mum. I heard you. Today's the day." He spoke out loud to the silent room, then jumped up and headed downstairs to put the kettle on and have a shower.

CHAPTER 41

As he left, Mary watched Jeffrey's hunched frame pass the lounge window, and her heart ached. It ached for herself and for Jeffrey. He had given up so easily, and what was that cold hand-shake about? After everything that had happened, all the progress they'd made, and all the signs she'd been *sure* she'd seen, he'd shaken her hand like a stranger's. Mary felt her eyes filling up and reached for her hanky. She didn't want Duncan to see her cry.

She'd watched Jeffrey earlier, kneeling there in front of her, looking so earnest. She'd wanted to speak but, at that moment, she couldn't help but think about him so easily leaving her be-hind. He hadn't called from Rome until he was practically on his way home, and now there he was, asking her to explain things to him. Despite her hurt feelings, she'd wanted to lean over and wrap her arms around his neck, but then there was Duncan. He was a kind and thoughtful man who'd not only saved her life but had also been there for her when Jeffrey hadn't. Her conflict had all but choked her and so, for safety's sake, Mary had kept quiet.

Duncan had taken the cups and plates into the kitchen, and she could hear him washing them up. She listened to the clinking and splashing and hoped he'd stay out there a little longer, long enough for her to gather herself.

Clearing her throat, she called out.

"I could do with a fresh cuppa, Duncan, if you can be bothered?"

"Aye, no problem."

Mary turned her attention back to the window. As Duncan clattered around in her kitchen, she watched the empty street. She couldn't stop herself hoping that she'd see Jeffrey's familiar form out of the window, a determined look on his face and a spring in his step. But he didn't come. Instead, Duncan brought her fresh tea and she did her best to sip it, feeling as if she were swallowing needles with every gulp.

After a few minutes, Duncan rose and walked towards the hall.

"Well, I'd better be off."

Mary, realizing that she'd been staring out the window silently, flashed him a big smile.

"Thanks for popping in, Duncan. I really appreciate it."

Duncan leaned over and took her hand.

"I could come in tomorrow, after my shift?" He looked hopeful, his big red cheeks and watery eyes sparking sympathy within her.

"Um, that'd be nice." The words were out, and Mary instantly regretted them. Backtracking, she added, "Perhaps we can see how it goes, I mean, if I'm feeling up to it?" She felt her smile falter, but Duncan was already facing away from her, pulling on his mammoth overcoat.

"Aye, OK. I'll talk to you tomorrow then, eh?" He looked at her and nodded.

"OK, then." She nodded back and lifted a hand to wave as he headed down the hall.

"You get some sleep." The deep voice faded away as Duncan went outside, and then she heard her front door click closed.

Damn you, Jeffrey Mere. If it didn't hurt so much to cry, she'd have given in to the tears of disappointment that were pushing up inside her throat. *Damn you.*

CHAPTER 42

———◆———

J effrey paced along Willow Street, a jar of honey from his bees in one hand and a bag holding the silk scarf, pannetone, and Italian sweets in the other. He bore gifts along with his new plan. Inside his coat, beneath his sweater and flannel shirt, his heart raced with a flurry of determination. He would win his ladylove back, man-mountain or no.

Having thought through their encounter the previous evening, Jeffrey understood how Mary could have misinterpreted his initial silence as indifference. Meanwhile, Duncan was muscling in, making tea, telling him Mary was tired, making him look bad. He would not let that happen again. He'd take charge, tell Mary what was in his heart, and be done with all this indecision.

The afternoon was bright and cold, and Jeffrey inhaled the smell of neighborhood fireplaces and the comforting scent of home cooking as he made his way down the road. He'd always enjoyed the few days between Christmas and the new year. The gap in time felt like a holiday to him, and although many of his former clients had worked through it, he had always taken the days off to spend with Agnes. It made sense to him to stretch the festive season out as far as possible, and he and his mother had often gone into Perth or Edinburgh to eat nice lunches, attend a concert, or take advantage of the January sales that usually started well before January.

The Subramanians' house was still as he passed, the windows dark and no tiny twins occupying the back of the sofa. Perhaps they were away? He wondered if Hindus put up Christmas trees. Funny, it wasn't something he'd ever thought about before, but as he walked briskly along, he decided to research it when he got home. It was time he became more outward-looking. He should invite the family over for lunch, try to get to know them a little. They certainly seemed like good people, and everyone needed good people in their life.

As he passed Mary's lounge window, he saw the tree lights glittering. Reaching up, he banged on the knocker, then stepped back to wait. As a few moments passed, Jeffrey suddenly felt a tiny crack of doubt appear in his newfound confidence. What if that Duncan opened the door again? He hadn't considered the possibility that the big man had not, in fact, gone home last night. Feeling slightly sweaty, Jeffrey loosened his scarf.

Eventually, the door cracked open and Mary, propped up on crutches, stood behind it.

"Oh." Her eyes were wide. "Jeffrey."

"Is this a bad time?" Preoccupied with the disturbing thought of Duncan in Mary's bed, Jeffrey sounded unintentionally abrupt.

"No, not at all." Mary was smiling. "I'm not getting out much, as you can imagine." She nodded down at her foot.

Jeffrey swallowed. What was he thinking about Duncan for? Mary looked tired but still happy to see him.

"Can I come in?" He smiled shyly.

"Of course, come in." Mary turned awkwardly and made her way into the lounge.

Jeffrey followed her slowly, watching as she struggled to control the unwieldy metal legs. He wished he could just pick her up and carry her, but that wasn't really something he would typically have done.

The crutches were cumbersome and hurt Mary under her armpits, but at least they allowed her to move around a little. As she caught a glimpse of herself in the hall mirror for the second time that day, she wished she'd been able to wash her hair. The health visitor had made a bit of a fuss when she'd been in the previous afternoon, saying she wasn't prepared for that and it would take too long. Mary had said that she supposed it could wait another day, despite the fact that the lank, greasy locks were driving her mad. What must she look like, to Jeffrey?

Settling herself in the armchair, Mary sighed. Jeffrey hung his coat on the rack, then set the gifts on the coffee table. Leaning over, he gathered the crutches from Mary's hands and propped them up against the fireplace.

"Can I get you anything?"

"No, thanks. I've not long had lunch. Takes me a while to get organized. But make yourself something." Mary nodded towards the kitchen.

"No, I'm fine, really." Jeffrey shook his head and sat down on the sofa, adjusting the cushions behind his back. "Oh, I brought you these." He pointed to the paper bag and the jar of honey.

"Thank you. What's in the bag?" Mary smiled broadly, and the joy in her face made Jeffrey feel a little less nervous.

"Have a look." He jumped up and handed Mary the bag and the little pentagonal jar. As he sat back on the sofa, the clock ticked loudly and the sound of a car stereo thumped as it passed outside the house.

"Young folk. I don't know how they don't all go deaf." He grinned and shrugged.

Mary nodded and smiled. "I know."

Jeffrey watched her adjust the pillow under her leg and shuffle the jar and bag in her lap.

"Can I help you?" He stood up and walked across to her.

"It's fine." Mary shook her head. "I'm getting used to it now."

Unable to stand the crackling silence and forced politeness any longer, Jeffrey perched on the edge of the coffee table, took the gifts from her, and gripped her hand.

"Mary. I owe you an apology." He searched her face for some sign that would give him hope.

"For what?" Her voice was tight.

"For so many things." His eyes slid to the floor.

"Well, I'm not going anywhere." Mary's smile was warm this time, and she let him take her hand.

Just as he was going to lean in and kiss her, the doorbell rang — a sharp, intrusive ring that sent the hairs on his arms to attention.

Mary looked startled and glanced up at the window. She wasn't expecting anyone until dinnertime, when Matilda had said she might drop by.

"Who's that?" Jeffrey stood up and walked towards the hall.

Behind the glass panel in the door, he saw a large, dark shadow. Damn, it was Duncan.

"Shall I tell them to go away?" He called down the hall hopefully.

"Well, see who it is first." Mary sounded nervous.

Jeffrey opened the door to see Duncan's massive form squeezed into a dark blue suit that looked like it might have fitted him ten years and three stones ago.

"Hello." Jeffrey's voice was flat.

"Um, hi. Jeffrey, is it?" Duncan stepped back from the door-step and blushed.

Jeffrey nodded. "That's right." He breathed deliberately slowly. The big man looked uncomfortable. The tables had turned; this time Jeffrey was inside and Duncan was out. This time, Jeffrey resolved, Duncan would remain on the outside, permanently.

"I've come to see Mary." Duncan wasn't giving up that easily.

Jeffrey exhaled and stepped back.

"I'll just see if she is OK for you to come in." He turned his back on Duncan. Not quite having the heart to close the door fully, as Duncan had done to him, Jeffrey left it slightly ajar as he walked away.

Mary sat forward in her chair, the jar of honey in her hand.

"It's Duncan." Jeffrey shrugged, his hands thrust deep into his pockets.

"Well, he'd better come in, then." Mary looked up at Jeffrey, her eyes wide. "You can't leave him on the doorstep." She smiled at him.

"No, I suppose not. Although I'd like to." He pulled his mouth down at the edges and crossed his eyes comically.

Mary laughed and, on a reflex, put her hand up to her mouth to cover her amusement.

"Now, now. Be nice." She shook a finger at him and nodded toward the hall. Jeffrey trudged away reluctantly to let his opponent in.

The threesome once again sat around the room. Conversation was stilted, with neither man backing down nor beating a retreat. Mary did her best to mediate, playing piggy-in-the-middle. They talked about Christmas, the New Year's party in Pitlochry, her leg, and her recovery. After an hour, a pot of tea, and plate of bourbon biscuits, they started on the weather, and Mary knew it was time to draw this to a close. Looking at the two men on her couch, she was deeply conflicted, her heart lying with Jeffrey, her sympathy and gratitude with Duncan.

Mary involuntarily yawned; then, embarrassed by her obvious display of fatigue, she blushed.

"Sorry, I'm a wee bit tired." She leaned over and reached for her crutches. "It's been lovely to see you, though." She spoke to no one in particular.

Duncan heaved his bulk off the couch and helped her out of the chair, while Jeffrey grabbed the crutches and slid one under each arm.

Duncan stepped back and waited, a frown on his face, as Jeffrey helped her balance herself.

"Are you OK there?" Duncan's big red face was wrinkled with concern, his huge hands hovering behind her, ready to catch her if she fell.

"I'll stay and help her." Jeffrey eyed Duncan, challenging him to protest. "I've got her."

Mary smiled broadly at Jeffrey. His words meant so much more to her than perhaps Jeffrey realized. He'd 'got her'?

Seeing the expression on Mary's face, Duncan's shoulders slumped inside his too-tight suit.

"Well, I think I'll be going then, Mary." The big man shuffled his feet awkwardly, tucking his shirt back into his trousers where it had worked loose.

"Thanks for everything, Duncan." Mary felt another wave of sympathy for this kind man who'd come to visit her, concerned that she might be alone over Christmas.

Jeffrey, suddenly feeling uncomfortable about his victory, steadied Mary against the mantelpiece and followed Duncan into the hall. As his adversary reached the front door, Jeffrey extended his hand towards him.

"I don't know how to thank you for what you did for Mary." Jeffrey's voice was genuine and thick with emotion.

Duncan peered down at the smaller man for a few seconds then, as if realizing that he was looking at the true object of Mary's affection, simply nodded.

"Take good care of her, OK?"

Jeffrey nodded, his eyes filling up with embarrassing tears.

"I will. You can be sure of that."

With Duncan gone, Mary, to Jeffrey's delight, said she didn't need to rest right away. He settled himself in the armchair with Mary next to him in the wheelchair, her leg propped up on the coffee table. She told him to pour himself a dram, and then he stoked the fire, piling on some more logs. The room was pleasantly warm, and the pair sat in companionable silence, each one appreciating the presence of the other without having to speak to acknowledge it.

Jeffrey sipped the amber liquid, enjoying the burn on the back of his tongue. There was nothing like a wee dram, especially on a cold winter's evening.

At Jeffrey's gentle questioning, Mary slowly began to talk. She explained about her trip to Perth, her Christmas shopping, and her journey home. She talked about the terrifying accident in a clear, calm voice. Jeffrey, however, could sense how afraid she'd been, trapped in the car, bleeding, broken, with no idea of when someone might find her, if they found her at all. He reached out and took her hand as she spoke, winding his fingers around hers. His larger hand swallowed her smaller one whole, and it felt right. This was where he was meant to be.

Having finished her tale, Mary exhaled and shifted again in the chair. Her ribs and leg were aching, and as she leaned over to scratch her toes, she noticed the clock on the mantle. She'd missed her pills with all the excitement. No wonder her pain was mounting.

"Jeffrey, could you please pass me those pills?" She pointed to the bottle on the sideboard. "I've missed a dose, and everything's starting to hurt." She grimaced theatrically.

"Of course. Here you are." Jeffrey opened the bottle and handed it to her. "I'll get you some water." He padded into the kitchen and filled a glass.

"Can I make you some dinner?" he asked as he handed her the water.

Mary swallowed two pills and gave him back the bottle.

"Matilda left a shepherd's pie in the fridge. We could have

some of that." Mary smiled up at him. He was obviously planning on staying around this evening. She felt her heart skip as Jeffrey clapped his hands together and rubbed them like the hungry giant having just spied Jack climbing the beanstalk.

"Brilliant. I'll heat it up and we can have some here, by the fire, on trays." His smile was beatific as he lifted a soft blanket from the back of the couch and tucked it carefully around Mary's hips.

"You sit here and stay cozy. I'll get things going and be back in a jiffy."

"I'm not going anywhere." Mary winked at him and settled herself in the chair.

She hadn't felt particularly cold, but the rug did feel good over her now. The fire popped, and she inhaled the peppery wood smoke. It made her muscles relax and her head feel lighter. She pictured the medication she'd just taken swirling through her bloodstream and attaching itself to the bones in her leg, the tendons in her arm, and the framework of her rib cage, easing out the throbbing pain.

She'd just close her eyes for a few minutes to rest them, and then she and Jeffrey would have a lovely dinner together. Things were definitely looking up.

CHAPTER 43

————◆————

Their empty dinner plates sat on the coffee table. Mary's back was to the fire, and the scarf with the wisteria blossoms on it lay on her lap. Her eyes were like saucers, and in the silence, Jeffrey could hear her breathing. The weight of his story hung heavy in the atmosphere, and he began to wish he hadn't told her.

"He had a knife? He took everything?" Mary's voice cracked. "Why on earth didn't you call me, tell me what happened and let me know once you were safe?"

"I didn't think. I wouldn't have wanted to worry you, anyway." Jeffrey squirmed on the couch. "Besides, you didn't tell me about your accident, either." He stared at her accusingly.

Mary let out a yelp of indignation.

"Well, that's true, but you weren't here, Jeffrey Mere. What could you have done?" Mary shrugged. "Perhaps we both need to do a better job of sharing things with each other?"

Jeffrey nodded.

"So the hotel let you stay until it all got sorted out?"

"Yes. The manager, Mr. Giacomo, was a very decent sort. He helped me get everything organized. I liked him, actually. A very accommodating man, for a foreigner." Jeffrey winked at her in an attempt to lighten the mood.

Unamused, she dipped her head towards her lap and folded the scarf carefully into a diamond, then leaned over and laid it on the table.

"It's not funny, Jeffrey." As she raised her head to speak, he saw her eyes glistening. Was she crying?

"I called the hotel, you know? They phoned your house while I was there, feeding Ralf. They said you hadn't arrived and that they were going to give your room away."

Jeffrey was aghast. He had no idea she'd tried to reach him. Not having contacted her now felt more like an injury to her than an oversight on his part.

"I'm sorry, Mary. I didn't know." His voice faded.

"It's OK. I called back the next day and they said you'd checked in, very late. So I knew you were there." She turned and stared out the window.

Mary sniffed and reached into her pocket for her hanky. Dabbing at her nose, she suddenly looked very young to him, vulnerable. Jeffrey felt a wrench to his heart. She cared for him, truly.

"I'll never not tell you something again. I promise. Scout's honor." Jeffrey held three fingers up to his forehead. "I'm sorry."

Mary sniffed again and tucked the hanky away.

"Well, you be sure to keep that promise. I don't want to lose you, now that..." Mary blushed, her sentence fading into the space between them.

"Now that what?" Jeffrey waited.

"Now that you're back here again. I mean, now that you're..."

Jeffrey stood up and walked towards her. Perching on the edge of the coffee table, he took both her hands in his.

"Mary. I'm not going anywhere without you, ever again." He watched her lovely face, and to his surprise, it crumpled before him.

Mary's final speck of strength disintegrated, and she let herself slump back in the chair. Her breath came in big gulps, and hot tears welled up in her eyes, rendering her blind. The gasping hurt her ribs, but she could not stop herself. A sob broke free, hanging in the air like a lead weight, then another followed, and then another. So many years of pain, fear, and loneliness were escaping from her that she was powerless to stop the momentum.

Jeffrey shifted forward and put his arms lightly around her, afraid to hurt her, letting her cry into his woolen shoulder. He understood that this was not simply about him leaving her behind or his being abducted, mugged, or in danger. It wasn't even about her accident or painful injuries. This was so much more than that.

He stayed very still until her sobs began to ease. Mary made no attempt to pull away from him, and that small gesture of trust made Jeffrey's heart soar. She was letting him in, letting him know how much he meant to her. There was no going back now.

As he held her, Lucia's words came back to him. *How can you do love wrong?*

This exact moment in time, sitting in her little lounge, with the fire burning, the Christmas tree lights twinkling, their stomachs full of Matilda's excellent shepherd's pie, Mary's leg in a cast, and his coat hanging on the rack, felt like the epicenter of the universe. There was no better time or place to speak his mind, tell her what was in his heart.

Jeffrey sat slowly back and brushed the hair gently away from her eyes.

"Mary Ferguson. I love you."

Mary wiped her nose again with her hanky and looked at him. Her green eyes had cleared and were focused directly on his. Jeffrey's smile quivered, and he swallowed. Surely she would say something? Surely she wouldn't leave him hanging here?

Just as Jeffrey began to have a moment of panic, she smiled.

"Well, that took you long enough, Jeffrey Mere."

Jeffrey let out a laugh and leaned in.

"Can I kiss you?" He looked at her shyly.

"If you don't, there'll be trouble." Mary laughed, her eyes filling up again.

He pressed his mouth to hers, feeling her soft lips under his. This was home.

CHAPTER 44

———◆———

Finding the right time to tell Mary about Lucia had been tricky, but Jeffrey had resolved to have no secrets from her. *Start as you mean to go on* was what Agnes had often said, and Jeffrey intended to follow his mother's lead.

They'd been out for a walk, well, more of a push than a walk, with Jeffrey steering the wheelchair along Willow Street and Mary tucked under a rug. It was New Year's Eve, and Mary had felt particularly cooped up that morning, so they'd layered on their woolens and ventured outside.

The streets were quiet, most of the residents preparing for their Hogmanay celebrations. Mary had been fretting about losing her Christmas shopping in the accident, as the bags from her car had not been recovered. Jeffrey agreed to take her to the shops so she could buy the Subramanian children something small. She was excited to see the high street after being cooped up for a week.

The morning was dull and cold, the sky scattered with dark,

ominous clouds. Jeffrey hoped they could make it out and back without getting wet. He didn't fancy pushing the wheelchair in the rain.

"Can we go to the bakery and get a coffee, maybe a mince pie?" Mary looked back at Jeffrey as he navigated the pavement, avoiding a small pothole.

"Why not? We deserve it." He laughed. He'd have taken her anywhere she wanted. "We can pop into the chemist and pick up my photos, if you like? We'll take them home and go through them after lunch." Jeffrey was formulating a plan.

"Great idea. I can't wait to see them." Mary nodded enthusiastically.

As they crossed Atholl Road, Mrs. Fraser spotted them and came out of the sweetshop. She was carrying a small paper bag and waved wildly as she trotted towards them.

"Well, hello, you two. How's the leg, Mary?" The cheery woman leaned down and patted Mary's gloved hand.

"It's not bad, thanks, Mrs. Fraser. Getting there." Mary smiled.

"Oooo, it's chilly, right enough." The big woman shivered and rubbed her hands up and down her wide arms. "Don't you get cold, now."

Mary nodded obediently.

"Well, here's a wee half pound of barley sugar. Great for healing, so I'm told." The woman pressed the paper bag into Mary's hand. "You can let him have some, if he's good." She winked and jerked a thumb towards Jeffrey.

"We'll see about that." Mary blushed under her hat and winked back at Mrs. Fraser.

"Are you coming to the street party tomorrow?" Mrs. Fraser

hopped from foot to foot, her thin cardigan and wool skirt not enough to protect her from the bitter wind that was picking up.

"I'm not sure," Jeffrey replied, looking down at Mary for a cue, just as Mary also replied, "We'll be there."

The threesome laughed in unison.

"So, we'll be there." Jeffrey shrugged, admitting defeat.

"Lovely, well, see you then. Get yourselves off somewhere cozy, it's bitter out here." Mrs. Fraser turned and waved over her shoulder as she went back inside the small shop.

Mary bought two chocolate selection boxes and a set of coloring books and pens for the twins. In the supermarket, they chose a bottle of wine and some chicken breasts for their dinner, and Jeffrey put cat food, milk, and a newspaper in the basket. Ralf had become moodier than usual, since Jeffrey was spending most of his time at Mary's house these past few days. He felt bad about it, so, to make amends, he bought Ralf's favorite gourmet food, with salmon rather than sardines.

They walked up one side of the main street and down the other, stopping to talk to people who came out of the shops to ask after Mary.

The clouds seemed to be lifting, and a watery sun poked its head out from between the remaining shreds of vapor stretched above them. As they made careful progress, Jeffrey was amazed at the number of people they knew, between the two of them. It was heartwarming and surprising at the same time.

He briefly left Mary to chat to Mr. McLintock, the butcher, while he popped into the chemist next door to collect his photos. Having piled all their provisions into the string bag, which hung across the back of the wheelchair, Jeffrey headed back down the hill.

As they approached the bakery, Mary turned her head towards him. "Let's just get a mince pie and take it home. I'm a bit sore, to be honest."

"Right, OK." Jeffrey was relieved, as he had seen her face looking rather pinched when they'd been speaking with Joe MacFarlane at the mountain sports store.

The bakery smelled as wonderful as ever, and Mrs. Barnes, thrilled to see Mary out and about, wouldn't let them pay for their mince pies. With the little paper bag balanced on Mary's lap, the two headed home.

"Let's stop at the Subramanians' and drop off the chocolate." Mary spoke over her shoulder.

"Well, all right, as it's on the way." Jeffrey smiled indulgently. "Just five minutes, though."

As they left the gifts with the giggling twins, their graceful, shy mother offered Mary a plate of samosas that she gratefully accepted. Jeffrey and Mary walked down the remainder of Willow Street, smelling the aromatic golden triangles that lurked under the cling film. They stopped long enough to feed Ralf his salmon dinner, then continued on to Mary's cottage.

The still-warm samosas proving too much of a temptation, Jeffrey abandoned the lunch he'd planned and put them on plates. He settled Mary on the couch, tossed the chicken in the fridge, and made a quick pot of tea.

"Let's eat these and then, if you're still hungry, I'll make us some roasted cheese later."

Mary nodded contentedly as Jeffrey sunk his teeth into the corner of a heavenly, crisp pastry. The curried vegetables were hot on his tongue and he could taste potato and peas wrapped in a delicious tangy sauce.

With their meal finished, Jeffrey gave Mary her painkillers, then retrieved the envelope of photos from his coat pocket.

"Ready for a photo extravaganza?" He waved the envelope at her and widened his eyes comically.

"Sure, let's see them." Mary shifted on the couch to make room for him next to her.

Jeffrey sat down, opened the envelope and began to hand them to her one by one.

"This is the Trevi Fountain. The one that's in the film *Three Coins in a Fountain*."

"Beautiful." Mary nodded, holding her hand out for the next one. "It's full of coins, isn't it?"

Jeffrey nodded and explained about the daily collection for charity.

"This is the hotel. It was really something, Mary."

"Gorgeous. Look at those pillars. And they're indoors, as well?" She shook her head in disbelief.

"Oh, this is the Christmas market, in Piazza Navona. That's where I got your scarf."

"I love it." Mary smiled up at him. "So, is this market only on at Christmas time?"

"Yes, apparently." Jeffrey's discomfort was rising, his voice sounding a little choked.

"Here's me outside St. Peter's Basilica, in the Vatican." Jeffrey felt his heart rate pick up a little. As he went through the timeline in his head, he knew the photo of him with Lucia was coming up soon.

As he handed Mary the next photo, the one in front of the Obelisk, Jeffrey caught sight of Lucia's dark head close to his. He hadn't realized how tall she was. She was leaning in towards him and smiling, her head inclined towards his shoulder. Jeffrey saw himself grinning, with his chest thrust out like a peacock, and for a second regretted his decision to show Mary the picture. He could have just fished this one out and thrown it away. She'd have been none the wiser. What she didn't know couldn't hurt her, right?

As it was too late to withdraw it, Jeffrey relinquished the picture as Mary's hand grasped it. She stared down at it silently for what felt like an eternity.

Jeffrey couldn't breathe. Why wasn't she saying anything?

"Who's this? A tour guide?" Without looking at him, Mary turned the photo over, as if expecting a clue on the back as to the identity of this elegant woman in the gorgeous coat and boots.

"That's Lucia." Jeffrey hoped his voice sounded normal, indifferent.

"Lucia?" Mary looked over at him, her eyes clear and wide.

"Yes, I met her the day I got my replacement passport and money. I'd been to buy some new clothes and we had to share a table in a café."

Mary nodded, once again looking at the back of the photo before flipping it over.

"She's lovely looking." Her voice was quiet.

"She's a good person, Mary. She's a wise person who's been through a lot. She helped me get my sea legs in Rome, so to speak." Jeffrey swallowed. That had come out wrong.

"What do you mean?" Mary's voice had an edge to it that Jeffrey had not heard before.

"I mean that she was kind to me. Helped me see that it was OK to stay on and see a wee bit of Rome, rather than come rushing home after my mishap." Jeffrey crossed his legs and leaned back against the cushions.

"Uh huh." Mary was obviously not pleased.

"The truth is, Mary, it was Lucia that helped me see how much I... I mean, that I was..." Jeffrey's voice cracked.

"That you were what?" Mary dropped the photo onto the coffee table and leaned away from him, trying to focus on his face.

Jeffrey saw her brow crinkle. Her lips pressed closed, and she folded her arms across her body protectively. That was not a good sign. He'd read that somewhere in a book about body language. He needed to retrieve the situation, and quickly.

"She made me realize that I was in love with you." Jeffrey reached for Mary's hand.

At his words, her eyes softened. She scanned his face and saw how nervous he'd become. It was more than she could do to make him suffer. After all, this was Jeffrey Mere, not some gigolo who'd gallivant around with any random Roman woman at the first opportunity.

"OK. So explain *how* she did that, please." Mary nodded expectantly, trying not to sound too stern, but indicating that he should go on.

As Jeffrey explained his relationship with Lucia for exactly what it was, a companionship, a meeting of kindred spirits, Mary's tension eased. She asked questions about the mystery woman, and the more Jeffrey spoke, the less concerned she became. Eventually, Jeffrey felt it safe to venture a question of his own.

"So, you understand? She was a friend when I needed one, nothing more." Jeffrey looked hopefully at Mary, who had let him take her hand in his and was now leaning against his shoulder.

"Yes, I think so. If you tell me that's how it was, then I believe you." She patted his hand and sighed. "You may be many things, Jeffrey Mere, but you are not a liar."

Jeffrey exhaled, relief flooding his chest.

"I didn't want to hide it from you, Mary. I want no secrets between us." He kissed the top of her shiny red curls.

"I appreciate that, love. I do." Mary turned her head and kissed his shoulder. "Thanks for telling me."

He nodded, hoping she wouldn't move, wouldn't break this critical and deep connection he felt with her right at this moment.

Mary, feeling the same way, sat still until her breathing fell into sync with Jeffrey's, and the only sound in the room, aside from their breathing, was the clock ticking on the mantelpiece.

CHAPTER 45

———◆———

The registry office was full to bursting. Their friends from Willow Street, Mary's fellow nurses from the home, and many of the town's folk sat on spindly chairs, shoulder-to-shoulder, waiting for the registrar to appear. The mild January sun shone bravely into the wood-paneled room, and a sense of excitement hovered over the gathering.

As Jeffrey scanned the lines of familiar faces, he smiled shyly. Imagine him and Mary having this many people who cared about them?

Among the crowd were the Subramanians, with the twins, who, dressed in matching sailor's outfits, were climbing along the backs of their chairs like lithe little cats. Joe MacFarlane, from the mountain sports store, raised a hand and waved. He and his wife sat next to Frank Duff, Jeffrey's old landlord, who tapped his heels together excitedly under his chair.

Mrs. Fraser, Agnes's good friend from the sweetshop, beamed

and gave him a double thumbs-up. Then she leaned in and whispered something to Mrs. Barnes from the bakery, who enthusiastically nodded her agreement with whatever had been said.

Jeffrey was touched to see so many faces from his past, and now, in front of him, Mary glowed, her face representing his future. He was a lucky man.

Mary had carefully tucked her one remaining crutch up under her arm, and the smaller boot she was still required to wear for two more weeks was not visible under her dress. Jeffrey had said he'd be happy to wait to get married until she was walking without the crutches, but, to his delight, she hadn't wanted to delay this day any longer than necessary.

"You can push me into the registry office in a wheelbarrow, if necessary, but we're doing it as soon as possible." She'd laughed.

He'd proposed on New Year's Day, after the street party, and Mary had wrapped her arms tightly around his neck, right there in Atholl Road, and kissed him deeply. Jeffrey had never been kissed like that in public. He'd rather liked it, too.

Soft violin music now played in the background, courtesy of Fred's portable CD player, and the scent of the soft pink roses in Mary's bouquet filtered along the rows, reminding everyone why they were here.

Fred and Matilda stood proudly at the front of the room next to Jeffrey and Mary. Jeffrey had asked them to be their witnesses, and Fred had surprised Jeffrey by getting quite choked up about it.

"It'd be an honor, Jeffrey, so it would." He'd coughed, his nose becoming an alarming shade of crimson as his eyes glistened. "Your mother would be so proud."

Jeffrey knew that Fred's words were true.

Matilda had gone to Perth and bought a new dress and a blue straw hat with a bunch of cherries and a feather on the brim, despite Mary telling her it was a very simple affair and that she needn't trouble herself. Fred was in his Rotary Club blazer, with a smart shirt and tartan tie. His Sunday-best trousers were pressed with sharp precision, and he beamed from ear to ear.

Mary wore a cream chiffon dress with a wide boat neck and long gauzy sleeves. A line of tiny lily of the valley was embroidered across the bodice, trailing mysteriously away over one shoulder. Her glorious red curls were caught up in a loose bun, and a tiny pearl shone in each ear lobe. Jeffrey thought she looked ethereal, like a wood nymph, pure perfection in her lovely dress.

He had decided to wear his kilt, Mary having said that the Bonnie Prince Charlie jacket and black bow tie made him look regal. His father Angus's sporran had been carefully brushed and the *sgian dhu* polished before being tucked into Jeffrey's sock. It had felt important to wear these things of his dad's today, and he was grateful that Agnes had given them to him a few years before. As a tribute to his mum, his Tues-Day socks lurked underneath his formal kilt socks. It made him feel close to her, which was comforting, despite the fact that two pairs of socks did make his brogues a little tight. Mary had pinned a sprig of white heather to his collar on the way in, and even though he knew he didn't need to, he reached up to touch it for good luck.

He'd been thinking about Agnes so much since Mary had consented to marry him. His mother's absence had been a tangible and painful presence during the planning and mounting excitement over their special day. Jeffrey knew that Agnes would have been thrilled at their union and would have danced into the

303

night, "yeuching" and "wheeching'" if her little body had been able.

Mary, who missed Agnes a great deal too, had suggested they pick some of her favorite songs to play at the reception in the private function room above the Old Forge Inn.

Tuesday's menu, for the former Jeffrey, would normally have been Scottish pie with beans. However, since he and Mary had started eating together almost every evening, things had changed for the better. For their wedding day, they'd chosen local smoked salmon and then roast beef with all the trimmings. A ceilidh band was coming out from Perth, and the room was booked until midnight, so the liveliest amongst them could dance.

Jeffrey was most excited about the honeymoon. Despite his suggestion to Mary that they wait until her cumbersome boot was gone, she was determined to travel, so they were to leave in three days. He had insisted on keeping it a secret, telling Mary only what she needed to pack. He'd helped her get her passport, so she knew they were leaving the country, but she had no idea of their destination.

"I suppose I trust you, Jeffrey Mere." She'd laughed at his obvious excitement over the surprise. She wouldn't spoil that for him by insisting he tell her what he had planned.

At last the registrar came into the room, and the low rumble of voices halted. He was a stubby little man with half glasses and a dark suit that had seen better days.

"Good afternoon, good afternoon. Welcome, one and all." His face split into a wide grin, revealing enormous teeth with a wide gap between the two at the front. Jeffrey instantly liked him.

"It's time to begin."

The ceremony went by quickly, and before Jeffrey knew it, Fred was handing Jeffrey the ring that he had kept carefully for him in his pocket. As Jeffrey slid the gold band onto Mary's finger, his heart was so full he thought it might burst.

She looked up at him, her eyes shining, as a bright light seemed to pulse all around them, fading out the faces of the guests. Jeffrey looked down at his new wife and marveled at the way the world worked. A few months ago, he'd been lonely, bored with his routine life, and scared by his impending retirement. Then he'd climbed a mountain, lost his dear mother, saved a neighbor from a burning house, retreated into a cold depression, then packed his bags and gone to Rome, afraid to spend Christmas alone.

There he'd had the most frightening experience of his life at the hands of a young Italian con man, been helped by a compassionate hotelier, met a strong and wonderful woman who had taught him a lot about life and who had helped him see that he was, in fact, in love. Now, here he was, at sixty-four years of age, standing at the threshold of an entirely new life. If only his mother could have been here to share this moment.

Fred patted him on the shoulder, jolting Jeffrey back into the room.

"Congratulations, pal. Well done." Fred's voice boomed.

Matilda wiped her eyes and then hugged Mary. "And to think I was the first to know about you two." The little woman giggled and winked at Jeffrey conspiratorially.

"Can you help me, darling?" Mary was speaking to him.

"Yes, sorry." Jeffrey held out his arm to her and Mary, leaning on him, hopped slightly, adjusting the crutch under her arm. They moved across to a long wooden desk where the big leather register lay, waiting for their signatures. Fred and Matilda duly signed their names as witnesses and the registrar then handed Jeffrey the marriage certificate. It was official.

Turning to face the crowd, the newlyweds linked arms and smiled widely.

The registrar spoke clearly from behind the table. "Ladies and gentlemen, may I present Mr. and Mrs. Jeffrey Mere."

The happy crowd clapped and cheered. Fred, taking on the role of witness-cum-best-man, ushered Jeffrey and Mary towards the back of the room and then addressed the crowd.

"Folks, the reception starts in half an hour. See you all at the Old Forge Inn."

Jeffrey walked slowly so that Mary wouldn't have to rush.

"Take your time, love." He looked down at her. "Don't trip."

"I'm fine. Don't worry." Mary squeezed his hand and continued her lopsided progress towards the door. As they passed by, their friends were reaching out to shake Jeffrey's free hand and patting Mary on the shoulders, the joy palpable in the room.

Reaching the door to the street, Jeffrey stepped forward and opened it, allowing Mary to pass through ahead of him. As he followed closely behind, he glanced to the left, where a shadow near the long hedge caught his eye. His heart jolted. No. It wasn't possible, was it?

Jeffrey turned his head and scanned the garden. Where had it gone? Had he really seen it? There, close to the end of the drive, near the street, sat the dog. Its big matted head was level with the top of the hedge, and with its huge paws planted firmly in the grass, the animal sat motionless. He felt his stomach twist. Surely he was seeing things?

Stepping away from Mary as well-wishers slowly engulfed her, he moved carefully towards the big creature. The dog waited for him, its long, dirty tail swishing across the short damp grass. As he reached it, Jeffrey knelt down and wrapped his arms around the broad-shouldered mutt.

"Oh, my god. It *is* you." He felt his eyes blur. "You made it."

The dog's eyes glinted and it pressed its bony chin onto his shoulder, snorting softly against his hair. Jeffrey inhaled deeply, smelling the same odd odor that he'd tried to identify each time he'd come across the animal. This time he definitely had it. It was cabbage and ginger snaps. But there were traces of damp wool, lavender, and honey too. Was that coffee? It was grass and furniture polish, freesias and river water, whisky and stew. It was all the smells that had made up his life, to this point, combined into one heady perfume. It was Agnes.

CHAPTER 46

———◆———

Jeffrey packed the remaining clothes he wanted into his suitcase and crammed the lid shut. Looking around his room, he realized that as soon as they got back from their honeymoon, he needed to start packing in earnest. He and Mary had decided that they'd live in Mary's house, and as Jeffrey looked out of the bedroom window, a big white "For Sale" sign swung in the breeze at the end of the driveway.

A nice young couple from Perth was moving in, and planned on decorating his spare room in pink for the baby they were expecting in the spring. Jeffrey liked the idea of a wee one in his house. Children brought life and happy chaos, and he hoped that the new family would be very happy here.

He'd thought he'd feel worse about leaving his cottage, having spent the best part of 30 years living in it. When it came down to it, though, he'd happily live in a shed, as long as Mary was with him. This house now felt more like simple bricks and mortar, and while he'd been happy in it most of the time, he'd also been lonely. He'd lost Agnes while he lived here, and the pain of her loss seemed to have worked its way into the brickwork.

Besides, Mary's house was cozier, with the big soft couch and chair in the lounge and warm velvet curtains at all the windows. She'd bought a new, bigger bed, the thought of which made Jeffrey blush, even though he was quite alone. She'd also made room in her wardrobe for his clothes and shoes, and a new tooth mug sat in her bathroom, waiting for his toothbrush and paste.

When they got home from their trip, he planned on easing Ralf out of his lair and introducing him to Mary's place. Something told him that it might be an easier task than he imagined, getting the cat to accept its new home. Ralf really had liked Mary from the start. That daft cat certainly had good taste.

With his new passport and two plane tickets in his pocket, Jeffrey switched off the light and bounded down the stairs. He'd left a note with their contact information on the kitchen table for Matilda. She had his door key and would feed Ralf while they were away. He had turned down the thermostat and canceled the post, so now all he had to do was go and pick up his wife and wait for the taxi to arrive.

Mary had packed the night before, so excited that she couldn't wait to get her suitcase ready.

"Will I need suntan lotion?" She'd called down the stairs, her voice making him jump as he watched TV.

"Nope." He'd laughed and turned up the volume.

"Will I need a swimsuit?" Her voice was light and full of amusement.

"Definitely not. Unless you want hypothermia." Jeffrey chuckled, very pleased with himself.

"For heaven's sake, will you not tell me?" He heard her laughter tinkling down the stairs. Despite her questions, he knew she didn't mind not knowing where they were going.

"Pack layers, some light, some heavy. Take gloves and a warm hat, for sure. A nice dress or two would be good, and some comfortable clothes for exploring. OK?" He waited for a response.

"Exploring?" She hopped to the top of the stairs and looked down over the banister. "Really?"

"Well, not mountain climbing or cave diving or anything, but touring places, sightseeing." He grinned up at her.

Mary poked her tongue out at him.

"It'll not be long before I *can* climb a mountain, Jeffrey Mere. Just give me time."

"I don't doubt it," he said, nodding.

"Just watch me." She tossed her red hair and stuck her nose in the air playfully. "I'll do it yet."

"We'll do it together, my love." Jeffrey watched her hop away into the bedroom and thanked his lucky stars for his life.

EPILOGUE

———❦———

Mr. Giacomo was waiting for them when they entered the lobby. He grinned and opened his arms to Jeffrey as he might have to an old friend.

"Mr. Mere. Welcome back. And so soon?" He took the hand Jeffrey extended and shook it enthusiastically. "And this must be Mrs. Mere?"

"Yes, this is my wife, Mary." The words tasted so good in his mouth that Jeffrey wanted to say them again.

"*Benvenuti in Italia.*" The manager smiled at Mary and took her hand. "But what happened to your leg?"

Mary looked down at the boot and shrugged. "An accident. I'm on the mend, though."

Mr. Giacomo nodded and carefully led them to the reception desk. The severe-looking lady with the very red lips, the same one who had given his room away, stood behind it. As he watched her, Jeffrey remembered, to his shame, having shouted at her.

Embarrassed, he approached her, smiling sheepishly.

Mr. Giacomo spoke quickly to her in Italian and then turned to Jeffrey.

"Maria will make your keys. The honeymoon suite is ready for you."

The young woman looked down at the computer screen, tapped on the keys for a few moments, then reached over and handed Jeffrey two room keys.

"Welcome back to Grand Hotel Plaza, Mr. Mere." She met his stare.

Jeffrey took the keys and held her gaze.

"Thank you, Maria, and I owe you an apology, I think."

The red-lipped receptionist looked somewhat taken aback; then a big smile split her face from side to side.

"No, not necessary. But thank you." She nodded at him and then turned to Mary. "Have a pleasant stay in Roma, Mrs. Mere."

"*Grazie*," Mary replied and took the keys from Jeffrey's hand. There was a story there, obviously, but she'd ask him about it later. At the moment, all she wanted to do was stare around her, at this incredible lobby, and just soak in the grandeur.

The manager beckoned to the bellboy, who was loitering at the front doors.

"Take Mr. and Mrs. Mere to the honeymoon suite." The young man nodded, trotted to a nearby door, pulled a brass luggage trolley over, and loaded their bags onto it.

"Thank you, Mr. Giacomo." Jeffrey smiled at the younger man.

"*Prego, prego*. Please enjoy your stay, and you call me if you have any problems."

Jeffrey and Mary followed the bellboy to the lifts. As the big brass doors slid silently closed, Mary nudged him playfully with her elbow.

"Well, you obviously made quite an impression on *him*." She looked flushed, and a more than a little impressed.

"I'll tell you all about it, later." Jeffrey took her hand and kissed her fingers.

"Welcome to Roma, Mrs. Mere."

ACKNOWLEDGEMENTS

Heartfelt thanks to everyone who supported me in this undertaking especially my stellar editors, Bev Katz Rosenbaum, Amanda Sumner and Carol Agnew, who helped me fine-tune this novel. Their efforts enabled me to reach a place where I was happy to share Jeffrey with the world.

Special thanks go to Lesley Shearer, who was there for every paragraph, stoking the creative fire. Also to Rasheeda Syed, always honest and reliably correct, the wise and tireless Annie Augenstein White from whom I've learned so much, Sharon Erksa for her creative eye and to my parents, Bill and Emma Shearer, who kept me true to the Scottish soul of this book. Last but not least, to Bob Ragsdale, for his constant encouragement, endless moral and technical support and most of all for his unshakable belief that I could do this.

ABOUT THE AUTHOR

Originally from Edinburgh, Alison now lives in Virginia with her husband and two beloved dogs. Educated in England, she holds an MBA from Leicester University.

Tuesday's Socks is Alison's debut novel. For more information on upcoming books, and a selection of short stories, go to www.alisonragsdale.com.

8264571R00190

Printed in Great Britain
by Amazon.co.uk, Ltd.,
Marston Gate.